The

AMISH
CHRISTMAS
CANDLE

The
AMISH
CHRISTMAS
CANDLE

KELLY LONG
JENNIFER BECKSTRAND
LISA JONES BAKER

ZEBRA BOOKS
KENSINGTON PUBLISHING CORP.
http://www.kensingtonbooks.com

ZEBRA BOOKS are published by

Kensington Publishing Corp.
119 West 40th Street
New York, NY 10018

All Kensington titles, imprints, and distributed lines are available at special quantity discounts for bulk purchases for sales promotion, premiums, fund-raising, educational, or institutional use.

Special book excerpts or customized printings can also be created to fit specific needs. For details, write or phone the office of the Kensington Sales Manager: Attn.: Sales Department. Kensington Publishing Corp., 119 West 40th Street, New York, NY 10018. Phone: 1-800-221-2647.

Zebra and the Z logo Reg. U.S. Pat. & TM Off.
BOUQUET Reg. U.S. Pat. & TM Off.

First Kensington Books Trade Paperback Printing: October 2017
First Zebra Books Mass-Market Paperback Printing: November 2018
ISBN-13: 978-1-4201-4417-8
ISBN-10: 1-4201-4417-0

eISBN-13: 978-1-4201-4418-5
eISBN-10: 1-4201-4418-9

10 9 8 7 6 5 4 3 2 1

Printed in the United States of America

Contents

Snow Shine on
Ice Mountain

KELLY LONG

For Jordan—who sees

Prologue

His big body strained in the flickering candlelight. He was desperate to lose himself in the Englisch girl's hair, her scent, her mouth—even though he knew he'd pay for it later. And it didn't matter that he couldn't even remember her name. Anything was better than feeling the way he normally did—morose, broken, and definitely lacking . . . At least I'm not disabled at kissing, he thought ruefully when the girl sighed with pleasure.

"Oh, Gray . . . I never knew Amisch men could be so—so . . ."

He silenced her whisper by slanting his head and deepening the kiss. One part of his brain focused on her lips with infinite skill while another drifted, beyond his control, to the day he'd lost the use of his right arm.

He'd been fourteen and confident that he could manage the four-horse team for the spring planting. He hadn't counted on a nest of rattlesnakes or the horses spooking. Both of his shoulders were dislocated while he strained to maintain control. That pain had been minimal compared to the Englisch doctor's solemn words that followed.

"Nerve damage in the right arm. Irreparable, I'm afraid . . . Sorry, son."

Sorry, sorry . . . I'm so sorry . . . He blinked back sudden tears and tore his mouth away from the girl. He sucked in his breath with harsh gasps.

"What?" She looked confused, her mouth thoroughly kissed. "Why did you stop?"

He gave her a cursory glance. *Why is it that any kind of intimacy eventually makes me think of that awful day? Why, Gott . . .*

"You start kissing me and then pull away with no explanation?" she said hotly.

He muttered a pointless apology to the girl and shifted her car in gear with his left hand. Then he leaned forward and blew out the small fragrant candle she'd insisted on placing on the dashboard to make the situation "more romantic."

"I don't believe this." She flopped back against the passenger seat. "Are you taking me home?"

He could sense her pout, even in the dark, but didn't bother to answer. His mind was far away, in the heat of a spring day, while the sound of rattlesnakes echoed softly in his brain.

Chapter 1

December
Ice Mountain, Pennsylvania

"I tell you, *Fater*—it has to stop." Twenty-three-year-old Naomi Gish rarely raised her voice, but she'd had it up to her neck with her *daed's* manner of "business."

Bud Gish patted her hand in a soothing manner. "*Ach*, now, now . . . my *maedel*, do not trouble yourself." He gave a wheezing laugh. "Anyone would think you believe I'm ninety instead of a spry eighty-two."

"Eighty-three," Naomi said dryly, regaining her composure. "And far too *auld* to be running moonshine up and down this mountain."

"We've been over this before, Naomi. What would you have me do instead? His gnarled hand swept the orderly array of aromatic wax vats and dripping candles. "It's you who's the art maker here."

She couldn't deny the truth in what he said. Her

mamm had taught her as a little girl to love the wax, to see each candle as special, providing the light by which to do Derr Herr's work.

She turned her thoughts back to the situation at hand and looked appealingly at her *daed*. "There is much that you could help me with here in the shop, Fater . . . especially during this busy winter season." She made her voice sound wistful and the dear wrinkled face before her suddenly brightened.

"So, you're needing help in the shop?" he asked.

"*Jah*, but I—"

She turned when the small bell over the shop door rang out with cheer. Naomi glanced up and then suppressed a groan. *Amelia Troyer . . . one of the most committed gossips on Ice Mountain . . . and always too glad to point out that I'm not yet married.* "Frau Troyer, how are you?" Naomi kept her voice cordial, noticing that her *daed* had slipped discreetly through the burgundy curtain that led to their living space. *Smart man . . .*

Naomi longed for her own escape when Amelia began to tout the beauty of her daughter, Iris.

"I know she certainly is lovely," Naomi agreed. *On the outside . . . on the inside Iris is as mean as a pit of rattlers, probably as mean as her mother . . .*

"That's a dozen of the white candles." Frau Troyer's words recalled Naomi back sharply to the moment.

"Of course," Naomi murmured suitably and prayed that Gott would forgive her ill thoughts of the Troyer women. . . .

* * *

"So, will you do it, *buwe?*"

Gray raised a brow as he considered Bud Gish's offer. The *auld* man, carrying a lit lantern and looking like he had the world by the tail, had cornered him ten minutes ago at Ben Kauffman's general store and practically dragged him into a stray canned goods closet. Gray had thought the man *narrisch* but he had to admit, Bud did present an intriguing, if risky, proposition.

"You want me to work in the candle shop, and use that as a cover for delivering moonshine?" Gray clarified.

"Right!" Bud grinned. "Just remember, you have to keep my *dochder* in the dark, if you take my meaning."

"That might be a problem then. I've heard it said that she's smart. And a man has a tough time hiding anything from a smart woman."

Gray watched Bud's chest puff out with pride. "*Jah,* she is smart."

"Then how am I going to pull this off without her knowing?"

Bud leaned close and Gray smelled a confusing combination of liniment and bologna. "I've heard it said, Gray, that you have a way with the women."

Gray had to swallow a laugh at Bud's confidence. True, he had a way with women—a reputation he wasn't exactly proud of. But this was staid, frosty Naomi Gish. His instincts told him he'd probably get tossed out on his ear the moment he stepped through the candle shop door. He'd observed her on occasion at church service and other gatherings—her dark brown eyes and plain brown hair did little to add charm to her serious mouth and straight back.

But . . . there were some upsides to the idea. The

job of runnin' 'shine definitely appealed; he was intrigued by the dangers associated with the practice . . . And he'd also learn the art of candle making, which he privately appreciated . . . not that he'd ever tell Naomi or Bud or anyone else. Ultimately, it was the challenge of pulling a bit of wool over Naomi's brown eyes that had tipped his decision. "I'll take the job," he said, grinning.

Bud slapped Gray on the back, the lantern in his hand almost going out. "I knew I could count on you."

Gray nodded, clasping Bud's hand to seal the deal. All in all, it was a bargain with a lot of promise . . .

After the prolonged transaction with Frau Troyer, Naomi went inside and began setting the table. She was putting out the warmed plates when her *fater* returned through the back door. His wrinkled cheeks were rosy and his blue eyes were bright, which immediately put her on guard.

"Daed, where have you been?" she asked.

"Out and about. What's for supper? I'm starved."

"Beef brisket . . ." she replied slowly, trying to puzzle out why he seemed so happy.

"Sounds *gut* . . . And I want you to know that I gave some thought to what you said earlier. I'm going to do as you ask and relax here at home. No more runnin' 'shine for me . . ." He started to sit at the table when he snapped his fingers. "*Ach, dochder,* and I nearly forgot. I hired Grayson Fisher to help you in the shop until after Second Christmas."

"What?"

"Yep . . . I will not be runnin'—"

"*Nee* . . . about Grayson Fisher!"

"Hmmmm . . . *ach, jah,* the *buwe* is due to start to-morrow."

"But I—"

"It'll be fine. He's a *gut* worker. You'll see." He sat down and picked up his fork. "Now can we dish up? I'm starvin'."

Still stunned, Naomi brought the food to the table mechanically. Grayson Fisher was the stuff of which a woman's secret dreams were made, and she wasn't above admitting that she'd sometimes stolen a glance at the man. *But to have him in the shop . . . so very close . . .* How was she supposed to focus on her work with him in the shop? He was attractive enough from a distance, and not just his good looks. There was something about him, something mesmerizing and a bit . . . dangerous. As if he would sweep her off her feet, only to let her crash to the ground, all without blinking an eye.

She couldn't allow that. She'd kept men at a distance for years, not wanting someone who simply thought she would be a *gut* housekeeper or a *gut* potential stepmother. But Grayson Fisher had enough of a reputation for her to know that she had to keep him very, very far away. *I will simply tell him that I don't need his help . . .*

Yet she had to struggle to silence the quiet voice inside of her that said denying him might not be so easy.

"Mmmm, Gray . . . where is your mind this *nacht?*"

Iris Troyer linked her arms around his neck and he stared down into her pretty face. She'd convinced her *mamm* that she was delivering quilt squares when she was actually making out with him in the confines of his cold barn.

He tried to focus when she gave an insipid giggle, then furrowed his brow in thought. Suddenly, he was bored with pretty girls; the ones who wanted his kiss only because it meant something to them for the moment. He gently lowered Iris's arms, first one, then the other, and set her away from him.

"I expect I'm not feeling myself tonight. Sorry, sweetheart."

She frowned, tilting her full lips into a downward slant, one that was meant to express her displeasure but to also offer him a second chance. He remained unaffected. Instead, he recalled his own words from earlier in the day—*A smart woman* . . . Naomi was someone whose brain outmatched her beauty. Maybe when he was around her, he wouldn't be plagued by these memories of snakes and pain and loss . . .

He saw Iris hovering near the barn door. "I'm leaving now, Gray."

Distracted, he nodded. "I'll walk you home—"

"Don't bother," she huffed and left.

He should go after her. At the very least he should feel guilty that she was walking home alone, even though she only lived two houses down. But he didn't. It wasn't the first time Iris had gone home by herself, usually at her insistence. He rubbed his arm. It hadn't taken him long to figure out that Iris was only interested in him for one thing—and he gladly gave it to her. All the pretty women saw him as someone to have fun with . . . but not to take home to their parents, and definitely not worth considering having a future with. And he was okay with that. He wasn't interested in marriage either . . . and if a beautiful girl threw herself at him, he would happily catch her . . . then let her *geh*.

But not tonight. Tonight, all he could think about was his new job . . . and how it would put him in close proximity with the smart, smart Naomi Gish.

Chapter 2

The first thing she thought when she looked at him was what she always thought when she saw Grayson Fisher—he was big. He was big but he moved with a lithe grace, edging his way with ease round the high boxes of wax and the rows of dripping candles.

"Your *daed* hired me to give you a hand," he said and his mouth quirked as if he'd made a rueful joke. She inadvertently glanced at his limp right arm.

"I—I don't need any help, Herr Fisher." She spoke in cool tones, dragging her gaze up to his strange, rain-colored eyes.

"Gray," he said, almost absently.

"What?"

"Call me Gray."

She nodded, feeling like she was being offered an intimacy and unsure if she wanted to take it. Then she told herself that she was being ridiculous—it was only his name.

"All right. Gray . . . My *daed* is *auld* and set in his ways. I can manage the candle shop quite well on my own."

He half smiled, the lazy tilt of his firm lips bringing out a dimple in his cheek. "That's what your *fater* said you'd say."

"Well," she paused, flustered. "That's what I'm saying."

He approached the counter and leaned his left elbow on it, bending his head a bit so that she was struck anew by his handsome profile—dark hair, thick lowered lashes, a perfectly chiseled nose, and a strong jaw. Then he looked up and spoke softly. "Think of it as an early Christmas gift to a disabled man—a chance to earn some extra money and to have a temporary feeling of purpose."

"Do you not usually feel Gott's purpose in your life?"

She realized it was the wrong question when he frowned and reached out to run a finger down her pulsing wrist. "*Nee*—I don't. But you might be able to help me with that. What do you say, Naomi?"

He pulled his hand back and she felt a curious pounding in her chest and a sudden desire for him to touch her again. She opened her mouth slightly, appalled at her thought, and he laughed in gentle tones. "Unless, of course, you'd rather not work with a cripple . . ."

She straightened her spine and took the risk of leaning closer to him, staring into the perfect gray depths of his eyes. "I am not a snob, Herr Fisher."

"Gray." He smiled, revealing white teeth and a very slight overbite that somehow made his mouth all the more appealing. "Then I'm hired?"

She swallowed hard, wondering what it would be like to have this big man in such close proximity for a *gut* length of time. *I'll probably* geh *crazy . . . like some lovestruck* auld *maid . . .* But suddenly, she knew she wanted him around, to give her some memories to hug to herself in her lonely bed. She stuck out her hand and he took it with a firm, left-handed shake. "You're hired."

"*Danki,* you won't be disappointed. I promise."

And somehow, she had the idea that there were layered meanings to his comment that left her breathless and as stirred up as hot wax . . .

Gray felt himself shiver as he trudged home through the deep snow. It wasn't the cold . . . *Nee,* it was her . . . that staid, stiff-necked Naomi. After she'd hired him, she'd put him to work, first giving him a list of duties he'd be expected to perform each day when he arrived and then dealing out directions on what to do with an emergency fire. She was crisp, concise, organized . . . and would probably balk like a chicken if he tried to kiss her. *Kiss her . . . wait, whoa, slow down here. She's going to be my boss, not some dalliance.*

He hiked for a few more minutes, taking a short-cut through the tall pines, and then came upon a small cabin nestled pleasantly in the mounds of snow. He climbed the stairs, grateful, as always, for the warm glow of candlelight coming from inside. His eccentric Aenti Beth made home both a place in his mind and his heart. She'd raised him since his parents left the Amisch to divorce. His mother and father had both felt that he'd be best served by staying with the community in Beth's care. He pushed away the darker thoughts associated with his lack of control in this matter and knew he was more than grateful for his Aenti Beth. Her kindness had sustained him through his injury, though even all of her love hadn't been able to wipe away the memories.

He sighed, feeling the warmth of his breath mingle with the chill of the air; then he stamped his boots and went inside.

Aenti Beth was, as usual, cooking at the woodstove though she had a diaper-clad guinea pig balanced on each of her shoulders. Ned and Ted squealed their greetings to him and he replied in proper guinea piggish, raising his voice to imitate the two friends—"Aw ra, aw ra, aw ran!"

Aenti Beth smiled at him as he came forward to brush her elderly cheek with a kiss. Then he scratched the two pigs and went to the pump to wash his hands. He had to lift his right hand to the water and he thought inadvertently of Naomi when he touched his own wrist.

"Hope you're hungry, Gray!"

"What are we having?" he asked.

"Bacon corn chowder . . . great on a cold *nacht*. How was the candle shop?"

Ned seemed to ask the same question, wriggling a large black nose.

"Fine—it'll be fine."

"Well, it gives you something to do besides ordering seeds in the winter—might learn a few things too."

"I might at that." He plucked at Ted's white ear and hoped there were only a few hairs in his chowder. Then he thought of what he might learn from Naomi Gish and decided that whatever it was, it would probably hold the touch of Gott and that had to be worthwhile.

* * *

Naomi nestled beneath the quilts of her bed and watched the shadows from the great pine outside her window play with the dancing fall of a light snow. She couldn't help reflecting on the day and hugged herself at the thought of being so near Gray Fisher. The man was mesmerizing, though she held no illusions that he would ever be interested in someone like her. Nee . . . *he deserves a delicate flower of a girl— not someone* aulder *than he and better put on the shelf with the other preserves* . . . Then she chided herself for such a negative train of thought and pulled her pillow close. She thought she might dream of Gray Fisher that *nacht,* but she awoke to the dawn with nothing but the recollection of a deep and pleasant sleep in her mind. Then she reminded herself that she'd be seeing Grayson—*nee,* Gray—in the flesh that morning and she needed to get prepared with materials that would help her to instruct him.

She ignored the traitorous voice inside her head that whispered of hidden things that he might instruct her in, then put such foolery aside and rose to dress for the day.

Chapter 3

He tried to concentrate. She was explaining something about scenting the wicks of certain candles with oils of lavender and rosemary, but all he could see was the confident movements of her slender hands. And all he could think about was stroking her wrist the day before, surely an intimacy, and the strange feeling of peace that had come over him—a peace that rivaled anything he'd ever experienced with a woman.

"Do you understand about straightening the wick?" Naomi asked in a no-nonsense tone, and he dragged his attention up to her dark brown eyes.

He savored her words aloud. "Straightening the wick . . ." *Yeah, I get it just fine, painfully fine . . .* "*Jah,* I do."

"*Gut,*" she nodded. "Now, I should warn you that you might get burnt occasionally." She turned her right hand palm up and lifted it for him to see.

Gray raised his fingers to rub at a red mark in the center of her palm. He glanced down and didn't miss the hectic color that flooded her face at his action. But he didn't draw away. He couldn't. Touching her was like putting warm fingertips to clear ice—there was a curious melting sensation inside of him that he couldn't explain.

"It's funny," he whispered, still touching her.

"My burn?"

"*Nee* . . ." He felt himself flush and awkwardly tried to say what he was feeling. "It's funny how we can have scars on the outside and they can hurt but it's the wounds on the inside that give us the most problems."

"Because no one sees them?" she asked.

"*Jah* . . ." He lifted her hand close to his mouth, then felt as if he'd had a bucket of ice water thrown on him when she jerked from his grasp.

"Herr Fisher . . . um, Gray—it's Bishop Umble *kumme* shopping . . ."

He looked round, rather dazed, to meet the wise blue eyes of the spiritual leader of Ice Mountain and gave a brief nod.

The *auld* man smiled. "Glad to hear you're working here, Gray. I saw your Aenti Beth and Ned and Ted, of course, out for a walk—the pigs' new winter parkas look top notch."

"Um . . . *jah*," he agreed, but he felt off balance, like right after his arm had been injured and he'd had to learn to walk while maintaining his equilibrium with the dead weight of his limb.

He jerked his attention back to the moment and realized the bishop was talking with Naomi about a special order.

"I want something for my Martha, one of those carved candles or maybe a honeycomb type—what do you say, Gray?"

"That it's *gut* you still want to buy your wife gifts after being married as long as you have."

The bishop laughed outright. "Back in control now, *buwe?* Well, I'll choose the honeycomb and make it big enough to serve as a centerpiece."

Gray told himself that Bishop Umble always said things like he'd just done—*Like he can see into a man's heart and mind . . . It was enough to freak a person out . . .*

Gray watched Naomi's careful penmanship as she detailed the order in the book she kept by the cash drawer and he loved the intricate loops and circles of her lettering. *I am losing my mind here—being interested in a woman's letters and not her breasts . . .* Which thought, of course, made his eyes drop irreverently to Naomi's bosom. He realized it was charming. . . . *Like two high apples, just waiting to be picked . . .* He met the bishop's eye and tried to diffuse his thoughts but not before the *aulder* man spoke succinctly.

"Make it in a honeycomb style, Naomi, but *sei se gut,* make it apple scented, if you don't mind."

It took all Gray had not to choke as Bishop Umble gave him a sunny smile, then took his leave without a backward glance.

"Do you want me to show you the apple-infused oil?" Naomi asked Gray diffidently when the bishop had gone.

"*Nee,*" he whispered, feeling like a coward, but seeing no way out. "I—I really want to see the honeycomb candle making."

He spent the next hour trying to tear his gaze from her chest and thinking about apples . . .

* * *

Naomi knew instinctively that he was studying her and she wondered if her *kapp* was askew or if she had something on the front of her apron. But when she made to inspect herself with a discreet glance, he raised his left hand in dismissal. "There's nothing wrong, Naomi."

"*Ach . . . gut.* I—um—made some sticky buns this morning for Fater and me. Would you like one? I usually have something to eat as a midmorning break. We can *geh* into the *haus* and listen for the shop bell."

"Sounds good. I love sweet things."

Well, she thought. *That leaves me out.* Then she swallowed, telling herself she was being silly and led him through the curtain and into the living area of the *haus.*

Much to her dismay, not only had her *daed* finished the sticky buns and left the pan on the floor near his chair, but he was also snoring loudly in his long johns, sound asleep. Naomi was about to back Gray out of the room when she heard a rich chuckle from behind her. She turned and looked up at Gray, whose rain-colored eyes were warm. "Sorry." He laughed low again. "But a man's got to be able to relax in his own home, doesn't he?"

She was struck by the sudden image of what Gray would look like relaxing—maybe on crisp sheets, mellowed cream by candlelight—his big chest bare and finely muscled. He would be lounging back against the pillows with the sheets tangled about his hips and . . .

"Naomi!"

She snapped back to the moment and realized her *fater* had awoken and was trying to gain her attention. "Um . . . what?" she asked, knowing her face was red with heat generated by her thoughts. *I never knew I had such an imagination . . .*

"I said"—her *daed* rolled his eyes—"Gray went to answer the bell in the shop. Best *geh* help the *buwe*. . . . And, uh—if you might send him back in here when you're done . . . I'll get my clothes on and could use his help outside for a minute."

"*Ach, jah* . . . surely." She turned and reentered the shop through the curtain, only to find Gray exchanging easy conversation with Mary Lyons—the young and beautiful wife of the schoolmaster on the mountain.

They both turned to smile at Naomi as she joined them. She felt glad to see Mary, who was as straightforward and natural a person as she'd ever met.

"Naomi," Mary said brightly. "My *dochder* Rose is going on three now and has a plaguing interest in touching everything. Jude thinks it's wonderful and he wondered if you had any flat wax that she might play with?"

Naomi smiled in return. "Of course."

"What's flat wax?" Gray asked with obvious interest.

She led him over to a counter where sheets of wax paper separated literal flat wax pieces. "See?" Naomi held up a piece of bright red wax that she'd flattened and oiled between the wax paper so that it might be rolled into a candle or used for play.

She handed him a piece and watched the lean fingers of his left hand work the smooth material. She couldn't help but wonder what it might be like to have him touch her with as much intent.

"I'll take five sheets," Mary said and Naomi turned to concentrate on the wax.

She was discovering that the candle shop was actually a very sensual place when Gray was around and then told herself that she'd better focus more on her customers than her handsome employee . . .

"Now runnin' moonshine is simple—if you don't get caught or shot." Bud Gish pronounced the words to Gray with all the solemnity of reciting a prayer in church and Gray felt a shiver go down his spine.

"Okaaaaay."

They were standing in one of Bud's caches, a hidden panel behind Naomi's cellar pantry, and Gray couldn't help the faint pang that came over him when he thought of deceiving the girl. *She deserves better* . . . But he knew that if he was in for a penny, he was in for a pound, and he couldn't just back out now.

"So," Bud was saying. "You make the run tonight at midnight. And no lantern light . . ."

"What about a candle?" Gray asked dryly.

"Only for a few seconds. You potentially got two kinds of folks after you—the Englisch authorities and other moonshiners. You have to be fast and sure. Tonight's drop is simple—a satchel of 'shine for a bit of money and we split fifty-fifty."

Gray nodded. "All right. So, the 'shine goes under Stoulfus's Bridge and the money should be there in exchange. Do I know who the buyer is?"

"Never . . . you might have ideas but *nee,* never."

"You know," Gray said after a moment, "a fellow has to think if it's worth it . . ."

Bud laughed and clapped him on the shoulder. "Soon enough you'll stop thinking, *buwe.* It'll just

start to run in yer blood—the mystery, the thrill—
not to mention the easy pay."

"Right."

But Gray knew that other things ran in his blood—
things like warm wax and smart women and he wasn't
as thrilled with his secondary job as he thought
he'd be . . .

Chapter 4

Naomi went to bed that *nacht* thinking of a confusing mixture of candle making, rich scents, and Gray. She blushed beneath the quilts when she realized that she was trying to recapture his scent—perhaps his soap—maybe just the essence of who he was. It was intriguing really, that so much of her work at the candle shop involved intricate scents yet she struggled to put a mental finger on what was Gray . . . She turned over in bed and gave her feather pillow a *gut* thump. Then she drifted into an uneasy sleep.

"Home-ly Naomi, Home-ly Naomi!" The children's voices chanted in cruel unison and she would have loved to run from the taunting. But she stood her ground, straightening her spine—not even closing her eyes. She noticed a gaunt stray dog trying to skulk past the school when her tormentors recognized another form of amusement and began to throw rocks at the dog. She quickly ran to try and fend off the blows from the whimpering animal when suddenly she

was aware of a taut young voice and she looked up to see Grayson Fisher standing in front of her and the hund.

She'd never spoken to the buwe *as he'd started school on Ice Mountain only a few months beforehand but she remembered his odd Aenti Beth bringing him his first day. She'd handed him a lunch pail and removed a squirrel kit from it. Then Naomi had listened to the foreign whispered word* divorce *as it was hastily tossed about the classroom. There were subdued giggles when Grayson came in, his dark head bent, his young jaw set, and she imagined he looked much the same way now as he stared down each one of the class bullies. They melted into another part of the school yard and Grayson turned to stoop down near her and the dog. He ran practiced hands over the cringing animal and looked into her eyes. "I'll take him home to my Aenti Beth."*

Naomi nodded, then held her breath as he touched a bleeding scratch on the back of her hand. "It's nothing," she whispered.

"It means a lot—to give your blood for another creature." She watched in detached fascination as he bent his dark head and put his mouth to her wound, slowly sucking it clean. Then he lifted the dog and started to walk away, growing smaller with each step until she sat up gasping in her own bed. . . .

Gray reined in the big black gelding with his left hand and made a soothing sound from the back of his throat. His horse, Thorn, was one of the fastest on the mountain but also blended in nicely with the shifting shadows of midnight. He slid from the back of the animal and eyed Stoulfus's Bridge in the near distance. Beneath the light of a winter's full moon, the *auld* stone structure looked eerie, even with its dusting of snow.

Gray tied Thorn to a low-hanging branch, then carefully untied the leather satchels that held the canning jars filled with moonshine. He glanced once more at the sky, then laughed softly to himself when it hit him full force where moonshining got its name. He slung the satchels over his left shoulder.

He trod softly through the snow, feeling his heart beat loudly in his ears. He wet his lips as he neared the curved arch of the bridge and concentrated on the darkness below. *Should have brought a candle,* he thought grimly. Then a hoarse voice gave him a frightening pause.

"Put the white lightning down real slow."

Gray straightened his back and chose to stand his ground.

The awful click of a gun being cocked sounded deafening in the cold *nacht* air.

"Give me the money—I'll give you the 'shine," Gray said hoarsely. He felt as if he was watching himself from some distance and his thoughts flashed oddly to Naomi and touching her wrist . . . *Peace* . . . *so sweet* . . .

He heard the crunch of boot steps in the snow and the hoarse voice came again. "Drop the moonshine now, boy."

Suddenly he didn't want anything but to live—live for some kind of purpose. He dropped the satchels roughly to the ground and heard the distinct sound of glass shattering. He knew the alcohol was now seeping into the snow.

"Aw, now what did you do that for, Gray!"

The moonlight shifted to play over Bud Gish's stubby form and Gray wanted to sag in relief.

"Bud!"

"Never drop the 'shine. That's a rule!" the *auld* man cried.

"Never pull a gun! Talk about rules—you're freakin' Amisch—you're supposed to be peaceable!"

Bud waved the small pistol around and Gray resisted the urge to duck. "'Twas me *grossdaudi*'s. It's not loaded. I just wanted to give you a little test run tonight. Calm your nerves . . . that's all."

"Calm my nerves? You almost gave me heart failure and you wasted your own 'shine."

Bud ambled over to clap him on the back. "I've got plenty more and you'll do all right, *buwe*. Besides, I promise—no more tests."

"Yeah, right," Gray muttered as he blew out a breath of disgust and bent to lift the damp leather satchels from the snowy ground. . . .

Naomi tried to go back to sleep after her dream but she found it impossible. How could she remember something so long forgotten through the power of a dream? She knew that the Bible said that the Lord could speak to men's hearts through dreams, and certainly her heart had forgotten those moments when she was young and Gray had defended her and the *auld* dog.

She decided to continue her musings by going out to the kitchen for a glass of warm milk and she'd nearly gained the cupboard when her *fater* stumbled in, breathless from the cold *nacht* air.

"Daed!" she exclaimed.

"What?" he asked, clearly startled.

"You said no more moonshine!" She put her hands on her hips.

Her father lifted a placating hand. "So I did, Naomi. So I did. And I'm telling you that I was out for a breath of fresh air—nothing funny, I promise."

She frowned, unsure whether to trust him or not, but then he produced a single small pine branch for her inspection. "I even stopped to take a look at a possible Christmas tree—would you like short needles this year, hmmm?"

She rolled her eyes heavenward. "Daed, what am I going to do with you?"

He laughed and she knew she had to choose to believe him. After all, she herself couldn't sleep, and she willed her heart to say it had nothing to do with her dream about Gray Fisher.

Gray dreamed about Naomi that *nacht*. A frustrating, unsatisfied mesh of tight collars and *kapp* strings and apron ties—the trappings of an Amisch woman . . . all pins and proper. But then he saw her by candlelight, her hair down, the ends skimming the curve of her bottom and her dark sensitive eyes wide with intelligent purpose as she leaned forward to kiss him. He was swept up in a feeling of peace; intense pulsating peace that seemed to rivet him to his bed, then left him arching in supplication for the feeling to continue.

But he woke and hurried to dress after realizing that he'd overslept. He made to bypass Aenti Beth with a quick kiss but she seemed to have other ideas.

"Whatcha doin' at the candle shop today, Gray?"

"I don't know for sure and I'd better get—"

"Well, if Miss Naomi don't have other plans, I want a mold of your hand."

He stopped still. "A what?"

"*Jah.* I asked Bishop Umble if it was vanity and he said *nee.* I saw those wax hand molds at a fair last year and liked them real well. It's a memory sort of thing. It seems like you came here with such small hands and now ye're a man grown . . . And I want pink for your hand," she said succinctly. "It's my favorite color."

"Pink?" he asked helplessly as Ted and Ned began to squeal. He clucked back to them and grabbed his coat. "I'll see what I can do, Aenti Beth—I can't make any promises."

But he caught her look of disappointment as he half turned from the door and knew he'd be asking Naomi how to do a pink hand wax mold before the day was out.

Chapter 5

Naomi had decided that Gray wasn't coming back to work, that he found it too dull, when he opened the door to the candle shop and stalked inside.

"Sorry I'm late."

Naomi found her voice. "Well . . . um . . . just don't let it happen again." She knew she sounded prim but the man positively threw her off balance. She watched him as he nodded and turned to take off his coat and hat. His dark hair seemed ruffled and her fingers itched of their own accord to smooth it. She swallowed, then hastily glanced down at the order book when he turned back around. She did not want to be caught staring.

"What are we doing today?" he asked and she snapped her gaze upward, watching in fascination as he gave her a lopsided smile.

"Well, we've got a big order for candles for Christmas church service and"—she broke off when he seemed to look relieved and grew immediately curious. "What is it?" she asked.

"What is what?"

"You kind of—exhaled. Is there something else you'd rather be doing?"

"*Nee*, I'm fine and—"

"Gray?"

"Hmmm?"

"I don't believe you're being quite truthful."

His handsome face flushed with color and he shrugged. "All right, so I'm not."

"I knew it." She felt happy that she was able to read him so well. *Perhaps it has something to do with my dream . . .*

"Uh, Naomi?"

His deep voice, sounding sheepish, brought her quickly back to the moment.

"*Jah?*"

"What do you know about making wax hand molds? Pink, in particular . . ."

He felt ridiculous when Naomi stood, eyeing him speculatively, but he owed Aenti Beth a lot and she never asked for much to make her happy.

"We could—uh—talk about it later," he muttered.

"*Nee.*" She put a finger to her lips and patted them in thought. "Would you let me do your right hand?" she asked after a moment.

He stared at her, shocked that he could be so intrigued by the idea of her clever fingers touching the sleeve of his light blue shirt.

"I—I could help you with your sleeve." She made a gentle gesture toward his arm.

He looked at her hands intently and then drew a deep breath. "I never let anyone touch my arm," he admitted.

She nodded, clearly disappointed. "Of course."

"But you, Naomi," he went on in a soft tone, "I trust."

"Why?"

He smiled. Any other woman would have been interested in the power he'd given her by sharing his vulnerability—but not the delightfully smart Naomi.

"You don't know how *gut* it feels not to have to play games," he said, taking a step closer to her.

"Play . . . games?"

"You would call it something like social word intricacies, but as to your 'why' question—I trust you because you are what you are, straightforward, sweet, innocent maybe . . ."

"Maybe?"

She looked put out and his smile widened. "Sorry. Definitely innocent as a *maedel* can be. And I would be honored if you'd help me with my arm."

He couldn't help but notice the color that warmed her cheeks. "*Danki,*" she whispered.

He turned slightly, offering her the right side of his body and she swallowed hard. She lifted her hands to the wrist of his sleeve—slowly sliding out the two pins.

She began to roll the fabric upward and peeked up at him, sensing the tension in his big body. She wanted to make some soothing sound but knew it probably would go unappreciated. Her fingertips brushed his midforearm and she couldn't help but enjoy the warmth of his skin.

"This arm looks perfectly—uh—"

"Normal?" he asked.

"*Jah,*" she agreed miserably, feeling as if she'd broken some sort of spell between them, but to her surprise he continued to talk about his injury.

"*Jah*, I've had it examined twice since the original accident. The second doctor taught me some exercises that I could actually do using my left arm to lift and bend my right arm so there'd be little to no atrophy of the muscle."

"That's good and I thank you for sharing with me . . . Sometimes when a person has a wound or difference about them, it's hard to know what to say, what to ask."

He shrugged. "Ask whatever you like."

"Do you remember much about the accident?"

"Yeah—that it hurt badly but not half as bad as the day my parents told me they were getting divorced."

Naomi swallowed hard, not expecting this turn of conversation yet feeling that it was exactly right somehow. "Do you want to talk about it?"

He gave her a wry smile. "I never do, but now . . . We were living in the Lockport Amisch community, and one day, after supper, my *daed* told me that he and Mamm were getting a divorce. I was eleven but I don't even think I knew what the word meant. Then he said that they were leaving the Amisch and I was to *kumme* here and stay with Aenti Beth."

"And you don't—they don't *kumme* and see you?"

He shook his head, his gray eyes bleak. "*Nee*, not once. I don't even know where they're living now. Aenti Beth says they wanted it this way, that I'd be better off being raised by the Amisch."

"So they don't know about your arm?"

"*Nee*."

She could form no reply and she realized that

she'd rolled his sleeve up as far as it would *geh*. She stepped back with something akin to disappointment, longing to *geh* on touching him. But then she turned briskly to the wax vats heating on an elongated wood stove top and asked him to step closer.

Chapter 6

"You need to make sure the wax is only at medium temperature."

He watched her lift his wrist and imagined how cool and purposeful her fingers must be. He closed his eyes for a moment, seeing the peace flowing through him . . .

"Does everything feel all right?" she asked as she briskly rubbed cocoa butter on his damaged hand and wrist as part of the mold-making process.

He nodded and opened his eyes, struggling to concentrate as she explained each step.

"It really is a simple process. People often make wax hand molds at fairs."

"That's where my *aenti* said she saw it done," he said hoarsely.

"And pink is her favorite color?"

"*Jah* . . ."

Gray watched her dip his hand into the liquid wax up to his wrist and then dip it into an adjacent pail of water. Then she moved back to the wax again. She began to speak, almost hypnotically as she moved, and her words made him bite the inside of his cheek.

"There's a romance about wax; watching it move, drip, then languidly harden . . ."

He swallowed a groan but then let his gaze move over the pale skin of her face as she worked. *She has no idea what she's doing to me . . . she's just talking about the wax. Focus on the wax . . .*

"Where did you learn to make candles?" he asked softly.

"My *mamm*—she had me rather late, you know, and spent a lot of time with me before she died. . . . Candle making and crafting, quilting and cooking . . ."

She dipped his wrist once more, then pulled his hand into the space between them. "There," she said triumphantly. "Now, this is the tricky bit—I'll just let your arm fall slowly and then I'll slip the wax free from your hand . . . like so. What do you think?"

She was turning up the edges of the wrist of the mold and set it easily on the nearby work table. He eyed the pink hand with a lifted brow.

"It's a perfect-looking hand—I guess the wax doesn't tell all of the story though, does it?"

He could have kicked himself when the smile slipped from her lips. "I'm sorry, Naomi. I—I get bitter sometimes about my—injury. I apologize."

She shook her head and reached out to tentatively touch his left shoulder. He could feel the warmth of her fingers through his shirt. "Are you bitter toward Gott, Gray?" Her dark eyes were worried and he had to look away.

"Sometimes . . ."

"I understand. I—I know it's a vanity but I've always wanted to be beautiful in some way—but Gott made me plain, as our people are sometimes. Children used to call me 'homely Naomi' and I grew bitter toward Gott—"

"Wait," he snapped. "What?"

"I became bitter and—"

"I heard that part—I mean when you said you wanted to be beautiful in some way."

"*Jah?*" Her brow wrinkled in puzzlement.

He used his left hand to lift her chin and looked hard into her eyes. "Listen to me, Naomi. Don't you know that you are beautiful—your mind, your heart, your touch—dear Gott—your touch alone makes me . . ."

He broke off when he saw the confusion on her face. *She probably thinks I'm* narrisch . . .

"Look, just don't ever let anyone tell you you're not beautiful—including yourself. How can you 'love your neighbor as yourself' when you cannot love the beauty Gott creates in you?"

She shook her head and he saw a sudden light in her dark eyes as a smile came over her face. "I've never thought of things that way before."

He had the desperate urge to kiss her, once and hard, but she wasn't a woman to take kissing lightly—he could tell. So he pulled away from her a bit roughly as the shop door opened.

Naomi felt as light as thistledown; Gray's words and reasoning made her feel good inside, but his point about Gott was truly a blessing. So the face she turned to greet Priscilla King and her children was radiant with joy.

"Someone is filled with Christmas already," Priscilla teased with a smile, her bright red hair peeking out from beneath her bonnet.

"Is it me, Momma?" her seven-year-old *dochder*, Hollie, chirped.

"*Jah*, you too, little one. Though she's not so little anymore," Priscilla laughed. "She's a great big sister to this fellow, too."

Naomi smiled down at Little Joe, who was the spitting image of his *fater*, with dark hair and big blue eyes. Her smile deepened when Gray produced a handful of sweets and offered them to the *kinner*.

"Say *danki* to Herr Fisher," Priscilla chided in gentle tones.

"Why don't I take them out for a quick snowball frolic while you ladies talk?"

Naomi saw that Gray was already pulling on his coat and was grateful. They had talked when he had started about the need to keep *kinner* away from the potential dangers of the shop in innovative ways. *And I'd love to be playing in the snow with him as well . . . he'll make a* gut fater *one day . . .* Naomi almost jumped at the thought, then felt as though the warmth of a single candle glowed inside her chest. It was enough to distract her from her customer . . .

"Um . . . what was that? I'm sorry . . ."

Priscilla laughed as the shop door closed on Gray and the children. "If I wasn't married to Joseph and he wasn't the most handsome man anywhere, I'd be looking like that, too."

Naomi swallowed, wanting to hang on to her dignity. "I don't know what you—"

Priscilla gave her an arch look. "Uh-huh."

Then Naomi giggled, a sound she had rarely heard from herself and leaned closer to Priscilla. "All right. He's *wunderbaar* and kind too . . . but I'm older and—" She stopped trying to hold on to her new sense of beauty. "I'm—"

"You're *wunderbaar* too!" Priscilla said stoutly. "Don't ever think less of yourself when there are girls like Iris Troyer on the loose!"

"She is beautiful but rather less so on the inside. . . . And, we're gossiping."

"You're right," Priscilla agreed. "Let's think of more pleasant things—like the fact that I'm here because Joseph and I are hosting a small holiday social and we want you to come. You know that Joseph's *daed* loves your *fater* and we are inviting Beth Troyer and Ned and Ted, too, of course. Which means that Gray will probably *kumme* and you two could—make it a date!"

Naomi shook her head. "I don't know, but I do love the thought. *Danki.* When is the social?"

"This coming Saturday. I'll tell Gray on the way outside and you be sure and tell your *daed.* Don't worry about bringing anything—but Gray," Priscilla laughed. "Oops! I almost forgot, I wanted to order two dozen tapers."

Naomi helped her friend with color and scent but all the while the idea of going somewhere public with Gray made her heart beat fast and hard.

Chapter 7

Gray had completed his third successful moonshine run and he wasn't about to make the mistake of becoming complacent, but tonight it was especially hard to concentrate. Priscilla King had breezed by him outside the candle shop that afternoon with a merry invitation to the upcoming social. And she hadn't made any bones about giving him a broad hint that Naomi would be going as well.

But he'd hesitated as he'd bidden the *kinner* goodbye and gone back into the shop. Naomi was a serious, smart, strong woman and she didn't deserve to have her heart broken by someone like him. But she'd looked excited and expectant when he'd turned to her after taking off his coat, and the words were out of his mouth before he could think.

"Do you want to *geh* to the social with me at the King *haus*?"

A smile had played about her lips. "Did Priscilla put you up to this?"

He'd laughed out loud and moved forward to risk stroking her hand. "*Nee,* and I have to confess that girls don't usually respond to my requests with such suspicion."

"How do they respond to you—girls, I mean?"

He hadn't missed the mingled tones of curiosity and reticence in her voice. She both wanted an answer—straight up—and she didn't want one.

"I've only had my face slapped once, if that helps you, but the truth is—I don't care about what other girls do or do not do, Naomi. I'm asking you if you'll *geh* and that's all." He'd waited, breath held, counting heartbeats, until the tension in her frame slowly eased away.

"I'd like to *geh* with you," she admitted primly and he'd had to stop touching her hand for fear of losing himself in her and the peace she brought.

But now he focused on collecting the money from the cache, then deftly wrangled Thorn around the silent, snowy mounds and headed for home— while thoughts of Naomi danced like the falling snowflakes about his head.

As the day of the Kings' social neared, Naomi grew increasingly frustrated when she searched her wardrobe for something festive to wear. In truth, most of her dresses were either brown or gray in color, which didn't seem to match Gray's personality—*Not that I should be concerned about that, but I do want to look my best* . . . She finally decided that nothing else would do but to pay a trip to Ben Kauffman's Ice Mountain general store and get some material for a new dress to wear beneath her apron.

She decided to go after work and was nervous and fidgety for the latter part of the day, not wanting Gray to know about her endeavor. But finally it was

time to close the shop, and she bade Gray a distracted *gut nacht,* then went to get her pocketbook
and bonnet as well as her long dark cape.

"We're running low on bacon, Naomi," her *fater*
called and, knowing he was hard of hearing, she
hollered a response as she left the cabin.

"*Was en der weldt* are you yelling for?" Gray asked
close beside her and she started in surprise.

"Why aren't you at home?" she demanded, feeling her face flush.

"Just hanging about, looking for something to
do. Today is when Aenti Beth usually bathes the pigs
and that's a one-woman job as far as I'm concerned.
Besides, you seemed—distant this afternoon."

"Well, I was just thinking, that's all. So . . . all
right, I'm going to Kauffman's to get some—bacon.
Bacon for Daed."

"I'll walk with you."

"You can, but you can't *kumme* into the store. I
mean, you can but you can't, if you get what I mean?"

"Huh?"

She blew out a breath of frustration. "I sound like
a twelve-year-old. Look, just don't *kumme* into the
store while I'm in there, all right?"

She watched his handsome face clear and he
grinned. "Ahhh . . . Secrets? Okay, two can play . . .
you go buy what you want and then I'll hold on for a
bit to see who's winning the checkers game. Sound
gut?"

She had to smile. "*Jah.*"

Ben's store was an aromatic feast and Naomi
paused as she entered to breathe in the peppermint,
pine, cinnamon, and the myriad other scents that
made her think of Christmas. Ben loved to give the
local homemakers a chance to sell their wares, so

baskets of oranges stuffed with cloves, small houses made of cinnamon sticks, and brightly polished sleigh bells stitched onto leather straps all added to the merriment and excitement of the place.

Even at this late hour, the store bustled with business and conversation, leaving Naomi feeling rather at a loss. She was typically a homebody and did most of her socializing with people as they came to the candle shop. And, of course she shopped, but she preferred to do it during the evening hours, when there were fewer folks about. But the season would have its way and she decided she might as well join in the jolliness of it all as she made for the dry goods counter.

Ben Kauffman, the store owner, was a big, burly man with a kind heart. His numerous children ran about, helping in various capacities, but it was Ben himself who called out a greeting to her as he rang things up behind the large counter at the back.

"*Ach*, Naomi—our sweet lady of the candles— what is it you need? Fabric? Josiah will see to ya! Next!"

Josiah was a towheaded *buwe* of about ten— Naomi always lost track of the ages of the Kauffman *kinner*. But the *buwe* had his *fater*'s knack for selling and a charming, easy attitude with the customers so that Naomi felt as if she was being waited on by a cheery elf.

"You're wanting to make something new, Miss Naomi? I always think ladies with dark hair and eyes look *gut* in forest green. What do you think?"

"I think that you have better style sense than I, Josiah! *Jah*, let me see some greens, *sei se gut.*"

The *buwe* climbed the stepladder with nimble feet and slid two subtly different bolts of material off one of the higher shelves. Then he plunked them down on the wooden counter, which was notched with measurements, and opened a fold of each.

Naomi put her fingers out to touch the colors and bit her lip. "I don't know—perhaps these would do for someone a bit younger . . ."

She was nervous of drawing too much attention to herself and glanced wistfully up at the solid browns on the shelves. Josiah must have followed her gaze, because he gave a gay little chortle that seemed to make nonsense of her fears.

"Younger? Why, you're as young as your toenails, my *grossdaudi* often says—not that I know what's young about toenails, and I probably shouldn't say that to a lady, but you are young, ma'am."

Naomi gave in to this convoluted reasoning and nodded with a smile. "My toenails choose the forest green. *Danki*, Josiah."

The *buwe* nodded, brushed the other green aside and set to work deftly, his sharp shears cutting to her specifications.

She had paid for her purchase and had it nicely wrapped in brown paper when she remembered the bacon. Josiah had disappeared into the bustle of the crowd and she decided she'd *kumme* back the next day for the meat. She turned, intent on leaving, when she ran full-on into Iris Troyer. Iris was petite, making Naomi feel awkwardly tall, but she steadied the other girl and moved to pass her.

There was a glint in Iris's menacing blue eyes that Naomi remembered from school days. She wanted to avoid it, to get back outside to where Gray waited, but Iris spoke in a overbearing tone.

"Why, Naomi Gish—out so late? I've heard that Gray Fisher has taken up working for you—you sly girl. Is that why you're changing your muddy ward-robe for something green? *Ach,* I saw you buy the fabric. I think it's a little too late to be doing something so different with what you wear, don't you?"

Naomi squashed the sudden urge she felt to belt the blond-haired twit, then giggled aloud at the unusual idea. Iris was clearly not pleased to find that her barbs held no poison this *nacht,* as Naomi smiled down into her beautiful, but cruel, face. "I don't know what you're talking about, Iris, but if you're feeling especially sour, I bet Ben's got a lemon you might suck on to match your disposition. *Gut nacht!*"

Naomi felt a rush of adrenaline as she heard a few giggles behind her, knowing that folks were laughing with her and not at her. It was exhilarating and she fairly danced out the door to find Gray leaning against the porch rail in the deepening dusk.

"You look radiant," Gray observed. "I never knew bacon buying could be so much fun."

Naomi laughed. "I forgot the bacon but I just did something wonderfully bad."

She stepped lightly down the steps and he abandoned the store, following her, much intrigued.

"Well, are you going to tell me?" he asked. "And I can't imagine you doing anything very much bad . . . Did you taste a frosted grape without paying for it?"

"*Nee.*" She smiled up at him.

"Pull *auld* Ben Kauffman's beard? You know they say it's fake."

She laughed. "Nope."

"All right, then I give up."

She stopped and turned to face him, her smile wide and entrancing. "I told off Iris Troyer."

Gray stilled and swallowed. "Iris . . ."

She must have caught the look on his face because she stopped smiling and immediately put out a hand to touch his arm. "*Ach,* Gray, I'm sorry. Perhaps she's a friend of yours?"

"A friend . . . *nee.*" *But I've had my tongue in her mouth and now I deeply regret it . . . What a fool I've been.*

"*Ach, gut!*" Naomi exclaimed. "You looked strange for a moment. . . . Well, I'd best head home. I'll see you tomorrow." She dropped her hand from his sleeve and walked off with a shy, backward smile.

Chapter 8

Gray smiled back at her but felt sick in his soul. He had never had his sins illuminated so brightly as he did in the dusk of that *nacht* and it shook him. He started the walk home, thinking hard. He'd never considered that his callous behavior with other women might possibly hurt the one he finally came to love . . . *To love—am I* narrisch? *Naomi—I love her? I don't even know her . . .*

But he could not deny the resonating peace he felt in body, mind, and soul when he was with her. If this was love, it was a true gift. And love's peace— *Ach, it's as close as Gott, as mysterious as Ice Mountain itself, and something I know I can share with her forever . . .*

He entered Aenti Beth's *haus* and excused himself from supper, saying he didn't feel like eating much.

Aenti Beth eyed him intently as did Ned and Ted. "What's wrong with you, Gray?" she asked.

He shook his head, wanting to be alone with his thoughts but then something occurred to him. "Aenti Beth, do you think Gott wounds us for our sins?"

"Wounds?" Her *auld* blue eyes narrowed. "You mean like your arm?"

Gray nodded slowly. "Maybe . . . yeah."

Aenti Beth put her hands on her ample hips. "Well now, the only place I can think of wounding is that Bible verse that talks about Derr Herr being wounded for the things we have done wrong . . . He is wounded for us, not the other way around. Yer arm—*jah,* a loss, but Gott will yet bring ya joy, *buwe.* You watch and see."

Gray half smiled, then moved to catch his *aenti* and the pigs in a massive hug. "I love you," he whispered over the hump of Ned's body beside her aged ear.

She pushed him away after a minute, her eyes damp. "Go on with ya now, Gray. You'll have me droppin' tears in the stew . . . I love ya too, *buwe.* Don't ever forget it."

"You have my word, Aenti Beth."

He mounted the steps to his room, feeling better in his spirit and renewed in his soul at the idea of loving Naomi. *Now the question becomes,* he thought as he undressed, *could she ever love me?*

Naomi spread the forest green fabric out on her bedroom floor. She knelt down, resting on her heels, and chewed her lips thoughtfully as she considered the making of the dress. There was the liberty in her community to make sleeves a bit more puffy with pleats and she wondered if she dared to try it.

She was an excellent seamstress, thanks to her *mamm*'s training, and she knew she could have the piece ready by Saturday if she took time to stay up and sew each evening. In the end, she decided on the puffed sleeves, and, after cutting out the basic shapes and starting on the basting, she went to bed, exhausted but satisfied in the extreme.

"I tell you, Bud—I've got to stop," Gray whispered.

It was early morning and the two men were standing in Naomi's kitchen pantry. Gray was having a tough time trying to convince his moonshining employer that he wanted out.

"But why?" Bud shook his head. "Ye've got things down; it's *gut* money. What more do ya want?"

"Out. I can't explain why right now but I need to stop. And you should too. For your *dochder*'s sake."

Bud glared up at him. "Don't lecture me on my fatherly duties. . . . All right, you want out, but at least do the run Saturday *nacht* after the social. It'll be the last—I promise ya."

Gray sighed. "Fine. It's a deal."

"What's a deal?" Naomi asked and Gray started just as the *auld* man beside him did.

"Uh—I told your *daed* that I could make a better egg-and-bacon sandwich than he could, any day, hands down. And he wanted me to try," Gray said with a warning glance at Bud.

"Why are you both holed up in my pantry? I think there's more than egg sandwiches going on . . ." Naomi put her hands on her trim hips and Gray stepped forward to catch her arm and lead her back to the kitchen while Bud harrumphed around in the pantry.

"I just got to work a little early, that's all—now how about letting me fix breakfast?" He didn't mean to do it but the gesture came naturally to him and he bent forward and kissed her gently. "Please, Naomi?" he whispered.

He saw the dazed look in her eyes and wondered at it, but then she nodded. "*Jah* . . . egg . . . sandwiches . . ."

"Great," he said. "Now do you have any fresh mayonnaise?"

Later, inside the candle shop, Naomi glanced at Gray with a puzzled look on her face.

"What is it?" he asked.

"I'm just trying to hold on to how it felt."

"How what felt?"

She sighed, knowing he was concentrating on dipping green tapers into melted wax. *Probably he kisses girls all the time . . . Probably it meant nothing and I'm being silly and—*

"How what felt?" he asked again, this time moving to stand close to her.

"Uh . . . well, my first kiss."

"Your first—"

"You know. Maybe you don't remember, but you kissed me this morning before breakfast. That was my first kiss."

She couldn't understand the expression on his face or why his gray eyes widened as if there was a storm brewing in them.

"That was your first kiss?" he asked hoarsely.

"Mmm-hmmm. And I thank you for it." She felt shy and skittish as if her words were inadequate.

He came around the counter and stepped very near her, so close that she could smell his soap and that intangible scent that was uniquely Gray . . .

"That was not your first kiss," he said, staring down at her.

"But it was . . ."

He lifted his left hand to run a tan finger down the fragile bones in her cheek. "*Nee,*" he whispered. "I promise you, Naomi, that I can do much, much better at kissing . . . Please let me have another try."

"*Ach . . .*" She felt the pattern of her breathing change as her heart fluttered in her throat.

He bent his head and she instinctively closed her eyes. "Don't," he muttered.

"What? I—"

"Don't close your eyes. Look at me."

Somehow, he was even closer, rocking his lean hips forward, pressing hard against her.

She felt awkward and vulnerable staring up into his eyes. She raised her hands to his arms to steady herself and then his mouth was on hers—a whisper of a touch—but she sensed somehow that he wanted much more and the thought sent a shiver of excitement coursing down her spine.

"Relax," he breathed and she swallowed hard and gave a little half bob of her head. And then he was kissing her with all of the pent-up intensity that she could imagine; slanting his head, teasing her, teaching her, until she responded in a way that drew a harsh sound of pleasure from the back of his throat and she knew instinctively that he was as much aroused by the whole adventure as she was. . . .

He suddenly remembered the day he'd rescued her from those play yard bullies and marveled that he'd never realized she was that sweet girl before this. Somehow, Gott had kept those memories hidden from his mind and Gray thought how strong and brave she was—so much of everything he hoped for and believed in—even when he couldn't be those things himself. . . .

Chapter 9

She pulled away from Gray hastily and looked up as the door to the shop opened and in blew a large, unfamiliar customer along with the swirling snow. The man was not Amisch but wore a dark brown parka with a huge furred hood.

"Candle shop, right?" his voice boomed.

Naomi was about to reply when Gray's voice cut in sharply. "It is but who's asking?"

The big man laughed and threw back the hood of his parka to reveal long, well-combed brown hair and a giant moustache that curled at the ends. His blue eyes shone brightly in his craggy face and when he smiled, Naomi found herself smiling too.

"Name's Gabe. And you must be Naomi and Gray, right?"

Naomi nodded, though she noticed that Gray still seemed suspicious. But she spoke up cheerfully. "What can we do to help you—uh, Gabe?"

"Need a candle. Big. Bayberry. In time for Christmas. Think you can do it?"

"You mean bayberry scented, of course?" she asked.

"Nope. Has to be the real thing. I can promise that your payment will be . . . great."

"It's not that. Real bayberries in the amount needed to make a large candle are simply next to impossible to find."

"They usually grow by the sea," Gray offered and Naomi nodded in surprise at his knowledge.

"*Jah*, and Ice Mountain is far from the sea, as you can tell. And it normally takes six to eight pounds of berries to make one pound of wax—nearly impossible, I'm afraid."

Gabe laughed. "I say all things are possible with Gott—that's what you call Him, right?"

"Yes, but . . ."

"Good. I'll expect it delivered on Christmas Eve. I'm staying in the small hunting cabin above the cemetery over aways."

"That could be rough travel if it snows," Gray said.

Gabe waved a big hand in dismissal.

"The weather will hold. So, I'll be seeing you then. Thanks." He turned, pulled up his hood and was gone out the door before Naomi could get another word in about the problem of making the candle.

"Well, what do you think of that?" she exclaimed after a few moments.

"The guy's *narrisch*."

"But we have to try . . . maybe he wants it for his wife or *dochder* or . . . sweetheart."

Gray smiled cheerfully. He had apparently forgotten the passionate kissing they had been doing before the strange candle order.

"You're sweet, Naomi Gish. That's what. And you're also the boss. So if you want a real bayberry candle, that's what we'll make."

"Even if the customer is *narrisch?*" she teased.

"Even then."

"You *geh* on and pick up the gal. Me and the pigs will get there just fine."

Gray smiled as he surveyed Ned and Ted, their small, plump bodies suitably clad in cheery red-and-green matching outfits. And Aenti Beth looked *gut* as well; her blue eyes snapped with life and her cheeks were rosy.

Gray bent and kissed her. "You look *wunderbaar.*"

She giggled like a young girl. "*Geh* on now, Gray Fisher. Save yer pretty words fer someone like Naomi."

"All right. I will. I'll see you there."

He went outside to the small barn, led Thorn from his stall, and hitched up the sleigh. Priscilla and Joe's *haus* was within easy walking distance but he felt like making the ride special for Naomi, and the sleigh bells were merry.

He arrived at the Gish *haus* and went through the dark candle shop to knock on the doorframe of the main home. The burgundy curtain was closed and he waited, his heart thudding fast as he heard Naomi's quick footsteps *kumme* to open it.

"Hello," she said calmly, even though her cheeks were flushed with hectic color.

"Hello, you look beautiful." The words would have *kumme* easily to his lips with any other girl but now he felt the weight of their truth as he surveyed her bright brown eyes, the shiny parted brown hair beneath her *kapp,* and the rich green dress she wore beneath her black apron.

She bit her lip and looked up at him, accepting his compliment with a demure grace that was enchanting. "*Ach,* you look handsome as well—as always, I should say."

He reached out and took her hand. "Where's your *daed?*"

"Daed? *Ach,* still looking for socks without holes in them and that match."

"*Gut,*" he whispered.

"*Gut?*"

"*Jah,* because now we can do this . . ." He bent his head to kiss her and he was shaken by her ready response. She kissed him with a novice enthusiasm that brought the now-familiar peace of her roaring through his ears. He was somewhere on the top of Ice Mountain, winter winds whipping in clean strikes, and he was free so long as he was touching her, drinking of her and all that she was.

"Naomi?" The call was plaintive and she pulled away to answer her *fater.*

"*Jah,* Daed?"

Gray was pleased that there was a slight quiver in her voice and was glad to know that she was at least shaken a bit, while he had to hold on to the doorframe to keep from touching her.

"I need socks!"

"Excuse me, *sei se gut,* Gray. I—I'll be right back."

He smiled and nodded, about all he was capable of doing in the state he was in. He knew that the evening held special promise.

* * *

Abner King's *haus* was a sprawling place now that Joseph had added on to the original cabin to accommodate his growing family, and by the time Naomi and Gray had arrived, the *haus* was packed with members of the King family and their *kinner*. Naomi let Gray take her cloak and waited shyly until he hung up his coat. Then she turned in surprise to see that Gray wore a matching forest green shirt and she couldn't contain her blush. In their Amisch community, usually only spouses or courting couples wore matching colors to social events so she had no idea what people would think.

"Let them think what they like," Gray whispered to her cheerfully. "They might not be far off in their pondering."

Naomi was still trying to figure out what his enigmatic words might mean when Priscilla came forward to greet them. "Matching colors? I'm not saying anything but here's some punch for both of you. Your *Aenti* Beth and Ned and Ted are enjoying entertaining everyone with my *fater*-in-law and your *daed*."

She glanced over to where the three older folks had holed up by the woodstove, telling stories to any and all who would listen and share their laughter. Children raced in between the longer legs of their elders and the skirts of the ladies, and Naomi had to laugh when Priscilla grabbed one little scallywag up, squirming, into her arms. He was one of Sarah and Edward King's little *buwes* and his antics as he tried to escape his *aenti*'s hold were comical.

From there, Naomi and Gray were absorbed into the family circle to enjoy a buffet of baked ham, mashed potatoes, sweet corn, sweet potatoes, and more gingerbread cookies in multiple shapes than could be counted.

The evening went by too fast and Naomi could barely stop laughing and talking on the ride home when she noticed that Gray had grown quiet. "Is—is everything all right, Gray?"

"Hmm? Sure. It was a great time. The Kings are a wonderful family."

Naomi felt that there was something wrong and immediately had to resist going down the familiar sled path of believing it had something to do with her or her being inadequate somehow. He must have realized how she felt because he turned to her then and smiled as he managed the sleigh. "Nothing's wrong, sweetheart. I was just thinking of what it would be like to have such a large family—*kinner* all over and a wife to cherish."

Naomi spoke wistfully. "I know—I expect it would be such fun, especially at holidays and in the summer. Daed can get pretty boring sometimes as company. . . . Did—did you just call me sweetheart?" She savored the word, turning it over and back in her mind. "You say it so easily," she went on when he didn't immediately reply. "You say it to a lot of girls, don't you?"

He sighed aloud and she could feel the tension radiating from his big frame. "I am what I've been, Naomi. A rake, a scoundrel—all the bad things you could think to hurl at my head—I've probably been and done those deeds. But you make me feel—different."

"Is that *gut*?"

"Oh, you have no idea how *gut*, Naomi Gish. I—think I could be brand-new with you—with how

Derr Herr works through you . . . but again, I'm not exactly the kind of man a woman would—"

He broke off when Thorn floundered into a drift. "I'll have to lead him out . . . I've got some straw in the back to make the way less slippery. I'll be right back."

But it took a good half hour to get the horse out and by then she knew their conversation had been lost to the icy *nacht* air . . .

Chapter 10

Gray wasn't happy with himself as he waited at the usual bridge spot at midnight after the party. He felt like a cheat and knew that sometime soon he'd have to tell Naomi about the moonshine and even about girls like Iris Troyer, who thankfully, wasn't a close friend of the King family and had not been at the party. He had no doubt that Iris would take great pleasure in wounding Naomi by telling her about their barn meetings and he wanted to avoid that if he could. He slowly realized that loving someone meant wanting more for them than you could ever imagine—the agape love that Gott spoke of in the Bible—selfless and patient.

Thorn grew restless and Gray gauged that it was time and slid off the horse to take up the satchels and move forward toward the bridge. He'd grown accustomed to the shadows in the area and reached to place the moonshine carefully in its regular spot, prepared to take the money, which was usually delivered in its own oil cloth wrapping.

He felt around in the dark but couldn't locate any parcel. He sighed in frustration and decided to take the risk of lighting a candle. His heart had begun to pound and he half expected to see a state trooper waiting for him in the dark, but instead there was a fairly large gray wooden box.

He wondered who would take the time to nail their payment shut in a box and moved to try to open it.

"I'll need a crow bar," he muttered aloud, extinguishing the candle.

The box was also heavy and he decided to leave the liquor and get a rope around the crate. He used Thorn to drag the box a safe distance from the drop area, and then he managed to pry it open with his knife. He lit a second candle and stared into the box.

He could find no rational explanation for what he saw and knew he'd have some strange explaining to do with Bud. . . .

Naomi paced the confines of her bedroom, idly brushing out her hair, then stopping every few steps to consider the very real fact that Gray seemed to like to kiss her. It felt miraculous, but then, so did the feelings she had when she looked at him. It wasn't only his good looks; *nee,* there was something else that played upon her heart and mind and made her think of *kinner* and laughter and a willingness to share hurt and sorrow with him as well—throughout all of life . . . *All of life . . . A life of love . . .* The thoughts held wonder, and her bare toes found a crack in the hardwood floor and she jumped—simply for the fun of it. She landed softly and was about to continue her play when a thud from the vicinity of the candle shop seemed to echo back to her.

She immediately put her brush on the dresser and crept from her room. She could hear her *fater* snoring on the couch and moved toward the long burgundy curtain. She never locked the door to the shop—she couldn't really because it closed with a simple latch. Now, from the sound of it, someone was definitely fooling with the door. She gathered her courage and muttered a prayer under her breath, then thrust the curtain aside.

"Gray," she exclaimed as she recognized his tall shape in the gloom.

"Sorry, Naomi. I hoped to leave before waking you."

She lit a candle and moved to his side. "What are you doing out here at this hour?"

Then she noticed the open crate on the floor and got down on her knees to peer into the box. "Bayberries! Pounds of them," she cried. "Wherever did you get them?"

She looked up at him and they both seemed to realize at the same time that she was wearing only a flannel *nacht* gown, and her hair was spread about her like a brown curtain, spilling over his boots. He caught her beneath the elbow and pulled her to her feet next to him, and she shivered with excitement and the cold that radiated off his heavy black coat. . . .

He took the candle from her and placed it in a holder on the counter. Then he pulled her up close against him. "You're cold," he murmured as he bent to smell the fresh rose scent of her hair.

"And you sent for bayberries for that man's order—Gabe."

Gray shook his head and nuzzled her neck. "*Nee,* the bayberries were simply—provided. I can't explain it any other way." *Dear Gott, how I want to hold her like this forever; feel her wax and wane, her belly full of my child, knowing her peace* . . . But she was cold and he decided he'd lost his wits out in the blowing snow.

He began to put her from him when she made a soft feminine sound of protest that he couldn't resist. He bent his back and pulled her against him once more with his left arm, wanting her closeness even through the thick layers of wool that separated them. He found her mouth, and, for the first time, he traced the line of her closed lips with his tongue tip and she moaned softly in response. He wanted to take, taste, drink of her but, in her innocence she didn't know what to do and this chided him more than any rebuke.

He let her go then and had to steady her as she bobbled on uncertain legs.

"Why did you stop?" she asked in a small voice. "Was I—did I do it wrong?"

"*Nee,*" he said hoarsely. "It was perfect, but I can't take advantage of you in your *nacht* dress and with your hair down as only your husband should see one day."

He didn't understand the way she lowered her head, as if in defeat, and then she was gone—scampering through the burgundy curtain, leaving him alone in the shadows . . .

* * *

Naomi had prayed during the nighttime and had determined to put aside the feelings she had for Gray even as she set about the preparations for creating the bayberry candle together.

He came into work quietly, while she was boiling the blue-gray berries in a large pot. "Are you making the candle for Gabe?" he asked in a subdued tone.

"*Nee,*" she replied briskly. "We're going to make it together. I'm boiling the berries and if you come here, you can see that the heather-colored berries give off a pale green wax that floats to the surface." She ran her skimmer across the top of the steaming kettle and lifted the bits of wax to show him.

He nodded, then put his much larger hand over hers gently so that they held the skimming spoon as one. "Naomi, about last *nacht*... I wanted to—I shouldn't have—"

"I understand completely," she lied, trying not to notice how nice his hand felt on hers, but then he moved away a bit and she had to refocus on the wax. "We'll let it cool down and harden once more and then we can start on the candle itself." She busied herself arranging some tapers while they waited and noticed that he simply stood, watching her.

Then she went back to the wax and wicking material. "We can each dip one part of the main candle."

"So, the final product will be like a twisting together?" he asked.

"*Jah*—I thought it might be pretty, and bayberry burns very slowly so it should last for years if Gabe and whomever he gives it to only use it during the Christmas season."

She couldn't ignore how the scent of the bayberry wax, something like pine and blackberries blended together, filled the air and lifted her spirits. "It smells like Christmas," she finally had to say.

She didn't want to see his slow smile or the dimple in his cheek, but she couldn't look away either.

"So it does."

He stepped closer to where the vat of wax and berries was cooling and ran his finger over the surface of the warm wax. Without missing a beat, he turned to her and dabbed it on her cheek.

He moved back as if to consider the mark and she flicked her fingers in the wax, both surprising herself and splattering his burgundy shirt with fast-drying droplets of wax.

"Tit for tat." He grinned and she felt herself blush when he caught her close against him.

"Gray," she protested weakly, knowing she had no true desire to resist him.

"Praise Gott that you know how to play, sweet Naomi, but I want to play a bit too." He put his mouth to her cheek, where the wax was, and licked around the small perimeter until she couldn't think of anything but him and the heavy intent of his body.

She reached her arms around his shoulders and stood on tiptoe to receive his burning kiss, then remembered the wax and closed her eyes—wanting to forget about work and duty and promises and simply be alive with him. But, in the end, they created a twelve-inch-high candle with a flat bottom and flat top so that it stood upright on its own; a sturdy, entwined, beautiful work of art with two wicks . . .

He was haunted for the rest of the day by the remembrance of their work together. As he trudged home through the snow, he realized that Naomi was a woman, not only of character, but of creative energy, wit, and play. And he wanted to court her. But he had no idea if he could risk the asking.

"How's the candle shop?"

Gray had been thinking so hard that he nearly ran full tilt into Bishop Umble, who seemed to materialize out of nowhere in the snow.

"Uh—the shop is *gut*. Really *gut*."

"And how are you, Gray?" the Bishop asked with a benign smile.

Gray sighed. He had no desire to make social conversation but he also knew that the *auld* man was not simply asking about his health and the weather. *Nee*, the *gut* Bishop wanted a deeper answer and wouldn't settle for less.

"I'm screwed up—to put it bluntly."

The bishop nodded. "Why is that?"

Here we geh . . . *the part where I bare my soul, or worse yet, don't, but Bishop Umble still manages to make me think things are okay or something* . . . "I am probably a mess because of my arm, the fact that my parents abandoned me—I made out with too many girls; I was running moonshine, and I want to court Naomi Gish."

"But the latter is doubtful because of all the former?"

"Right."

Bishop Umble smiled. "Well then, I have a radical solution."

"What's that?"

"Tell Naomi the truth."

Gray stared at him, aghast. "I'd lose her or any chance with her."

"Mmmm—maybe. But evil has no power against the truth. Remember that. Telling the truth is incredibly freeing but also liberating and the two are not always the same thing."

"Uh huh . . ."

"Liberty is won," the bishop mused. "But true freedom can only be found in the truth of Gott." Gray considered this weighty thought and finally nodded with reluctance. "I'll ask her *fater* if he'll let me court her. He might say *nee* anyway."

Bishop Umble clapped him on the shoulder. "The truth, *sohn*. Remember."

"Right. The truth . . ."

Chapter 11

Naomi decided to set out early the next morning to cut some greenery for the shop windows. There was a fine nip in the air and snow blew lightly about her cheeks and nose, making her feel young and carefree. She drew her heavy pair of work shears from the sheath and bent to cut at the lower branches of a tall fir.

"Well, well . . ." a feminine voice purred nearby. "Who have we here?"

Naomi straightened abruptly, having thought herself alone in the woods so early in the day. She looked at Iris Troyer and blinked.

"Where's Gray?" Iris asked with a smirk. "I would have thought he'd be with you just about every place you *geh.*"

"Why would you think that?"

The other girl's eyes flashed, full of malice. "Word gets around. I heard you two wore matching colors to Abner King's get-together."

Naomi could not contain the flush that came to her cheeks but she kept her voice level. "So? I think

I'd better get on and find some more greenery—if you'll excuse me." She turned to go but Iris's words halted her steps.

"Has he kissed you?"

Naomi wet her lips and turned slowly back around. "It's really none of your business—"

"*Ach,* but I think it is, Homely Naomi."

The taunt straightened Naomi's spine and she clutched the shears she held tighter. "What do you want, Iris?"

The other girl shrugged. "Not much . . . Did he use his tongue like he normally does? All hot and sweet? It's really amazing how he can kiss—"

"That's enough, Iris." Naomi heard the quiver in her own words and wanted to run.

"I suppose it is . . . *Ach,* but he told me all about you and we laughed together. Kissing the homely candle shop owner—just to make her holiday season perfect. It really is funny, don't you think?"

Naomi whirled and gave in to the urge to move. She dropped the piece of greenery she held and ran back through the snow with Iris's laughter echoing in her ears.

"You want to court my girl?" Bud Gish was still half asleep and Gray chafed at having to repeat himself again.

"*Jah,* I want to court Naomi."

The two men were standing in the kitchen of the Gish cabin. Gray had waited as long as he could that dawn before trekking over to see Bud. He wanted to talk with the older man while Naomi was still asleep. Gray had thought a lot about the Bishop's words the day before and knew he wanted to share with Naomi a chance for real peace and happiness through truth.

Bud scratched his right ear. "So, you ain't runnin' 'shine no more, but the candle shop cover caught you my little *maedel* . . . I don't know what to say—"

"Well I do." Naomi's voice cracked like ice and Gray spun round to see her standing in the open kitchen doorway.

"Naomi, *sei se gut*, let me explain . . ." Gray began in desperation.

"*Nee*," she snapped, her chest heaving. She pointed at him. "You—get out!"

Gray saw that there would be no reasoning with her in that moment and slowly stepped across the kitchen.

Bud spoke up lamely. "It was I who talked him into it, Naomi."

Gray saw her brown eyes flash, then darken. "Well, that makes it all the worse." She stiffly stepped aside and Gray slid past her, wondering if he was losing her forever.

The days dragged by and Naomi struggled to do her work at the candle shop. She missed Gray dreadfully but each time she thought of his kisses and kindness, Iris Troyer's mocking words came back to haunt her. And then there was the moonshining . . . At the very least, she'd managed to *kumme* to peace with her *fater* when he'd sought to break the silence between them one morning in the kitchen.

"Dochder, with the Christmas season approaching us, can ya not find it in yer heart to have a bit of forgiveness toward an *auld* and tired man?"

Naomi had blown out a breath of sad exasperation because she knew she could not keep ignoring her *fater* forever. Gray, though, she'd thought with a sniff, was an entirely different matter . . .

"All right, Daed," she'd said, turning from the pump sink to face him. "Did you think me so stupid that I would not eventually find out? How could you do that to me?"

Her *fater*'s eyes had welled with tears and he'd rubbed his hands together fretfully. "I be deeply sorry, Naomi. I was ashamed of my own age—that I couldn't run 'shine like I used to and in that shame I hurt the one most dear to me."

A rueful smile came to her lips. She knew her *fater* loved her and that getting *aulder* must be no easy thing. In the end, she'd opened her arms to him and rejoiced in his bashful hug even as she mourned the loss of Gray.

Gray missed his work at the candle shop and a dozen times over would have tried to *geh* and explain to Naomi about his moonshining but felt in his heart that she was most likely far from wanting to see his face after the deception. So he went through his days and *nachts* automatically; not sleeping and heavy of heart.

One early morning, he was in the barn, muttering morosely to Thorn as he took care of chores, when a small sound made him stand up in sudden wariness. Iris Troyer stood just inside the sliding door and he frowned as she came toward him.

"Iris, I'm sorry but it's not a *gut* time."

She pressed boldly against him with wanton intent despite his cool tone. "*Ach,* but I can make it a *gut* time for you, Gray. You know I can."

"Iris, please—"

She stepped away from him and stamped a foot, making a display of putting her hands on her hips. "Please what, Gray Fisher? Please act as if I've got a poker up my back like your Homely Naomi does?" She gave him a small smirk. "I told her about us."

He blinked. "You what?"

"I told her that I knew how well you could kiss and that we enjoyed laughing at her stupid—"

She took a quick step backward and Gray knew his face showed the anger he felt.

"*Geh*," he said, low and harsh. Iris pursed her lips, then fled to the barn door, hastening to slide it closed behind her.

Gray understood now that the blow dealt to Naomi had been twofold and his heart ached for her. He knelt down in the straw of the cold barn and began to pray that Gott would intercede in Naomi's life and his with the light of a miracle.

Chapter 12

Christmas Eve day dawned with the advent of a powerful snowstorm settling over Ice Mountain. Gray went about his morning chores thinking deeply. When the old windup clock struck noon, he finished his dinner with haste, then turned to Aenti Beth.

"I've got something I need to do."

"Well, do it then, *buwe*. We've had it up to our ears with your moping about." The *auld* woman smiled softly at him and Ted gave a tender chirp.

Gray laughed for the first time in days. He bent to kiss her cheek, then pulled on his coat and hat. He turned up the collar of the black wool and went out into the breath-stealing blur of white. He turned determined steps to the barn and hitched up Thorn to a small cutter sleigh.

"All right, *buwe*. We've got a lady to catch . . ."

It took a precious half hour to make it to the candle shop but when he got Thorn under cover, Gray smiled in the blowing cold to see several candles, like halos in the dark of the storm, beckoning him on.

He knocked on the door and was nearly blown into the shop when Naomi lifted the latch.

"What are you doing here?" she demanded while he drew in harsh breaths of warm air.

"Taking you to that *narrisch* guy Gabe's cabin." He held up a hand when she opened her mouth to protest.

"I know. I know—I'm scum and a liar and a cheat but I'm not about to let you deliver that candle alone in a storm as bad as this. And don't bother telling me you weren't about to *geh*. I know you, Naomi Gish, and you've got the wrapped candle right there."

"I—I wanted to burn it, melt it down. I suppose I should have. . . ." Her words drifted off and the pain in her voice lanced through him.

Still, he hadn't *kumme* to try to reason with her so he kept his voice brisk. "Bundle up. It's going to be a cold ride."

He watched her as she hesitated, praying inside that she'd agree to *geh* with him. He exhaled when she nodded and moved past him to take her cloak from the peg near the door.

"Take your *daed*'s coat too. It's freezing out." He reached out his left hand to help her with the garment but she whirled away, clearly not wanting him to touch her.

Gray ignored her anger and helped her into the sleigh; then he folded his long legs to get in beside her. The cutter sleigh was meant for courting and Gray could not help feeling her pressed against his side, even through the bulk of their outer things.

"Remember that Gabe said the weather would hold," he practically had to yell over the blowing wind.

"It is holding—right at storm level," Naomi called back and Gray rejoiced in her small bit of humor.

"Are you all right?" he hollered every few minutes to her, not wanting her to fall asleep in the treacherous cold.

He felt her nod against his shoulder, then returned his attention to Thorn as the horse nearly floundered in a big dip, but the gelding hefted himself up and soon they had finally reached the hunting cabin above the Amisch cemetery. But to Gray's surprise, no welcoming candle or lantern shone in any of the windows of the *auld* place. In fact, even through the blur of the storm, the cabin looked deserted. He hopped out of the sleigh and went around to help Naomi out and lead her to the shelter of the porch. She clutched the carefully wrapped bayberry candle in her arms.

"I've got to get Thorn under shelter."

"I'll *geh* inside."

Gray helped her to the door and felt the latch give, then hurried back to the gelding, reluctant to leave Naomi alone . . .

Naomi realized that the cabin was deserted and sighed to herself. Carefully, stretching her cold fingers, she unwrapped the bayberry candle and placed it on what she thought was a table top. The white blur from the windows did nothing to aid her vision. Then she reached in her apron pocket and found her ever-present pack of matches. She lit the thick green candle's two wicks, then stepped back to eye the light dispassionately as the contours of the small cabin were revealed. She had no desire to be trapped in the snow with Gray. In truth, if she could have, she would have run. She couldn't face his lies and excuses.

She steeled her resolve as the door opened and Gray almost fell inside with a good bit of snow. She glanced at the candle, but the twin flames held despite the sudden burst of wind. She looked away when he took his hat off and began to pull off his coat. "So, no Gabe, it appears," he murmured. "But the candle smells *gut.*"

Naomi made no comment. She could not deny that the rich, aromatic scent stealing across the cabin was wonderful, but her heart was still broken.

"Naomi, I need to talk to you," Gray began and she shook her head.

"I don't want to hear it, Grayson Fisher. We will wait out the storm and *geh* back. That's all."

"Iris Troyer told me what she said to you."

Naomi felt unwanted tears spring to her eyes but said nothing.

She heard Gray sigh deeply. "*Jah,* Iris was someone I kissed, but it meant nothing in truth. I fooled around with girls to try to forget the pain in my life. But I never, ever spoke of you, Naomi. I never laughed at you. I give you my word, for what it's worth."

Naomi kept her focus on the twin flames of the candle and ignored the teardrop that slipped, unheeded, down her cheek. But Gray didn't . . . Suddenly he was right beside her, his lean fingers wiping away her tears.

"Don't," she gasped but he let his hand trail downward to find the contours of her neck and shoulder.

Even through the damp layers she wore, his touch sent her heart soaring, but she did not want to believe him.

"Don't touch, Naomi?" he whispered huskily. "*Ach*, but I cannot imagine ever stopping . . . not when the feel of you brings me peace inside such as I've never known. Peace, Naomi. Something I would never find with anyone else."

"You don't know that." The words had slipped out before she could help it and she saw his small smile out of the corner of her eye.

"I know it, and I can think of no better place than a candlelit room, smelling like Christmas, to tell you that I love you, Naomi. You are beautiful and so smart and so wise and there's a storm of peace raging inside of me that only you can create, sweet Naomi. A storm that rivals the one out there . . ."

Something flickered in her heart, fanned by the truth she heard at the center of his words. She half turned and looked up into the light of his gray eyes.

"I love you too," she said simply and she felt his big body shake as he rocked forward and pressed his legs into her. She bobbled off balance for a moment and bumped the table. Gray watched the large candle tip and start to fall, headed directly for her long skirts. He grabbed the candle without thinking, then set it back on the table.

"Gray!" she gasped.

"What? It's fine."

"*Nee* . . . you used your right hand. You used your right arm!"

He heard her words as if from far away and stared down at his right hand as he flexed his fingers with relative ease. He remembered with clarity Gabe's words . . . *"Your payment will be great"* . . . Then he looked into Naomi's peace-washed eyes and knew that the true miracle was her love for him.

Epilogue

One Year Later
Christmas Eve

"Is she asleep?" Gray whispered as Naomi returned from peeking into the small cradle that was warmly ensconced in the corner of their bedroom.

"For now." Naomi smiled, her face illuminated by the glow of the bayberry candle that sat on their bedside table.

Gray made room for her in the bed to snuggle close and he couldn't help but smile as he pressed his mouth against her neck, loving her shiver of delight. "You know, your *daed* told me he'd like a boy babe next time. . . ."

"He'll take what he gets," she said practically and Gray had to smile.

"Mistress of the candles of Ice Mountain and mistress of my heart, I love you, Naomi Fisher."

"I know." He heard the confident satisfaction in her voice, as pure as the shine of candles on snow, and began to prove his love for her once more. . . .

Please read on for a preview of Kelly Long's

next novel,

An Amish Match on Ice Mountain!

Coudersport, Pennsylvania, 1958

Stephen Lambert lay on his back in the inky darkness and tried to block out the unmistakable sounds of pleasure coming from the cot next to his.

"Mmmm, baby . . . you're so hot . . ."

Great, Stephen thought, wondering how Mike managed to get girls back to the fire station with stupid lines like that.

The girl's soft cries were harder to ignore—breathy little mewls of passion that set Stephen's teeth on edge.

Gott . . . he wanted to be the one kissing her. . . . He turned on his side and grabbed his pillow, ramming it over his head. He knew it was wrong but he was infinitely grateful when the alarm bell rang, clanging against any forthcoming sounds he might have heard.

He swung his legs over the side of the cot, pulled up his suspenders, and slid on the waterproof boots.

He ran down the hallway, falling into line with the other firefighters until they reached the engine room. Stephen was number seven and he methodically pulled on the heavy coat and plastic hat, tightened the chin strap and turned toward the truck, only to bump into Mike, the chief.

Mike was a different man when he wasn't romancing some local girl, Stephen thought. This Mike barked concise orders and soon had everyone on the engine in proper position, including the station's wolf dog, Midnight.

Coudersport was a small but bustling logging and coal town, deep in the mountains of Pennsylvania. But, because the town had grown up practically overnight, a lot of the local structures were not built well, and even some of the nicer buildings could become a fireman's nightmare.

The fire engine, Old Betsy, roared down the main street of town, following the dark plume of smoke that rose against the moonlit sky. It was a boarding house on the wrong side of town—a place where the poor congregated, sometimes living on the streets despite the cold.

The boarding house had gone up like kindling and the false front of the building had already half collapsed, spewing flames out into the late spring air.

Stephen began to pray automatically; maybe it was something to do with being Amisch, but it was natural for him to beg *Gott* for mercy for his crew friends and those inside.

The engine roared to a stop and Mike began to shout at onlookers to get out of the way. Stephen saw Midnight take up his post, prowling the perimeter of the building, looking for anyone in need. Other crew members were running out the hoses while Stephen and two other men took up ladders and tried to find a viable position.

It was strange but after a few fires, Stephen had begun to be able to separate sounds in his head—the cries of onlookers versus the screams of those inside. And now he heard it. A frantic female cry for help, coming from the second floor. His praying escalated as he grabbed the longer of the two metal ladders and moved toward the heat.

Joe, Stephen's big friend, shook his helmeted head. "Too risky, Steve. That whole false front is goin' to go any second!"

"I'll be down fast. You know I will!" Stephen ignored his friend's warnings and found a place near the far right of the structure that would allow him to get close to the window frame.

He could see her now, her long red hair hanging from the sill. Her young face looked terrified and sooty. He went up the ladder without fear, wishing for about the tenth time since starting this job that his company could afford a fancy breathing apparatus for each member of the crew. As it was, all he had against smoke inhalation was a damp neckerchief tied around his mouth and nose.

The girl saw him and ducked down inside the sill. It was a common enough reaction; victims of fire were often uncertain when rescue was near.

"Stand up!" he screamed. "Stand up."

Mercifully, the girl obeyed. He could tell now that she was older than he'd thought, but all of this went through his head in a rush as he felt the water pressure from the hose spray his legs and back. There couldn't be much time if they were wetting him down from below.

The girl's frantic gaze locked with his. "All right." He nodded. "You're going to have to jump!"

Ella Nichols stared in horror at the fireman. His black hat and yellow coat seemed to waver in the heat of the fire.

"I can't jump," she screamed back at him, terrified at the thought of falling.

"I'll catch you. You won't fall—I promise!"

Ella thought of how much easier her life might be if she simply sank to the floor and gave up. But then she thought of the unborn child she carried and straightened her spine. She slung one leg over the window sill, which seemed hot even to the touch.

She looked down and felt a wave of nausea.

"Don't look down!" he ordered, apparently watching her every move.

"All right!" She cautiously eased her other leg out, then grabbed the sill with her fingernails as a whoosh of flames flared up behind her.

"Jump when I tell you. On three."

He extended his arms, somehow standing on the high, swaying ladder with only his legs for support.

"One!"

I'm going to die.

"Two!"

I don't want this baby to die.

"Three!!!"

She closed her eyes and jumped. . . .

A Honeybee Christmas

JENNIFER BECKSTRAND

*To the strong women in my life, especially
Aunt Beatrice Pyne, the original Aunt B.*

Acknowledgments

As always, I want to thank my agent, Nicole Resciniti, my editor, John Scognamiglio, my prayer warrior, Tonya, and my dear family for supporting my crazy schemes. Most especially I'd like to thank my husband, who is my biggest fan and best friend. Love you, Gar!

Chapter 1

"This is *dumm, Dawdi,*" Levi said, making a big show of trudging through the snow as if it were as thick as molasses.

Yost Weaver forced a smile and tapped Levi's hat so it fell over his eyes. "You walk slower than an old lady with bunions."

Levi grinned in spite of his sour mood. "I do not."

"Maybe I need to light a fire under the seat of your pants."

"What are bunions, *Dawdi,* because I probably have them. I should go home and rest."

Yost chuckled. "No use dragging your feet. What needs to be done, needs to be done." He said it with more conviction than he felt. Yost would have done just about anything for the welfare of his grandson's soul, but setting foot on Honeybee Farm was almost too much to ask, even for young Levi's sake.

Bitsy Kiem owned Honeybee Farm, and Yost wanted nothing to do with her. He had wanted nothing to do with her for thirty-five years, and most of the Amish in the community felt the same way. They all tried to show her Christian charity, but Bitsy was irreverent, unconventional, and she dyed her hair all sorts of improper colors. Not only that, but Yost had heard a rumor that Bitsy liked to talk to *Gotte* right out loud, as if she were sitting in her kitchen drinking *kaffee* with an old friend. Was it any wonder that the Plain folk in the community were suspicious?

Even though she lived in his district, Yost had avoided Bitsy like the plague ever since she'd moved back to town with her three orphaned nieces fifteen or so years ago. But a meeting couldn't be helped today. Levi needed to learn a lesson, and Bitsy Kiem, no matter how odd, was the one to give it to him. Yost could only hope that Bitsy would give Levi the kick in the pants he needed.

The snow crunched beneath his boots as Yost glanced at his twelve-year-old grandson out of the corner of his eye. Levi slumped his shoulders, and his ears stuck out straight from underneath his hat. They were both dreading an encounter with Bitsy Kiem. "You're well nigh coming up to be a man, Levi, and men take responsibility when they've done something wrong."

"I know," Levi mumbled. "But why can't I just write her a letter? What if one of her cats attacks me? Or maybe she'll make me get a tattoo."

"No one can make you get a tattoo," Yost said, with a hint of tease in his voice, even though he wasn't so sure of himself. Bitsy plastered herself with temporary tattoos, and Yost suspected she had a real tattoo on some unmentionable area of her body. He clenched his teeth. Maybe Levi was right. Maybe a letter would be enough.

Nae. Levi needed to make restitution for his sins, and it couldn't be done in a letter.

Yost wouldn't leave Levi's side. How much damage could one woman with a loose screw do to his grandson in a mere few minutes?

Bitsy had jumped the fence and left the community when she was eighteen years old. Yost had thanked the *gute* Lord every day that he hadn't followed her to Green Bay or wherever it was she had ended up. Bitsy had spent twenty years as an *Englischer,* and no doubt, she'd gotten herself into all kinds of trouble. Yost had always been very grateful he'd chosen to stay in Bienenstock, raise a family with Ruth, and work the land. Ruth had been gone for almost four years now, and Yost had many happy memories of their life together. He wouldn't have traded that for any kind of life in Green Bay. Even when he felt days of excruciating loneliness or when his daughter Hannah said he was boring, he didn't see that anything needed to change in his life or that he should have done anything differently.

They paused briefly at the sign that marked the entrance to the Honeybee Farm. The sign had all sorts of flowers painted on it and three words in bold black letters.

"Beware the Honeybees," Levi read. "What does that mean?"

Yost didn't say what he was really thinking. The sign only meant to warn people about the many beehives that Bitsy kept on her property, but it was also an apt warning about the woman who lived there. The gossip was that she sometimes painted her fingernails. Black. Yost wouldn't be surprised if Bitsy owned a pair of fancy shoes. He smiled at his grandson so Levi wouldn't suspect that Yost was worried about finger-nail polish. "Bitsy has lots of beehives on her prop-erty. She doesn't want anyone to get stung." He had to admit that it was a very thoughtful sign. Maybe Bitsy's niece Rose had come up with the idea.

For all her strange and rebellious habits, Bitsy had done an adequate job of raising her nieces to be devout and proper Amish girls. Bitsy's sister and brother-in-law had died several years ago, and Bitsy had raised her three nieces as her own. Yost was hon-est enough to give her credit for doing a *gute* job where Lily, Poppy, and Rose were concerned. As far as he knew, none of them colored their hair or had a tattoo, and they had all married godly Amish men a little over a year ago.

Yost and Levi crossed the small wooden bridge that spanned an even smaller pond at the front of the property. The pond was frozen over, even though it was only two days after Thanksgiving. A body of water that tiny probably froze in mid-October.

A dozen beehives stood under a line of bare trees across the field of snow to the right. "I don't see any bees," Levi said. "Do they fly south for the winter?"

Yost raised his eyebrows. "I don't know. Maybe you should ask Bitsy." He grimaced. He'd rather not spend any more time with Bitsy than they had to. It would be best for everyone if they could be in and out of her house in three minutes. Yost scrunched his lips to one side of his face and scratched his cheek. Was it possible for Levi to make restitution in less than three minutes?

Probably not.

Maybe Yost could pay Bitsy for Levi's damages and then let Levi work off the debt on Yost's farm. That was an excellent solution. Three minutes would be plenty of time.

They ambled up the snow-packed lane, both lolly-gagging for their own reasons. The lane curved to the right past more beehives, a couple of outbuildings, and a country-red barn and stopped at a flagstone path that led to the house. Bitsy's house was a mossy green color with white trim and a wide covered porch. A strand of pine boughs hung over Bitsy's front door with two bright red ribbons tied at the corners. Bitsy had already done a little decorating. At least she still believed in Christmas.

To Yost's surprise, Levi slipped his hand into his as they trudged up Bitsy's porch steps. At twelve, Levi had made it very clear that he wasn't a child anymore and didn't wish to do childish things like hold *Dawdi* Weaver's hand or get a kiss from his *mamm* before he left for school. The closer Levi got to thirteen, the more surly and withdrawn he became, as if it offended him that he had to get up every morning. Yost didn't like the change in his happy-go-lucky grandson, but he hadn't really expected anything different. He knew enough about teenage boys to understand what could happen if a young man didn't have a firm hand to guide him through the teenage years.

Yost hung back, and Levi tapped lightly on the door, as if hoping Bitsy might not hear him and he'd have an excuse to leave.

The door opened about five inches and a mangy black and white cat darted outside, hissing and growling as if there was something very frightening on the other side of the door. Levi jumped back as the cat ran between his legs. A second cat, orange marmalade and smaller, shot out of the house and chased down the porch steps after the first one. Just when Yost thought they were done, a third kitty with a brown striped coat strolled out of the house, brushing her thick fur against Levi's trousers as she passed. Levi glanced up at Yost and grinned. Yost's heart melted, and he smiled back. Levi wasn't too grown up yet not to take delight in a parade of cats.

Bitsy Kiem opened the door wider and looked past Yost and Levi as if they weren't there. "Don't come crying to me if you freeze to death, you *dumm* cats."

Yost couldn't help but chuckle. Bitsy had her fingers wrapped around the barrel of a shotgun while the butt of the gun rested on the floor, and she leaned on it as if it were a cane. Her prayer covering, or *kapp,* sat askew on her head and one of the pins that held the *kapp* in place stood straight up, perpendicular to her scalp. Any sudden movement and she would skewer herself. Her salt-and-pepper gray hair was tinted a light shade of periwinkle purple and more than one strand poked out from beneath her *kapp* as if she and her cats had been having a pillow fight.

A quick glance told Yost she wasn't sporting any tattoos, at least on the skin he could see. He cleared his throat. No good would come of thinking of the skin he couldn't see.

Even with lavender hair, Bitsy didn't look especially wicked or even particularly unpleasant. His gut clenched. He saw her every other week at *gmay.* He knew exactly what she looked like. Why did it feel as if he were seeing her for the first time?

Bitsy was fifty-three, exactly two years younger than Yost. They shared a birthday—a fact that had made them instant and unlikely friends years ago in school. The years had been good to her. A few wrinkles congregated around her eyes, but the lines were softer around her mouth. There was good humor in her face, even though she was scowling fiercely in the direction of the cats.

Yost tried for a friendly lilt to his voice. "How many cats do you have?"

Bitsy waved her hand as if swatting her cats into the trash bin. "*Ach!* Too many. People call me 'the cat lady' behind my back. I'd let you take one home, but Rose loves those cats, and it would break her heart if one or two of them disappeared mysteriously in the middle of the night." She cocked an eyebrow, tilted her head to one side, and looked at Levi. "*Gute maiya*, Levi Weaver. You've grown an inch since *gmay* last Sunday. If you'd pull your shoulders back, you'd probably clear five feet."

Levi didn't like being told what to do, but he straightened his spine slowly so that Bitsy might not notice he'd taken her advice.

Bitsy tilted her head to the other side and studied Yost like a lice-infested horse. Her eyes sparkled with amusement and maybe a hint of something else. Annoyance? "Well, Yost Weaver. This is the first time you've set foot on my farm in fifteen years. It must be a special occasion."

Why did he feel as if she were accusing him of something, and why did guilt niggle at the back of his throat? He hadn't done anything wrong, and he certainly didn't regret any behavior where Bitsy Kiem was concerned.

She folded her arms across her chest. "It's no use trying to apologize after all these years."

"Apologize? You want me to apologize?" Every

muscle in his neck tensed. How had the woman with shocking blue eyes and purple hair managed to raise his hackles in a matter of seconds? This was Levi's confession, not his.

Bitsy blew an errant strand of hair out of her eyes, and by the look on her face, Yost half expected her to scold him for slouching. "I've long since gotten over it, Yost. I dare say I haven't given you a second thought in three decades, and the last time I asked *Gotte* to smite you with a dread disease was thirty-five years ago." She drew her brows together and peered at him as if she were trying to read his mind. "You didn't happen to get chicken pox right after I left town, did you?"

She looked almost hopeful, and Yost had no idea what to say. Bitsy had asked *Gotte* to give him chicken pox? Was that allowed in the *Ordnung*? "I . . . I had the chicken pox when I was three," he said, not sure why he'd told her that. His childhood diseases were none of her business.

"What about heat rash? Have you ever had a *gute* heat rash?"

Yost shook his head slowly.

Bitsy looked up at the ceiling. "Lord, you said to ask and I'd receive. How will I learn to believe if you won't answer my prayers?"

So the rumors were true. Bitsy prayed to *Gotte* right out loud. That discovery shocked Yost into silence. He'd be wise to stay far away from this one.

Levi, on the other hand, seemed quite taken with Bitsy Kiem. His eyes widened and his lips parted in a bewildered smile, as if Bitsy Kiem knew a wonderful secret that Levi could discover if he just gazed at her long enough. Yost nearly yanked on Levi's suspenders to drag him down the steps. Someone as brash and un-apologetic as Bitsy Kiem shouldn't be allowed around impressionable *kinner.*

Yost expelled all the air from his lungs. Didn't Jesus say that inasmuch as ye have done it unto one of the least of these, ye have done it unto Him? If nothing else, this encounter with Bitsy would teach Levi that some people were chosen by *Gotte* while others were not. He nudged Levi forward. "My grandson has something he needs to tell you." In an instant, Levi seemed to lose four inches of height.

Bitsy raised her eyebrows, tucked a piece of hair behind her ear, and leaned the shotgun against the wall. She slid her arm around Levi's shoulders and tugged him into the house. "What you need is a mug of hot cocoa and a slice of oatmeal cake. *Cum reu* before all the warm air goes out with the cats."

Yost followed Levi into the house and closed the door behind him. The tempting aroma of cinnamon and sugar met his nose and made his mouth water. Bitsy and her nieces were known for keeping bees and baking all sorts of *appeditlich* desserts and good-ies.

Bitsy's kitchen stood to his left, with shiny wood floors, a butcher-block island, and an ample table di-rectly in front of him. The kitchen chairs were sturdy, but one of the chair slats had duct tape wrapped around it. The sitting room was to his right, with a sofa half covered in duct tape, two overstuffed chairs, and a rag rug—also crisscrossed in duct tape—on the floor. It looked like a comfortable house, except for the abundance of duct tape.

"*Hoch dich anne,* sit down," Bitsy said.

They took off their hats, and Bitsy pulled out a

chair at the table for Levi. He slumped into it and fiddled with his suspenders. Yost took a chair next to him.

Bitsy pulled two plates from the cupboard and some mugs from the shelf. "Do you like cinnamon in your cocoa, Levi?"

"*Nae.*"

"Do you like marshmallows?"

Levi perked up at the thought of marshmallows. "Have you got little ones?"

"I have four sizes. Jumbo, normal, miniature, and tiny."

Levi nodded, and a smile might have played at the corner of his mouth. "Tiny, please."

"Would you like tiny marshmallows too, Yost?"

Yost sort of flinched. Bitsy had admitted she'd prayed for him to get chicken pox. He hadn't expected her to offer him marshmallows. "*Nae, denki.*"

"Do you want a jumbo marshmallow?" Bitsy said, propping a hand on her hip as if she was waiting for him to come up with a cure for warts.

He worried that marshmallows would soften him up, and though he didn't know why, he thought maybe he shouldn't let Bitsy soften him up. No marshmallows. "*Nae.* I don't need marshmallows."

Bitsy smirked. "No one *needs* a marshmallow. You could just as well eat a teaspoon of sugar for all the good it does."

She poured three mugs of cocoa and dropped tiny marshmallows into two of them, then brought the mugs to the table with a fourth mug filled with nothing but marshmallows. She gave Yost a shrug. "Just in case you change your mind." She nudged Levi with her hand. "Or if you want extra."

Steam rose from the cake sitting on the butcher-block island. It was almost as if Bitsy had been expecting company and had just pulled the cake from the oven for them. Maybe she'd made the cake for someone else. Without asking if they wanted any, she cut two slices and scooped them onto two small plates. "Do you like oatmeal cake, Levi?"

"I've never had it."

"Almost thirteen years old and never eaten oatmeal cake?" She put the plates on the table and gave Yost and Levi each a fork. "If you don't like it, you can give it to Farrah Fawcett. She might be willing to eat it."

Levi perked up a little more. Not only did he get cake and hot cocoa, Bitsy was turning out to be more interesting than he'd probably expected. "Farrah Fawcett?" He took a gulp of cocoa, and a marshmallow stuck to his top lip.

Bitsy turned and gazed at a fluffy ball of white fur lounging on the window seat. The ball of fur had a pink, upturned nose and mustard-yellow eyes. "My cat. Well, one of my cats, though Farrah Fawcett likes to pretend she's the only cat in the family. The others are beneath her notice." She sat down on the other side of Levi. "Do you like it?"

"Mmm," Levi said, stuffing a large piece into his mouth. "I brrg id."

Bitsy nodded. "It's a *gute* recipe."

Yost gave Levi one of his firm looks. "Don't talk with your mouth full." He glanced doubtfully at Bitsy. "Aren't you having any?"

Bitsy shrugged. "*Ach*, I can't eat that. If I get chubby, I won't have the energy to chase my worthless cats." She tapped her chin. "Although, if I couldn't chase them, maybe they'd run away—all but Farrah Fawcett. She wouldn't run if the house was on fire."

Yost took a bite of cake while he studied Bitsy out of the corner of his eye. She was wiry but sturdy, someone who worked hard enough to never catch up on her eating but wouldn't be blown over by a stiff wind either. With her high cheekbones and full lips, she was really quite pretty when she didn't scowl. "This is *gute*," he said, tempering his show of enthusiasm. Bitsy didn't need any encouragement, even if her cake tasted like a plate full of heaven.

"Eat as much as you want," she said. "My nephew-in-law Luke is coming over tonight, and it would do him *gute* to see that he is not entitled to all the food in the house." Bitsy laced her fingers together and propped her elbows on the table. "Now, Levi. You have something you want to say to me?"

Levi froze with his mug halfway to his lips, as if he'd just remembered why he'd come in the first place. He put his mug down, stuck his finger in the cocoa, and pushed the remaining marshmallows around. Yost almost scolded him, but the poor boy was just about to experience the wrath of Bitsy Kiem, and even though Yost didn't know exactly what that would be, a woman who painted her fingernails and might or might not have a tattoo wasn't likely to show much Christian charity. But it had to be done. Levi needed to learn that actions had consequences and that if a boy lost his integrity, he had nothing of value left.

Levi kept stirring and staring faithfully at the three remaining marshmallows in his mug. "I . . . I wanted to start my own beehive to earn money to buy a scooter."

Bitsy scrunched her lips to one side of her face. "Believe me, Levi, a beehive won't make anybody rich."

"I borrowed three bee board things from your shed—"

"*Stole* three bee board things from my shed."

Gute. Bitsy wasn't going to let Levi get away with making it less than it was.

Levi frowned. "Okay. I stole three bee board things from your shed, and you didn't notice."

Bitsy leaned back in her chair. "I don't know why you think I didn't notice. They went missing August tenth or maybe the eleventh. And they're called *frames.*"

Levi widened his eyes. "I guess you noticed. I put the board things—the frames—in a cardboard box and set the box right in the middle of the Chidesters' sunflower patch, where no one could see it. I wanted to catch some bees for my hive."

Bitsy didn't smile, but she seemed to grow more and more amused with every word that came out of Levi's mouth. "You wanted to catch some bees?"

Levi lifted his chin. "I'm not a *dumkoff.* The bees would come if I had more boxes. I just need to start earlier. In the spring."

Bitsy smirked. "Just because you're named after a pair of pants doesn't give you permission to be too big for your britches, Levi Weaver. You don't know the first thing about starting your own hive."

Levi deflated like a balloon. "It doesn't matter, because they're ruined now."

Bitsy narrowed her eyes. "Ruined?"

"I put the box in the barn for the winter, and our horse stepped in it. Dat found the smashed frames and got wonderful mad."

"I don't wonder that he did," Bitsy said.

"But Dat don't have time so *Dawdi* brought me over to say I'm sorry."

"And to pay you back," Yost added, to be sure Bitsy knew they meant to make it right.

Bitsy pinned Levi with a stern look that carried a hint of compassion with it. "You're the oldest in your family, aren't you, Levi?"

"*Jah.*"

"Your *mamm* is busy with eight little ones, including a new set of twins."

Levi nodded.

"Do you help her with the babies?"

Levi stirred his cocoa with his finger again. "Sometimes. Mostly she says I'm underfoot and to go find something else to do. She barely notices me. I thought she would like it if I caught some bees."

Bitsy rested her chin in her hand. "Do you help your *dat* on the farm?"

Levi shrugged. "I guess. He's gone a lot working on houses. Amos and me milk the cow and muck out."

Bitsy nodded. "Your *dat* works construction out of town sometimes. And cuts wood for the mill."

Yost pressed his lips together. Reuben, his son, wasn't home very often. Maybe Levi needed his *dawdi* more than they all realized.

"He once got a splinter two inches long," Levi said, maybe hoping that Bitsy would feel sorry for him.

Bitsy looked up at the ceiling, and Yost thought she would launch into prayer at any moment. It did look like she was having a conversation with someone up there because she frowned and rolled her eyes and scrunched her lips together, but she didn't speak out loud so Yost couldn't be sure.

"Well, Levi," she finally said, "I've needed some excitement in my life for months. I've thought about getting a real tattoo or cutting my hair short or even buying a television so I can watch *The Bachelor,* but what would really be fun is starting a candle business. What do you think?"

"I suppose."

"What do you mean *you suppose?* I've already bought some candle molds. I've got bears and bee-hives and honeypots. I went crazy online at the library and bought a skull mold too. The excitement never stops around here."

Yost didn't know where she was taking this strange little story, but they'd been here way past three minutes, and he didn't want to prolong the agony, especially now that she had started talking about skulls. "If you tell me how much the frames cost, I will pay you the money and then Levi can work off his debt on my farm."

Bitsy's mouth fell open, and she squinted as if try-ing to see him clearly. "That's a terrible idea."

Well, he wouldn't have to guess what Bitsy thought. And he grudgingly admitted to himself that she was right. It was a terrible idea, born out of convenience and the wish to get out of there as soon as possible.

She turned to Levi and ignored Yost, probably hoping he wouldn't think of any more bad ideas. "As I was saying, I want to start a candle business, but I need an assistant to help me melt and pour wax and clean up and do candle-making things. Would you like to help?"

Levi stopped stirring, but his finger still dangled into his cocoa. "I guess. I don't know."

"You've got to be more decisive than that, young man. Boys who can't make a decision get led around by the nose by persuasive friends." She leaned closer to Levi and rested her elbows on the table. "You help me pour wax three days a week, and I will let you sell all the candles at the community craft bazaar in two weeks. And you can keep the money."

Levi jerked his finger out of the cocoa, and chocolate splattered across Bitsy's already-unruly *kapp*. She didn't even flinch. Levi pretended it hadn't happened. "You mean you'll let me keep the money we make?"

Bitsy reached up and pinched a drop of cocoa that was threatening to drip from a strand of hair. "But you'll have to come three days a week after school, and when you leave, you'll have to carry a cake or a casserole home to your *mamm*. What do you say?"

"I say yes!" Levi shoved a bite of cake into his mouth.

Yost loved seeing his grandson so happy, but he couldn't let such a silly notion go unchecked. "But there's no penance in making candles if he gets to keep the money. Levi still needs to pay for the broken frames."

Levi pressed his lips together and glanced at Bitsy. He obviously thought she could solve the problem for him. Hadn't she just offered to make him rich? Well, as rich as a twelve-year-old Amish boy could hope to be.

Bitsy took a swig of her cocoa that had gone untouched until now. "*Ach,* he'll earn his keep. He'll make candles and run errands and feed the chickens and the hog. Is that good enough?"

Yost couldn't see anything wrong with Bitsy putting Levi to work, especially when he wasn't much help at home and Bitsy would make sure he learned how to work. There was only one thing that worried Yost. Three minutes had turned into weeks. How bad of an influence would Bitsy be on his grandson if he were here three times a week?

"If you do a *gute* job, I'll give you one of my extra hives and even send away for a queen in the mail. You can start your own hive when it gets warmer."

Levi jumped from his chair, waved his hand in the air, and whooped like a peacock. "I get my own hive. I get my own hive."

Bitsy grabbed his hand and pulled him to sit. "Don't go counting your chickens before they hatch. I'm very strict, and if you don't do a *gute* job, you won't get a thing. Except I might decide to give you one of my cats."

Levi stuffed another piece of cake into his mouth. "I'll do a *gute* job. Mamm says I'm one of her best workers when I keep my head out of the clouds."

Bitsy pointed her finger at him. "I don't want any heads in the clouds. That wax will burn your fingers if you don't pay attention."

"I will." Levi's smile faded, and he eyed Yost. "Can I do it, *Dawdi?* She'll give me a beehive."

Yost cleared his throat. How could he say no when Levi seemed happier than he'd been in months? With his *mamm* occupied with so many babies and his *dat* often away from home, Levi tended to get lost in the crowd. Maybe a candle business was just the thing he needed.

Yost searched Bitsy's face, and warmth spread through his body until he felt as toasty and mushy as a bowl of tapioca pudding with raisins. Why would she do this for a boy she barely knew from a family that didn't have much to do with her? It would certainly be more of a burden than a help to have an awkward boy in her kitchen, knocking things over, dropping dishes and candles, and complicating the process that she could surely do more efficiently herself. But Levi needed this, and Bitsy, for all her faults, was mindful enough to see it.

Yost's throat got sort of thick, and he was a little ashamed of himself. He'd judged Bitsy harshly. Amidst the praying aloud and the purple hair, Yost had almost forgotten. Bitsy Kiem was not only an excellent cook, but also a woman of many good works. When Ruth went through her chemo, Bitsy had sent over something delicious from the Honeybee Farm at least once a week. She was known to be someone who was always first to a sickbed or a funeral, and now she was offering to take in a boy who needed some extra attention. Who would Jesus say was the true Christian?

Yost didn't know why he had expected anything less. Bitsy had a rebellious streak, for sure and certain, but she had been kind to everyone in school, except for the boys who picked on the little kids.

"Can I help Bitsy with her candle business?" Levi said.

Yost nodded slowly. "If I come with you."

Bitsy squinted and scrunched her lips together, but she didn't argue. Yost would come with Levi every time he came to Bitsy's. There were still rules to follow, and Yost was the only one who could make sure Bitsy followed them. For Levi's sake.

Black fingernail polish and tattoos were not going to be allowed.

Chapter 2

How did Bitsy always seem to get herself into these messes?

It was because she couldn't bear to say no to someone in trouble. It was definitely one of the burdens of being such a nice person.

She simply wouldn't turn her back on a little boy who needed a little bit of attention and a wonderful lot of guidance. The beeswax candle idea had come to her out of the blue as she had been sitting at the table trying not to stare into Yost Weaver's interesting eyes. It had been a *gute* idea, just not an incredibly convenient one. She had cleaned and rendered several pounds of beeswax earlier in the year, and it sat in her pantry in thick blocks, just waiting to be made into candles. She and Levi would have a wonderful *gute* time melting it down and forming it into candles. She was looking forward to that part. Levi was a sweet boy, even if he fancied himself more clever than he really was. Boys that age always thought they knew more than anyone else in the world.

But she was dreading the *dawdi*. Yost Weaver

wouldn't think of leaving his grandson alone in the same room with wicked Bitsy Kiem in case she talked Levi into a pierced ear or a Mohawk.

Hadn't anybody in the district noticed that Bitsy had done quite an adequate job raising three girls to be very nice and devout Amish women? It was as if her neighbors thought she'd drag them to hell if they got too close. Some days, Bitsy was sorely tempted to wear a pair of horns to church with a pair of red high heels. If they thought she was so wicked, she might as well play the part.

She pulled three saucepans from the cupboard and frowned. She wasn't being exactly fair to her neighbors. Most of them offered unreserved friendship, even if they had their private reservations about her. The people like Yost Weaver were the exception. The Amish were notoriously set in their ways. Bitsy couldn't blame them for avoiding what they couldn't understand.

Those people gave Christians a bad reputation. Although, many of her neighbors thought she was the one who gave Christians a bad reputation, so she couldn't really point out the mote in their eye. They were wrong, and she was right, but there was no way to convince them of it. She simply couldn't give up coloring her hair and wearing earrings. She loved how the dangly ones tinkled when she moved her head, and the hair colors gave the neighbors something to gossip about. Why should she spoil their fun?

She heard a noise at the door and opened it. Billy Idol, the ugliest cat in the world, stood on the mat, his paws caked with snow. Leonard Nimoy and Sigourney Weaver, two more of Bitsy's cats, were covered head to toe with snow. They'd obviously been having some sort of battle, and Billy Idol looked as if he'd gotten the better of them.

"Billy Idol, you've got to stop picking on Leonard and Sigourney. You'll soon have no friends left." Who was she fooling? Billy Idol didn't have any friends at all—except for maybe her nephew-in-law Luke. Billy Idol and Luke seemed to get along just fine. Probably because they were so much alike.

Bitsy spread a towel on the floor, and the cats rolled around on it to dry off.

It was too bad Yost felt the need to babysit his grandson. Or maybe it was her he thought he had to babysit. She shouldn't have fed him. It was always a mistake to feed a man. They'd keep coming around like stray cats, and Bitsy had no patience for stray cats. She had no patience for any cats. Why in the world did she have four?

Yost was like an attack dog left to guard the cookie jar, watching every move she made, waiting for her to sin so he could report to the bishop or the deacon just what Bitsy Kiem was up to. He was a horrible nuisance. Good-looking, but still a nuisance. He hadn't let himself go like so many Amish husbands did at his age. Bitsy hadn't been able to detect an ounce of fat around his middle, and his arms had obviously seen some wonderful-heavy lifting. It wondered Bitsy why Yost hadn't remarried. Ruth had been gone three or four years, and surely every widow and old maid in the community had set her cap for him. Well, every old maid but Bitsy. Ever since she had moved back to Bienenstock with her nieces, Yost and his family had made a point of steering clear of her.

She had told Yost that she'd gotten over it, but in truth, she still held a grudge. It was a small grudge, because time had certainly made it less important, but it was there in the back of her mind all the same. She couldn't see how the grudge hurt anybody, and carrying the extra weight on her shoulders probably burned a lot of calories, so she'd never tried to get rid of it. Still, she felt a little down this morning knowing that Yost and Levi were coming, so she had put on her dangliest pair of earrings first thing— partly to make herself feel better and partly to get under Yost's skin.

She never blamed Yost for choosing not to go to Green Bay with her. His parents loved him, he loved them, and he was happy at church. He had no reason to leave. But she did fault him for not having the courage to at least look her in the eye and tell her he wouldn't go. She had waited for him on that abandoned road and had never before or since felt so utterly alone.

She should probably forgive him—not that *he* cared one way or the other. Bitsy had a *wunderbarr* life with three nieces who loved her, and she didn't regret one decision she'd made. Well, almost. She looked up to heaven—or at least as far as the ceiling. "Dear Lord, I'm sorry about dyeing my hair that urine color. *Denki* for trying to warn me. It took months to fade. And I regret the Milli Vanilli concert." She took a deep breath and expelled it slowly. "And, Lord, I would appreciate it if you could help me forgive Yost Weaver. I shouldn't hold his past sins against him. You didn't give him the chicken pox, but I'm assuming he had a heat rash or two. *Denki* for that."

A knock on the door made her jump, and she quickly closed her prayer. Yost need never know about Milli Vanilli.

She opened the front door to find Levi grinning from ear to ear and Yost wearing a look of deep, deep concern. She shook her head slightly so her earrings tinkled. Yost's concern became an abyss.

"*Hallo,* Bitsy," Levi said, strolling into the house without being invited in. Somebody needed to teach that boy some manners.

"*Cum reu.* If you step on one of the cats, you have to take it home." Bitsy grabbed the corners of the towel where the cats were sitting and pulled it from in front of the door. Yost looked like he might break if he tried to sit down. Bitsy's niece Rose always said that anyone could be softened up by a cat. Bitsy scooped up Leonard Nimoy and handed her to Yost. "Here," she said. "Try this."

If anything, Yost stiffened even more. "What do I do with this?"

"You hold it and cuddle it and give it some love."

He grimaced. "I don't want to give it some love."

Bitsy sighed. "Some people just aren't cat people." She took the cat from his arms and handed it to Levi. "You like cats?"

Levi shrugged. "I like dogs better, but cats don't poop in the yard."

"Would your *mamm* let you take this one home?"

"*Nae,*" Yost practically shouted.

He was so adamant that Bitsy had to laugh. "Don't worry, Yost. I won't make anyone take a cat home today."

"Today?"

"I want to soften you up first."

Yost frowned. "I'm never going to get that soft."

Bitsy had to agree. Those rock-hard arms were testament to the fact that Yost was a hard worker, and that tended to be a lifelong habit. "I have a way of wearing people down," she said. "Be on your guard."

She could tell he didn't know whether to smile or go back to looking deeply concerned. "I will."

Bitsy shrugged off Yost Weaver. It was Levi who needed her attention. "Okay, Levi. That's enough holding the cat. We're going to make three candles today. I hope you can keep up."

Levi set Leonard Nimoy on the window seat next to Farrah Fawcett, who seemed very offended at the invasion of her privacy. "For sure and certain I can."

"Okay, then. Fetch a block of beeswax from the shelf in the storage room. Your *dawdi* will have to help you."

"Why?"

Bitsy made a point of not looking in Yost's direction. "They're heavy. He might as well make *gute* use of those muscles."

Levi and Yost went into the storage room, and Levi came out carrying a beautiful orange-yellow block of beeswax that Bitsy had rendered a few months ago. "I'm strong enough," Levi said. "*Dawdi* didn't even have to help."

Bitsy shrugged. What did she care if she got to see Yost's muscles in action or not? "Okay, then. Don't get too big for your britches."

Levi ran his finger along the smooth top of the wax. "It looks like an orange cake."

"It's pretty, isn't it? Beeswax orange is my favorite color. But don't eat it or you'll throw up." She retrieved her sturdy grill turner from the drawer and handed it to Levi. "Use this spatula to break the sheet of wax into smaller pieces that will fit into the saucepan. Do you know what a double boiler is?"

"*Nae.*"

Yost leaned against the counter to watch as if he were supervising the entire operation. His presence was slightly annoying and, for some unexplainable reason, more than a little unnerving. She tried not to scowl at him. Why should Yost Weaver *ferhoodle* her? She didn't care one whit about him or his piercing blue eyes or the little bit of gray that mixed with the chestnut brown of his horseshoe beard.

Levi cut the wax into smaller pieces while Bitsy readied the double boiler on the stove.

Yost sneaked up behind her, like a cat on the prowl. Bitsy tensed when he got close. She didn't like cats. "What's that?" he asked.

"A double boiler," she snapped, as if his question irritated her. She pressed her lips together and tried to soften her tone. "You heat up the water in the bottom and put the bowl on top. The wax melts but doesn't burn." She forgot one of the burners was out and tried to turn it on. When it didn't light, she groaned and switched to the back burner.

She clenched her teeth when Yost leaned over her shoulder and she smelled leather and strong soap. "Is it broken?"

"*Jah.* Josiah, one of my nephews-in-law, tried to fix it with duct tape and nearly burned the house down."

Yost chuckled and pointed to the duct-taped sofa. "Josiah fixed your couch, I see."

Bitsy grunted her displeasure. "And my porch. And my kitchen chair. He was desperately in love with Rose and I didn't want to discourage him, so I let him fix anything he wanted to. I suppose it's what I get for being so nice."

Yost put his finger on the burner cap and wiggled it back and forth. "I can fix your stove."

"Without duct tape?"

He nodded. "I'm very handy. I plumbed my whole house myself, including pipes underneath the floor for heat."

"But is there any chance of my house exploding?"

"Not a chance," Yost said, blooming into a smile that would have persuaded her to agree to almost anything.

She held her breath and tried to act her own, grumpy self. Yost need never know that his smile had some sort of power over her. "Okay. You can fix my stove, but after Levi and I make candles."

She showed Levi how to put the candle molds together with rubber bands and hang wicks over the molds. They melted the wax and used a turkey baster to transfer the wax to the molds. Levi dripped wax everywhere, but Bitsy could see he was trying to be careful so she didn't scold him. She would make him clean it up when it cooled, and if she had to go back and clean it again when he left, she hadn't expected anything different when she offered Levi a share of the candle business.

When they finished pouring wax into the molds, she directed Levi to scrape the rest of the soft wax back onto the block of hard beeswax to use another day. They cleaned up the mess, with Yost insisting that he wash the dishes. He didn't do it well, but at least he was willing to help. It was like pulling teeth to get her nephew-in-law Luke to help. Bitsy used to be a dental hygienist, but she'd never liked pulling teeth.

"That was fun," Levi said, drying his grimy hands on one of Bitsy's good towels. She made a mental note to pull out the rags for next time.

She resisted the urge to ruffle Levi's sandy-brown hair. He seemed like the kind of boy who would want to be treated like a man. Instead, she folded her arms across her chest and made a show of surveying the full candle molds and the clean kitchen. "Your *dat* would be pleased with the fine job you did. Would you like to make a candle for your *mamm* next time?"

Levi gave her a crooked grin. "Okay."

"Well, then. No more lollygagging. It's time for you to muck out Queenie's stall."

Levi groaned and dragged his feet across the floor but didn't seem all that put out about it.

Bitsy wouldn't let him get away with even that little childishness. "I can't abide a whiner, Levi Weaver. You'll find the shovel and pitchfork hanging on the wall of the barn. Put down clean straw for my horse."

Levi closed his mouth, squared his shoulders, and put on his coat and hat. He marched out the door, seemingly determined to take his medicine like a man. Bitsy turned to see Yost gazing at her with a strange look in his eye. A thread of liquid chocolate made its way up Bitsy's spine. She wanted to throw something at him. What did he think he was up to, getting under her skin like that?

"*Denki* for caring about my grandson," he said.

Well.

Yost Weaver had never approved of her. She hadn't expected him to be grateful.

"He's lonely and only wants for a little bit of attention." She cleared her throat and frowned persistently. "And a bath. Have you talked to him about hygiene? He needs it, especially coming up on puberty."

A shocked laugh burst from Yost's mouth. "I've never heard anyone say 'puberty' out loud."

"Well, why not?"

"Don't you think it's a little awkward to talk about?"

His expression pulled a smile out of her. "*Nae*. If we don't talk about it, the children will grow up stinky. It's got to be said."

He chuckled and gave her that melted chocolate smile again. "There's nobody quite like you, Bitsy Kiem."

"*Ach, vell.* I'm sure the bishop is very grateful there's only one of me."

Yost stared at her for a second too long then cleared his throat and lost his smile. "That is why I ask that when Levi comes to your house, you don't wear earrings or tattoos or fingernail polish and that you do not pray out loud. I'm only thinking of my grandson."

"You're afraid I'm a bad influence on him."

"I'm sorry. For sure and certain I don't mean to offend you."

Bitsy folded her arms and eyed Yost like he'd just said something very *dumm,* which he had. "Yost, I would never do anything to hurt your grandson. Do you believe that?"

He leaned back and propped his hands against the counter. "I know you wouldn't do it on purpose, but children are like sponges. They see and soak up everything. He likes you. He shouldn't look favorably on a woman with purple hair."

"Why not?"

"Because coloring your hair is worldly and fancy."

"Martha Glick colors her hair. Treva Yutzy colors her hair. Even old Susie Borntreger dyes her hair, and her husband was bishop for thirty years."

Yost's brows inched together. "She does not."

Bitsy had to laugh at the look of utter disbelief on Yost's face. "*Jah,* she does."

His mouth fell open. "Susie Borntreger . . . are you sure?"

"Seventy-five-year-old women do not have shiny, jet-black hair, especially when it was brown twenty years ago. And Suvilla Hoover lets her roots go too long. If it's wrong to color your hair, then you'll have to admonish at least five other women in the *gmayna.*"

Yost seemed to have been struck dumb. Unfortunately, only momentarily. "Black is better than purple." His lips twitched as if he wasn't sure he should just smile and surrender the argument.

Bitsy let out a long I'm-barely-putting-up-with-you sigh and marched to her bookshelf. "You said that coloring my hair was a fancy thing to do. You didn't say only certain colors are acceptable." She pulled her well-worn Bible from the shelf, went back to the kitchen, and shoved the book toward Yost. "Show me."

"Show you what?"

"Show me in the Bible where it says I'm not allowed to color my hair."

He glanced at her doubtfully before opening the book and leafing through its pages, almost as if he believed he'd find it. He pulled a hundred-dollar bill from between Lamentations and Ezekiel. "Lose some money?"

She grabbed the bill from him and slid it back between the pages. "I don't believe in banks."

"So you keep your money in a Bible?"

"No thief is going to steal a Bible."

He must have decided it was okay to smile. "Unless he knows that's where you keep your money."

He was searching the New Testament so earnestly she almost felt sorry for him. She gazed upward. "Dear Lord, please let Yost find something. Men get so downhearted when they're proven wrong."

He looked up long enough to roll his eyes at her while he searched through the writings of Paul. "Here's something," he said, as if he'd already lost the argument. "*But if a woman have long hair, it is a glory to her.*"

Bitsy couldn't help but tease him. "But if a woman have long purple hair, it's even better."

He let the Bible fall shut. "Okay. I'll let you win that one for now. But what about the earrings and the tattoos?"

She tilted her head to one side, causing her earrings to tinkle annoyingly. "It would do Levi good to experience another culture."

She was doing her best to be contrary, but to her surprise, Yost laughed. "Bitsy, you are not another culture."

"Of course I am." She took the Bible from him and returned it carefully to the shelf. That was her propane money for the next three years.

Yost didn't seem convinced, although he looked slightly less inflexible. She grabbed his wrist and led him to the table, where she set the example and sat down. With a bewildered look on his face, he slid into the chair next to her.

"Yost," she said, propping her chin in her hand, "what do you think of my girls?"

"Paul Glick says Lily cheated him out of some honey. His *dat* is a minister, so it's not a light thing to disregard what he says."

Bitsy thought her head might explode. Paul Glick used to be Lily's boyfriend, and he was still—and forever—bitter that Lily had jilted him. Paul was like a popcorn kernel stuck between Bitsy's teeth—small, troublesome, and annoying beyond endurance.

Yost's brows inched together. "Regardless of what Paul says, I haven't seen anything but that they are faithful, godly women who do much good. Lily and Dan work at his *fater*'s dairy, and Lily helps at every quilting bee and canning frolic in the neighborhood. Poppy has a heart for the downtrodden, and she seems to take very *gute* care of your parents. And no one who knows Rose would give her anything but the highest praise. She does many good works and never says a bad word about anybody. Josiah just drew the lot for minister in the district, so *Gotte* must certainly approve."

Bitsy nodded. "Do you think those girls raised themselves?"

"*Nae.* I suppose not."

"Or maybe you think they turned out well in spite of me."

He sighed. "I'm willing to give credit where credit is due."

"They grew up exposed to my butterfly tattoos and my colorful hair and an occasional Van Halen song, and are still *gute* Amish girls. Very *gute* Amish girls."

"But what about the praying aloud, Bitsy? It's prideful, plain and simple."

She grunted. "I don't pray to be seen of men, Yost. I started talking to *Gotte* when everyone else failed me, and I haven't stayed quiet since. *Gotte* has never abandoned me. He is the only one I can depend on. You can't shut me up."

He stared at his hands, and a smile played at his lips. "That's for sure and certain."

He jumped when she snatched his hand and squeezed it. "You try it."

"Try what?"

"Praying out loud. It will do you *gute*."

He let out a shocked exclamation and shook his head hard enough to fan up a breeze. "*Nae*, Bitsy Kiem. I'd just as soon paint my fingernails."

"That can be arranged," she said. His eyes got wider. That man had no sense of humor. She closed her eyes and squeezed his hand tighter. "Dear Heavenly *Fater*." She opened one eye and nodded her encouragement. "Say it."

Yost pressed his lips together so tightly they turned white.

She'd just have to show him how it was done. "Dear Heavenly *Fater*, please bless my grandson Levi to know he is loved by all of us." She opened her eyes to slits. Yost's lips were still clamped shut, but his head was bowed. "Bless Levi's *mamm* and *dat* with their quiver full of children that they won't misplace any of them or forget their names. And help me—and by *me* I mean *Yost*—to be more open-minded and less arrogant, although as a man, I can't very well help it."

"Oh, *sis yuscht*," she heard him mutter.

Bitsy stifled a giggle. "Please help me to be humble enough to see that Bitsy Kiem is always right, and *denki* for sending her like an angel from heaven into Levi's life. Amen." She opened her eyes and looked up.

He gave her the stink eye.

She let go of his hand and patted his arm. "That wasn't so bad, was it?"

He folded his arms across his chest. "Bitsy Kiem is always right?"

"You asked me to help you. If you don't like what I said, do it yourself next time."

"I didn't ask for your help."

"You needed it." The look on his face made the laughter bubble up inside her. She couldn't help herself. Amish men weren't used to being teased or countermanded. It was a sign of Yost's good nature and even temper that he laughed with her.

Bitsy remembered herself and jumped to her feet. She had better things to do than sit and stare at Yost Weaver all day.

What a complete waste of time.

"Now that's settled, you can make yourself useful and look at my stove."

"Nothing is settled, Bitsy. What about Levi?"

"It will do him *gute* to make candles and muck out my barn, and you know it. Besides, he needs to understand that actions have consequences. I know you still want him to learn at least that one lesson. There's no use arguing about it. I've made up my mind, and that's all there is to say about it."

Yost leaned back in his chair and mulled that over for a few seconds. "The man is always supposed to have the last word." He smiled when he said it, so she didn't take offense, even though she wanted to.

Bitsy pinned him with the stern look that she

might have bestowed on Luke, her most aggravating nephew-in-law. "You have some ridiculous notions in that head of yours, Yost Weaver."

The man had a lot to learn. Maybe Levi wasn't the only one who desperately needed what Bitsy Kiem had to teach.

It was exhausting being so indispensable.

Chapter 3

Yost zig-zagged through the crowds looking for the table Bitsy said would be halfway down the second row, right next to the fudge display, and his heart did a somersault at the mere thought of Bitsy's name.

What was that about? He was well past being a teenager.

They'd spent five days last week and four days this week getting ready for the community crafts bazaar. The bazaar gave local *Englisch* and Amish craftspeople a place to sell their wares to eager Christmas shoppers. Of course, the Amish didn't think Christmas should be commercialized, so it wasn't even called a Christmas bazaar. But most shoppers got the idea.

Levi and Bitsy, with a little help from Yost, had spent their time together pouring beeswax candles, trimming the wicks, and tying them up with cellophane and red ribbon. Yost had helped tie ribbons in between fixing Bitsy's stove, her leaky faucet, her lopsided table, and the broken slat on her kitchen chair that her nephew-in-law Josiah had tried to mend with duct tape.

They'd also spent a lot of time laughing because Bitsy liked to be stubborn and Yost liked to contradict her. She really was very pretty when she scowled at him.

He thought he heard strains of "Silent Night" playing over the loudspeaker, but it was too noisy to make out much of anything. Gaudy Christmas lights hung over almost every booth, even the Amish ones, as Amish and *Englisch* alike tried to attract the attention of buyers looking for Christmas gifts or decorations. The crowds were big, especially for Bienenstock, Wisconsin. Yost prayed that someone, anyone, would buy Levi's candles.

He caught sight of Bitsy's green-tinted hair under her white *kapp* and curled one side of his mouth. Bitsy had colored her hair green because it was a Christmas color, and she said it would attract more buyers to their candle table. He flinched when he saw what looked like a plump red bug crawling up Bitsy's neck. It turned out to be a tattoo of something Christmas-y, like a ribbon or a flower. Yost couldn't be sure, and for sure and certain he wasn't going to stare at Bitsy's neck long enough to find out. He could only hope it was the temporary kind.

Bitsy and Levi stood behind a folding table covered with a red tablecloth and stacked with beeswax candles, smiling at anyone who would make eye contact with them.

Well. *Levi* was grinning from ear to ear. Bitsy was trying for a pleasant look on her face. Cheerfulness didn't come easy to her, and she wasn't one to pretend. Yost watched as an *Englisch* man approached the table and asked Levi a question. Levi's smile got wider, if that were possible, and he picked up one of his candles to show the man. The *Englischer* pulled his wallet out of his pocket and handed some money to Levi. Levi in turn gave the man a beehive shaped candle and a toothy grin.

Yost melted like a July snowman. Any amount of hardship with Bitsy Kiem was worth that look on Levi's face. Yost eyed Bitsy. Behind her persistent frown, her eyes were alight with something akin to pride—the *gute* kind of pride—no greater than if Levi had been her own grandson.

Levi saw Yost and waved with his whole arm. "*Dawdi*, we sold four candles already. I made sixteen dollars."

"Not so fast, young man," Bitsy said, reaching under the table for a candle from their box. "You need to pay me for ribbon and cellophane expenses. You've only made fifteen dollars."

Levi nodded as if every word that came out of Bitsy's mouth was the gospel. "Okay. Fifteen dollars. How much does a beehive cost?"

"A lot more than that. Don't count your chickens before they hatch. Or your beehives."

Yost took the candle from Bitsy and set it on the table, replacing the one they'd just sold. "Do you need help?"

"Levi doesn't even need *my* help," Bitsy said.

Levi smiled. "You can stand behind the table with us, *Dawdi*. It's fun to try to get people to buy candles."

Yost nodded. "Okay. But I'm not very *gute* at talking to strangers."

"I'll do the talking," Levi said. "People still think I'm a little kid. They like buying something from a little kid."

Yost mutely stood next to Bitsy for the next half hour, watching Levi sell candles and trying not to think about how good Bitsy smelled, like vanilla and honey with a little beeswax mixed in. The bazaar would go all afternoon and into the evening, and Levi and Bitsy had sold more than half their candles already.

Yost noticed Mark Hoover and Peewee Davie Zook before they noticed him, which wasn't surprising because Mark and Peewee never noticed much past their own upturned noses. Mark couldn't have been more than twelve, just like Levi, but Peewee was fourteen and as Bitsy would say, too big for his britches, even though he was shorter than Mark. They strutted down the row of Christmas toys and food as if they owned the whole market. They were in Yost's district, and Yost had never really liked them much, but they were both young and it wasn't too late for them to grow out of being *dumm.*

The problem was that cocksure boys like that tended to appeal to boys less confident, and Levi thought Mark and Peewee were more *wunderbarr* than a whole dish of *yummasetti* hot from the oven.

Levi caught his breath and straightened to his full height as soon as he saw Mark and Peewee. His eagerness set Yost's teeth on edge.

"You selling candles?" Peewee said. He had never been too bright.

Yost pursed his lips. Uncharitable thoughts about Peewee Davie Zook were beneath him. He was fifty-five years old and had been a *deerich* young man once. Peewee would learn, and probably the hard way.

"*Jah,*" Levi said, glancing back at Bitsy. "Bitsy Kiem and I made them."

Peewee looked directly at Bitsy and grimaced as if he'd drunk a whole jar of pickle juice. He leaned forward and cupped his hand around his mouth, whispering loudly enough so people three tables down could hear. "Look at her green hair and that *hesslich* tattoo."

Bitsy smirked in Peewee's direction. "You must be an orphan or your *mater* would have taught you some manners."

"I'm not an orphan," Peewee said, as if she'd insulted his entire family. He narrowed his eyes at Levi. "Are you going to jump the fence like Bitsy? My *dat* says she doesn't follow *Gelassenheit*."

Yost pursed his lips. *Gelassenheit*. Yielding to a higher authority. Humility. It was what every Amish member strived for. But Peewee didn't know a thing about Bitsy. She was more devoted to *Gotte* than many others in the *gmayna*. Yost had to put a stop to such talk, especially in public.

"Peewee," Yost said, but Levi interrupted him.

"I'm not going to jump the fence," Levi said, taking two steps to the side so he wasn't as close to Bitsy. That brought him closer to Peewee.

Peewee raised his arms and jumped back as if he'd been burned. "*Ach*. Don't touch Levi. He's friends with the tattooed woman. We'll catch a disease." He turned and strolled away, casting a self-righteous glance behind him as he went. Mark followed him.

Yost put a hand on Levi's shoulder. "That was very rude. They should know better than to behave like that."

Levi looked up, and there were tears in his eyes. "They think I'm going to jump the fence. I would never jump the fence. None of the people in the *gmayna* will buy a candle because Bitsy has a tattoo."

Yost glanced at Bitsy and then gave his grandson

a warning frown. "Now, Levi, it's because of Bitsy that you even have candles to sell."

"But they think I'm going to jump the fence."

Bitsy wrapped her arm around Levi's neck as if she were going to choke him. That was probably her version of a hug. "Sit down, Levi."

There were two chairs next to the table. Levi sort of lumbered to one of them, and Bitsy took the other. She turned her chair so that she and Levi were knee to knee and propped her elbows on her legs. "Levi Weaver, you're a fine boy and a *gute* candle maker, and you don't upbraid me for having pierced ears like some people do."

Yost found it hard to swallow. At the moment, he didn't like being one of the "some people."

"You have worked hard and should have a say in how we sell our candles. Would you feel more comfortable if I covered up my hair and my charming poinsettia tattoo?"

Levi stopped sniffling and eyed Bitsy as if trying to decide if she was serious. Then he nodded.

"Okay then," Bitsy said, slapping her knee and standing up. Without making a fuss about it, she grabbed a thick red scarf from under the table and tied it like a bonnet around her head. It covered up her green hair and the tattoo on her neck and looked absolutely ridiculous.

Yost was sufficiently horrified. Levi, on the other hand, wiped his nose with the handkerchief from his pocket and burst into a smile. "You look like a Christmas ornament."

Nae. She looked like she had a red pillow tied around her ears. If she needed to take a nap, she'd be comfortable resting her head anywhere.

Bitsy bent her head in Levi's direction. "What did you say? I can't hear you."

Yost choked back his laughter. Bitsy was willing to make a fool of herself to help Levi feel better. She hadn't been willing to take off her earrings for Yost, but she'd been willing to cover up that hair she loved so much for Levi's sake.

Yost would never, ever say a bad word or think an unkind thought about Bitsy Kiem again. In truth, right now, not one bad thing was coming to mind. Bitsy was thoughtful and charitable and Christian, and he had misjudged her.

Badly.

She'd never been more beautiful, even if she looked as silly as a horse in a pair of pajamas. If they had been alone, he would have taken her into his arms and kissed her.

Something hard stuck in his throat. How had that thought ambushed him? It was intriguing and horrifying at the same time.

Yost was desperately trying to catch his breath when all three of Bitsy's nieces ambled up to the candle table. Lily, the oldest, was in a family way and looked to be due very soon. Poppy pushed a stroller with a chubby baby inside. Rose didn't have any babies and didn't look to be with child. Bitsy went around the table and immediately picked up the baby. "Luke Junior must have his papa's appetite. Either that or you're feeding him buttermilk."

Yost smiled as best he could, but he still couldn't breathe properly. *"Hallo,"* he said. "It is *gute* to see all of you and I don't want to be rude, but I need to go outside to get some air." He stupidly nodded to Bitsy as if seeking her permission. He didn't need her permission. He didn't need her for anything.

He hurried outside, grabbed a handful of snow from the nearest snowbank, and pressed it to the back of his neck. The ice dripping down his back did nothing to help him think more clearly, and now he had a wet shirt.

The sooner Bitsy Kiem was out of his life, the better.

Who needed the aggravation of wet shirts and extra laundry?

Bitsy and her girls moved away from the candle table so they wouldn't block anyone's view of the candles.

"Oh, *Aendi* Bitsy," Rose said. "The candles are wonderful-*gute*. I love the beehives."

None of the girls mentioned the thick red scarf tied around her head, but they were used to her being a little different and nothing she did surprised them anymore—at least that was her goal. It was hard to hear the conversation and even harder to cuddle Luke Junior, but that didn't keep her from trying. She pressed her lips to Junior's cheek and gave him the biggest hug a woman wearing a scarf headdress could give.

"Levi Weaver looks very happy," Lily said, resting her hand on her growing abdomen.

Bitsy had always thought there was nothing more beautiful than a woman who was going to have a baby. Lily was glowing. "He should be. He's making all sorts of money off our beeswax."

Lily smiled and looked in the direction Yost had disappeared. "I've always liked Yost Weaver. Only the best kind of *dawdi* would go to so much trouble to see that his grandson learned a lesson."

A line appeared between Poppy's eyebrows. "He likes you, I think."

"Of course he likes me. He's lonely, and he needs a woman's influence. His *mater* is beside herself with little ones."

Poppy's lips curled mischievously. "I was talking about Yost."

Poppy shouldn't say such things if she didn't want Bitsy to drop the baby. "Yost? Yost doesn't like me. We barely put up with each other." She frowned. Despite his objections to her hair colors, Yost had done a lot of smiling at her in the last two weeks. He still had all his teeth, which was very important to a former dental hygienist, and one of his top front teeth was slightly crooked, which made him seem more interesting than he probably was. She had to admit he made himself useful by fixing things around the house. There was considerably less duct tape than when he'd started coming over. She enjoyed irritating him with her vocal prayers and her tinkling earrings, and he seemed to enjoy finding money in her Bible as he searched for verses about earrings and fingernail polish.

But Yost certainly didn't like her. And she most certainly didn't like him.

How could Poppy plant such an idea in her head?

Oy, anyhow. It was going to get stuck there.

Chapter 4

Yost and Levi walked up Bitsy's porch steps, and Yost's heart knocked against his rib cage as if it were trying to get out of his chest. It was only a Friday, and she was only Bitsy Kiem. His heart shouldn't be doing an *Englisch* tap dance.

Every time Yost came to Bitsy Kiem's house, he wondered if he should do some sort of penance for simply being there. Should he talk to the bishop about sitting idly by while Bitsy prayed out loud? Should he ask *Gotte's* forgiveness for adoring the way Bitsy's newly dyed blue hair accented her eyes?

Bitsy had refused to take off her earrings when Yost asked her to, but the second Levi was in trouble, she was willing to do anything to make him happy— even wear that bulky scarf that made her head look three times too big for her body.

Yost had never been so touched. Or so dismayed. How could a man like him even think about having feelings for a woman like Bitsy? They were as different as asparagus and cinnamon.

What made everything worse was that he enjoyed,

even took pleasure in being with Bitsy and her unconventional opinions, which made him feel even more guilty and more in need of repentance. It was a vicious circle, like a merry-go-round that he saw no hope of getting off.

They had searched the Bible for passages about earrings and tattoos and even something called Van Halen. She had taught him a ridiculous song—*There ain't nothing I can do, a total eclipse of the heart*—and prayed out loud on his behalf several times. He had laughed more in the last three weeks than he had laughed in the last four years, and he was so happy, he caught himself whistling Christmas songs while milking the cows. Bitsy was a puzzle and a delight and a frustration all at the same time.

Every minute he spent at Bitsy's house was the happiest, best time of his life. And the worst.

Was it possible to feel guilty about liking someone?

Not just liking her, but spending every waking hour thinking about her, every night dreaming about her, every beat of his heart hoping she'd smile at him—or give him one of her exasperated frowns.

This was not normal, and he should feel very guilty. *Did* feel very guilty. But what could be done?

He'd already admitted to himself that he liked Bitsy. Unfortunately, Levi liked her too, and Yost couldn't cut off contact simply because he was uncomfortable in her presence. Levi was blossoming. He didn't slouch at the dinner table anymore, and Yost's son, Reuben, said Levi had been given the biggest part in the school Christmas program because the teacher had noticed that he was trying harder at his schoolwork.

A week ago, Yost had considered sending Levi by himself to Bitsy's, but the thought of not seeing her made him depressed. Maybe after Christmas, when spring came, he'd be too busy and have an excuse to cut Bitsy Kiem out of his life.

It was a sad thought at Christmastime.

Levi could barely contain his excitement as he knocked on Bitsy's door. Yost was having an even harder time containing his. Hopefully, Bitsy would be just as excited as they were.

She opened the door with that endearing frown on her face and a long sparkly pair of earrings in her ears, the same pair she'd been wearing the first day they'd come to make candles. She'd colored her hair blue a few days ago, and it matched her eyes and clashed with her pumpkin orange dress. Who wore a pumpkin orange dress? Her outfit was like the remains of a pumpkin pie splattered against a blue linoleum floor.

Except, she looked too pretty for words.

How was that possible?

"It's about time you got here," she said. "I grew three new gray hairs while I waited."

Levi did his best to contain his smile. "We had to get a surprise."

The lines around Bitsy's mouth deepened. "I'm not fond of surprises. It's not another cat, is it? Because if it is, you can turn around and march right back home." She pursed her lips and squinted. "Although, I'd like to name it before you go. How does Snoop Dogg sound?"

"For a cat?" Levi said.

Bitsy cocked her head to one side and made her earrings jingle. "Well, *cum reu.* You're letting all the cold air in. I thought we could make a candle for your *mamm* for Christmas."

Levi and Yost stayed firmly planted on the porch. Levi looked up at Yost with a glint of animated anticipation in his eyes. "We're taking you for a ride."

Bitsy looked from Levi to Yost and back again. "I don't like the sound of that."

Levi laughed with all the sincerity and joy of a child, then reached out and tugged on Bitsy's hand. "Dawdi brought his sleigh, and we're going to take it along the back roads. We can go fast."

"As fast as Rocky is able to go through the snow," Yost added, just so Bitsy wouldn't expect too much.

Bitsy looked sufficiently impressed and shot Yost a look that might have made a weaker man's knees give out. Yost had *gute* knees. "I'm always up for a sleigh ride," she said. "Let me get my coat."

"Can we bring the cats?" Levi asked.

Yost peered at him and raised an eyebrow. He'd obviously been planning on asking.

"Please?" Levi added.

Bitsy wrinkled her nose in disgust. "I suppose, but they'll be nothing but trouble. Wait here." She closed the door—to keep the cold air out—and reappeared a short minute later with a wicker basket almost the size of a small bathtub. Inside was a fluffy pink blanket and all four of Bitsy's cats. The white one, Farrah Fawcett, looked positively insulted at being carried in a basket. Billy Idol hissed at Yost with barely contained rage. Leonard Nimoy and Sigourney Weaver looked more excited than even Levi did at the possibility of a sleigh ride. Leonard Nimoy jumped on Farrah Fawcett, then on Billy Idol, and when neither of them would play with her, she settled for pawing at Sigourney Weaver.

The basket had a sturdy handle, and Bitsy hooked it over Levi's arm. "Don't drop it. Rose would never forgive me if you just happened to leave the basket somewhere by the side of the road."

She went back into the house and closed the door. Levi folded the edge of the blanket over Farrah Fawcett's rump. Farrah Fawcett looked excessively ungrateful.

When Bitsy came back outside, she wore a brown beanie that had two felt eyes and a black felt nose sewn onto the front with big brown pompoms on either side of the top. That Bitsy owned a bear beanie was surprising enough, but that she had the gall to wear it in place of her *kapp* was more shocking yet. Yost was quite without words.

Should the bishop know about this?

Her earrings poked out from under her beanie, and Yost nearly swallowed his tongue. What would Levi think?

"Dawdi says we Weavers don't wear beanies. Straw hats are *Gelassenheit*."

Gute boy.

Bitsy didn't seem offended in the least. "Your *dawdi* is absolutely right to be concerned, but I wear this beanie to scare the bears away. There's nothing that scares a bear more than the sight of another bear."

Levi's eyes widened to saucers. "Do you think we'll see a bear?"

"Probably not, but you can never be too careful." Bitsy snapped her fingers, which didn't make a sound because she wore mittens the same color as her beanie. "I forgot something." Back into the house. She came out carrying a round plastic container with a lid and handed it to Yost. "I made Bicnenstich Cake this morning. We might as well take it with us. The only thing better than a sleigh ride with cats is a sleigh ride with cats and Bee Sting Cake. And . . ." She returned to the house and emerged with a leather strap laced with jingle bells.

Yost cleared his throat. The beanie was one thing, but he'd have to put his foot down about jingle bells. "*Nae*, Bitsy. Bells are fancy. They draw attention."

Bitsy puffed her cheeks out and blew a loud gust of air from between her lips. "Stuff and nonsense. Marty Troyer has jingle bells on his buggy, and his son is a minister."

Yost frowned. "Are you sure?"

"I may be old, but I'm not feebleminded." She disappeared into the house again and came back with the jingle bells and her money-stuffed Bible. "Show me where it says we can't put jingle bells on the sleigh."

Yost shook his head and cracked a smile. "It says nothing about jingle bells in the Scriptures."

"*Gute*," Bitsy said. "I was beginning to think I missed something."

"Though it does mention tinkling cymbals."

"Two completely different things." She closed her door, grabbed one side of Levi's basket handle, and shook her bells all the way down the steps. She attached the jingle bells to Rocky's harness and climbed in the seat next to Levi.

Yost turned the horse around, and the sleigh glided down the lane of Honeybee Farm. Bitsy started singing "Jingle Bells" the minute the sleigh hit the snow-covered dirt road. She had true pitch, but she made her voice warble and soon had Levi laughing hysterically.

The sound of Levi's laughter loosened some sort of strap that had tightened around Yost's heart when he'd seen that beanie. Bitsy was odd and rebellious and unconventional, but she cared deeply about Levi. Yost could mostly overlook her many flaws. She had a heart of gold, and it covered a multitude of sins.

They rode north, staying to the back roads. They were snow-packed so Rocky had an easy time pulling the sleigh. Yost snapped the reins and spurred Rocky into a trot. He had to press his hat down over his ears so it wouldn't blow off his head. So did Levi. He looked over at Bitsy and smiled. She held on tight to the side of the sleigh and smiled back. He lost the ability to breathe, and flying over the snow had nothing to do with it.

Bitsy's hat stayed tightly on her head, which was one of the advantages of a beanie even though Yost frowned on them. The bells attached to Rocky's harness jingled merrily and made Yost feel like laughing out loud.

Bitsy laid her cake on the floor of the sleigh and raised her hands high over her head. "Woohoo!" she called.

Yost's laughter finally escaped. "What was that?"

"It's a roller-coaster trick I learned," Bitsy said. "It's more exciting if you don't hold on."

Grinning like the cat who ate the canary, Levi secured his hat firmly in one fist and raised the other hand high over his head. "Hooray!" he yelled. The sleigh suddenly lurched forward, and Levi caught his breath and grabbed onto the dashboard. "It is funner," he said, as if he was completely astonished, "but a lot more dangerous, especially if you don't want to fall out. You try it, Dawdi."

Yost shook his head. "I'm the driver."

"*Cum,* Yost. Don't you want some excitement in your life?"

"*Nae.* My life is exciting enough."

Bitsy snorted. "Nights spent reading *Die Botschaft* newspaper do not count as exciting."

How could Bitsy know that? He was going to have to install some blinds in his front room window. "Sometimes they have recipes," he said, trying to keep the sulk out of his voice.

"And poetry." She gave him a look that said he wasn't fooling anybody.

"Come on, Dawdi," Levi said. "I'll hold the reins, and you lift your hands in the air."

It seemed harmless enough. Yost couldn't think of anything in the *Ordnung* that would forbid having a little extra fun on a sleigh ride, and Levi would be fine with the reins for a few seconds. "Okay," he said, carefully transferring the reins to Levi's outstretched hands. "Take her nice and easy with a light grip."

"I can do it, Dawdi." Levi held the reins as if he had a baby rabbit in each hand. Rocky slowed to a trot. Even better.

Yost made a big show of tightening his Velcro gloves. Just to prove to Bitsy that he was at least as exciting as any fifty-five-year-old and braver than men half his age, Yost threw caution to the wind and stood up. Surely it was safe at ten miles an hour. He lifted his hands high into the air while a strangled whoop clawed its way out of his throat.

Levi eyed him with awe written across his face, as if his *dawdi* had done something amazing. Yost couldn't help but be proud that he could still impress his grandson. He raised his hands even higher and waved them back and forth as if he were trying to fan up a breeze. Then he leaned from side to side, showing off his exceptional balance and amazing courage. He grinned at Bitsy, who raised an eyebrow as a signal she knew he was showing off, and gave a loud whoop to the sky.

Unfortunately, just as he turned his face upward, the sleigh glided over a bump in the snow that catapulted Yost into the air and out of the sleigh before he even had a chance to react. His landing was soft, except where his nose hit something hard just underneath the snow. Oy, anyhow! It stung all the way to the back of his head.

Levi yelled and stopped the horse as Yost pushed himself from the ground and sat up, not even caring that the snow was soaking through to his backside and blood was dripping from his nose onto his shirt. He definitely needed to stop seeing Bitsy. His laundry pile was growing bigger and bigger.

Levi and Bitsy jumped from the sleigh and ran in his direction. Well, Levi ran. Bitsy trudged slowly toward him, doing her best to suffocate a smile that persistently tried to take over her face. He should have been offended that she took so much amusement in his misfortune, but one look at her face and the laughter bubbled up inside him. He'd made quite a fool of himself.

Bitsy's smile finally broke free. "You flew ten feet into the air."

Yost chuckled. "You don't seem to care that I might have broken my nose."

She waved away his scolding. "*Ach.* You didn't break your nose. You'd be flat on the ground writhing in pain if you'd broken your nose. You're fine."

"Are you okay, Dawdi?" Levi said, kneeling in the snow next to him. "Your nose is bleeding."

Yost shot a glance at Bitsy. "I think it's broken."

Bitsy pulled a handkerchief from her coat pocket. "It's not broken. He'll be fine unless he freezes to death." Bitsy laid a hand on Levi's shoulder and pinned him with a dramatic look. "You should never sit in the snow. You'll catch your death of cold."

She handed the handkerchief to Yost. He took it and tried to mop up the blood on his face. It was fortunate his coat had been unzipped. The blood on his shirt would wash out easier than blood on his coat. There were a few drops of blood in the snow and several impressive spots on his shirt, but the bleeding had already slowed considerably. His nose was definitely not broken, and they wouldn't have to cut their sleigh ride short to go to the hospital.

Levi stood and reached out his hand. "Here, Dawdi."

Yost took Levi's hand, although if he actually put any pressure on his grandson's hand, he would have pulled him into the snow with him. He pushed himself from the ground with his free hand and stood with a groan. He had landed in the snow, but that didn't mean he wouldn't have a bruise or two by the end of the day. "I'm too old for this," he said, rubbing a particularly hard knot in his lower back.

Bitsy stepped back, folded her arms, and studied him like she might regard one of her cats. "*Jah,* you are. I don't know what you were thinking, standing up like that. It was wonderful foolhardy."

Levi frowned, forced a smile onto his face, and tried to be encouraging. "You were so brave, Dawdi. And then you sort of flew like a bird."

Bitsy pursed her lips and nodded. "You're right, Levi, and I'll give credit where credit is due. Any ballerina would be proud of your graceful landing, Yost. And you haven't even had any formal training."

"Ballerina?" Levi said.

"A dancer. Someone who is trained to jump high into the air and land without hurting herself."

Yost rubbed another sore spot farther up his spine. He was going to ache for days. "I'm glad you admire my talents."

"I wouldn't go that far," Bitsy said. "But at least you didn't die or break your neck. It would have been hard for Levi and me to load your body in the sleigh. And what a chore to keep the cats from licking you."

Pain traveled down his spine when he laughed. "Please, if I ever die at your house, keep the cats away."

"I'll do my best."

With Levi and Bitsy close behind, Yost limped to the sleigh where the cats and the Bee Sting Cake waited patiently for them. For all the soreness in his back, the icy moisture seeping through his trousers was the biggest discomfort. They would have to cut their sleigh ride short. He wouldn't be able to guide the horse if he was shivering with cold.

Bitsy picked up the reins. "I think I'd better drive." She eyed his wet trousers and shook her head. "You've gotten yourself into a pickle. We'll have to head straight home before your trousers freeze to your legs."

"Aw," Levi whined, "do we have to? We were having so much fun."

Yost zipped up his coat and wrapped his arms around himself. "We should probably go. I don't want to get frostbite."

Bitsy jiggled the reins to get Rocky moving, then her eyes seemed to catch fire with excitement. "There is a small hunter's cabin not ten minutes north of here. We could build a fire and eat cake while you dry off."

Levi burst into a smile. "It would be like camping."

"I don't camp anymore," Yost said. It was uncomfortable and cold, and he always came home smelling like a campfire.

"We've got cake and a basket of cats. It might be an exciting afternoon adventure." Bitsy nudged Levi with her elbow. "Your *dawdi* needs some excitement or he's going to turn into a boring old man."

"I am not," Yost protested, although he wasn't so sure it hadn't already happened. He had made a *gute* life with Ruth. They had camped, played games, worked side by side, and raised children. Nowadays, he faithfully planted crops, worked the farm, went to *gmay,* and took a nap every Sunday afternoon. He made himself hot dogs and macaroni and cheese every other night for dinner, alternating with ramen soup on off days—except when Hannah or Reuben invited him over. He read *Die Botschaft* faithfully, including the poetry, trimmed his beard every morning after chores, and memorized Bible verses every night before he went to bed. He liked his life. What was wrong with being a boring old man?

He nearly told Bitsy to turn the sleigh toward home, just to be contrary, but maybe he wasn't quite finished with excitement in his life. He was only fifty-five. Not even one toe was dangling over the edge of his grave yet. There was nothing about camping forbidden in the *Ordnung*. "Okay," he said, tapping Levi's hat more firmly on his head. "But that cake better be worth the trip."

Bitsy nodded. "It is. Many a boy has fallen in love with a girl because of that cake. You won't be disappointed."

To his dismay and frustration, Yost's throat constricted. Why would he react that way just because Bitsy said something about love? For sure and certain, he wouldn't fall in love with Bitsy because of a cake.

He took a deep breath.

Nobody was going to fall in love with anybody over a Bee Sting Cake.

Bitsy guided Rocky between two trees at the edge of the road. The going was slower because the horse would have to plow through deeper snow. Bitsy glanced in his direction. "The cabin is stocked with matches and firewood. You'll be able to melt that ice off your beard in a trice."

Rocky pulled the sleigh through the woods until they came upon the cabin standing watch under a canopy of bare and massive trees. Well . . . *cabin* was quite a grand word for what stood in front of them. It was a hut, a small hut, not more than a dozen feet across and a dozen feet wide. Time and weather had worn the wood slats to a silvery gray, and they looked as if they would topple over with one *gute,* stiff wind—or even a gentle breeze.

"*Ach, du lieva!*" Levi said, not seeming to care that the cabin walls listed to one side. He jumped from the sleigh and jogged to the front door. "What a *wunderbarr* place! Look, Dawdi. It has a door knocker."

Yost smiled at his enthusiastic grandson, almost longing for the days when life and things like a rickety old cabin held so much promise, even if Levi would not be allowed to set foot inside that thing.

Bitsy tied the reins and picked up her basket of cats. "See if somebody's home," she said, obviously not caring about the danger.

Levi lifted the knocker and banged it hard against the door. No answer. None of them had expected one. Levi skipped around the cabin—hut—no doubt looking for something exciting lurking about in the bushes.

Bitsy eyed Yost with suspicion. Maybe she knew what he was thinking. "Don't sit there with your mouth open like a walleye. Let's go in and get a fire going."

"Who is going to pull me out of the rubble if the wind blows it over?"

Bitsy jumped from the sleigh with her basket. "Levi gets pulled out first. After that, I can't promise anything."

Yost planted his bottom more firmly on the seat, which was extra chilly with wet trousers. "Levi and I will stay here while you die in a cabin accident."

Bitsy attempted to look deeply offended, but she only managed to seem mildly irritated. "You'd let me die alone?"

"Someone needs to watch after Levi."

"I've stayed here with my girls at least a dozen times during the deer hunt. It hasn't fallen on me yet."

Yost's eyebrows nearly flew off his face. "You've been on a deer hunt with your girls?"

Bitsy hooked the basket handle over one arm and picked up the cake with her free hand. "*Nae.* We've stayed here during the deer hunt. I don't believe in guns."

"But . . . what do you mean? Did you hunt deer? What about your girls?"

Bitsy gave him her I'm-going-to-lose-my-patience-with-you look. "We used to come out here during the deer hunt and scare the deer away so the hunters couldn't kill them. But don't worry. We wore the bright orange hunting gear so we wouldn't get shot."

Yost didn't even know where to begin to make sense of anything Bitsy said. "You scared deer away?"

"We made a lot of noise. I urinated on several bushes, but the girls wouldn't do it with me. The deer catch the scent and run away."

Yost knew he should be horrified at the thought of Bitsy . . . he wouldn't even think about it . . . but before he could open his mouth to express his deep and appalled disapproval, laughter burst from his lips, and he couldn't do anything to stop it. He laughed hard and loud, so loud he probably scared not only the deer, but the hibernating bears, the badgers, and the bunny rabbits. "Bitsy," he breathed between fits of laughter, "you are the strangest . . . funniest . . . most lovable woman I have ever met."

She scrunched her mouth to one side of her face to stop the upward curl of her lips. "Everybody has to do their part to save the wildlife. Soon there won't be a patch of grass left in the whole state."

Yost glanced at Levi, who was busying himself collecting kindling under the snow for the fire they were not going to build in that tumble-down hut. He shook his head as his laughter subsided. "I am very glad my grandson didn't hear that."

Bitsy raised an eyebrow. "Why? Don't you want him doing his part to save the wildlife?"

Yost chuckled. "Not that part."

Bitsy turned toward the hut. "*Cum.* We don't want to disappoint Levi, and you will get wonderful cold without a fire and a piece of cake."

Yost tilted his head to one side and studied the cabin again. With his head tilted, the cabin looked more upright, but still apt to fall over. "It doesn't look safe."

Bitsy blew air from between her lips. "A man who doesn't have any more sense than to bleed on himself doesn't know what's safe and what's not." She raised her eyes to the sky. "Dear Lord, I'm usually very patient, but Yost will die of frostbite and stubbornness if you don't coax him into this cabin right now. Amen."

She was so determined and so obstinate, Yost had to laugh again. But if she was persistent enough to pray for him, he should be pliable enough to bend in her direction. He could bend when he had a mind to. And he didn't want to disappoint Levi.

Besides, the walls of the cabin were so thin that if they collapsed, they might get a splinter or two but no bruises.

He gingerly stepped down from the sleigh and took the basket of cats from Bitsy. It wasn't all that heavy, but she shouldn't have to carry everything. Bitsy lifted the door latch, and the three of them tip-toed into the cabin just in case a heavy step would make it fall down.

To Yost's surprise, the cabin had a wood floor, old and weathered, but tight and smooth. It didn't creak. That was something. The man who laid the floor had obviously not erected the walls.

A small window sat in the wall across from the door, and a shiny potbelly stove stood in the corner of the room with firewood stacked shoulder high in a neat row against the wall.

With eyes turned upward, Levi walked around the room as if he were taking a tour of a castle. "This is the best cabin ever," he whispered. "Is it yours, Bitsy?"

Bitsy set her basket on the floor. All of the cats but Farrah Fawcett jumped out and began exploring the small space. "*Ach.* My *dawdi's fater* built this cabin many years ago, but whatever hunter happens upon it is welcome to use it as long as they stock it with firewood and sweep up after themselves."

She set the cake on the floor and opened the stove. "My *dat* bought this stove not two years ago. The old one smoked something wonderful."

At least Yost wouldn't have to fret about a fire in addition to a collapse.

Levi helped Bitsy crinkle a few pieces of newspaper into the stove, and Yost crammed in as much firewood as would fit. They needed a big fire. Both he and Levi were starting to shiver. Bitsy pulled a box of matches from the top of the woodpile and lit the newspaper. It popped into flame, and they watched it until the fire took hold of the wood, crackling like a strip of bacon on the pan.

"There. We should be melted in no time," Bitsy said. "When it gets warm enough to sit down, we'll eat our cake and tell ghost stories. How does that sound?"

"No ghost stories," Yost said, smiling so Bitsy knew he wasn't cross.

Bitsy clapped her mittens together. "But now we need something to warm us up while the fire gets going. Levi, do you want to learn a song?"

"What kind of song?"

"An *Englisch* song. They sing it to get their blood pumping."

"Okay," Levi said.

Yost was too distracted by the soft glow of Bitsy's eyes to be concerned that her song might not be appropriate for Levi. Bitsy was a beauty, the contours of her face soft and smooth, the movement of her hands strong and graceful, the arch of her eyebrows captivating and maddening. He should have been more adamant about not setting foot in the cabin. It was too small, and Bitsy felt too close, but there was nowhere to go to get away from her because Bitsy filled the entire space.

"The words to the song are easy to learn. *Ice cream and cake, we like ice cream and cake. Ice cream and cake, we like ice cream and cake. Ice cream and cake, we like ice cream and cake.*"

Levi grinned from ear to ear. "I like it. But you're not really singing."

Bitsy nodded. "I'm talking. It's called rap."

"What is rap?" Levi asked, eager to learn anything about the *Englisch* world.

Bitsy shrugged. "It's a lot of yelling and people getting mad and words you can't understand. But the ice-cream-and-cake rap is just for getting warm. Do it with me." She slapped her knees to the rhythm and said the words while Levi tried to keep up.

"I don't know about this," Yost said.

"Now, Yost," Bitsy said, "you know perfectly well that there is nothing about ice cream and cake in the Bible."

"And you know perfectly well that the bishop would never approve a song about ice cream and cake, and knee-slapping might as well be dancing."

Bitsy didn't seem the least bit troubled. "There's no sin in keeping warm, Yost. And we can check with the bishop when we get back to town, but since he isn't here, we'll just have to use our best judgment. You want to stay warm, don't you?"

Yost felt as if he were being pulled slowly out to sea by a gentle but persistent current. He didn't even want to put his foot down. Levi's whole face was alight with happiness, and Bitsy was frowning at him as if she sort of liked being with him. How could he resist that?

While the fire slowly warmed up the rickety little hut, Yost, Levi, and Bitsy recited the Ice Cream and Cake song. Yost couldn't keep any rhythm to speak of, but Bitsy had plenty for both of them. Her earrings tinkled whenever she moved. She'd obviously done some dancing in her younger days. She and Levi kept a steady beat with their hands against their knees, and they made a game of saying the words faster and faster until they sounded like nonsense. All three of them ended up laughing, warmed through even before the potbelly stove got hot.

They sat on the cold floor of the cabin, and Bitsy cut them each a slice of Bee Sting Cake with Yost's pocketknife. Bee Sting Cake was altogether too messy to be eaten with their hands, but they didn't have plates or utensils, so they got very sticky and Levi had a wonderful-*gute* time licking his fingers. Yost had never tasted anything so delicious, fork or no fork. The soft, bread-like cake, the pastry cream filling, and the crunchy almond topping could have almost made him believe that someone could fall in love over a Bee Sting Cake.

Even him.

Bitsy gave each of the cats a taste of the cake, except Billy Idol, who probably considered himself too wild for something so civilized as a piece of cake. The two smaller cats chased Billy Idol around the room and pawed at him until he arched his back and hissed at them.

"Billy Idol," Bitsy scolded. "Be nice to Leonard Nimoy and Sigourney Weaver. They just want you to love them."

Billy Idol crouched as if he were hunting, squeezed through a hole in one of the floorboards, and disappeared.

"Where did he go?" Levi said.

Bitsy licked her thumb and wiped it down the side of Levi's mouth, swabbing off a smudge of cream filling. "Outside, for sure and certain. He doesn't like to be cooped up indoors for long, even in the winter."

He pressed his lips together. "Billy Idol is an unwanted cat, isn't he?"

Bitsy's posture stiffened but so imperceptibly that Yost wouldn't have noticed if he hadn't been staring at her, wondering what it would feel like to take her hand in his and trace his thumb around the graceful lines of her fingers. Something told him the Ice Cream and Cake song was to blame for the improper thoughts he was having.

"Why do you think Billy Idol is an unwanted cat?" Bitsy said.

"He's ugly, and you always complain about him."

"I don't like Billy Idol, it's true," Bitsy said, "but I wouldn't say he's unwanted."

Levi looked down and fiddled with the laces of his boot. "I'm unwanted."

It felt as if an earthquake passed through Yost's heart. Levi thought he was unwanted? "That's not true," Yost said, a sharp reprimand in his tone. "Don't you ever let me hear such things from your mouth again." He wouldn't stand for Levi to believe that about himself.

His eyes wide with innocence and hurt, Levi closed his mouth and nodded obediently.

Bitsy's glare could have seared a hole through Yost's hat or made the cabin fall down around their heads. "Yost Weaver, you're not usually one to speak without thinking, so I won't pray the measles down upon you, but just because you don't want to hear it doesn't mean it's not real. Or important. You might as well tell the sun not to shine as to tell someone not to feel something. Keep your mouth shut, and maybe you'll learn something." She looked up at the ceiling—probably hoping it wouldn't fall on him. "Dear Lord, please make Yost a little less thick in the head, and help him remember he has two ears and one mouth. He should listen twice as much as he talks."

Yost would have taken two steps back if he'd been standing. No woman had ever talked to him like that before. No Amish woman would have ever dared. He should have been righteously indignant. He should have grabbed Levi's collar, pulled him outside to the sleigh, and driven away without a second thought for Bitsy Kiem.

But a stunning realization paralyzed him. At that moment, he felt nothing but fierce gratitude for Bitsy. She cared about Levi—deeply. And not only cared about him but was unafraid to admonish a man for the sake of his grandson. He'd never seen the like of it.

While every fiber of his being seemed somehow attached to Bitsy, she turned her face from him and seemed to completely forget he was even in the room. "Why do you feel unwanted, Levi?"

Levi's gaze traveled to Yost and then back to Bitsy. He licked his lips and swallowed hard. "My *mamm* never makes cake anymore. Or cookies. She used to put a cookie in my lunch every day. Now she doesn't even make me a sandwich. She frowns when I come home from school and tells me to go outside and not bother her, even when it's wonderful cold outside. My *dat* only comes home between jobs and he doesn't hardly say three words to me except '*Did you muck out today?*' Or '*You didn't strain the milk so gute.*' " Levi's eyes filled with tears, and he blinked them away before they had a chance to run down his cheeks. "My *mamm* and *dat* don't love me anymore. They'd be better off without me, just like you'd be better off without Billy Idol. You already have enough cats."

Yost thought his heart might break. He wanted to yell, to tell Levi that of course his parents loved him but they were going through a busy time with baby twins and eight *kinner* under the age of thirteen. But he thought better of it and kept his mouth shut. Bitsy was doing a much better job of drawing Levi out than he ever could.

"Let me clear one thing up before I say the important things," Bitsy said. She pointed at Levi. "Billy Idol is an ugly cat, but you are not an ugly boy. You've got fine eyebrows like your *dawdi* and a face full of freckles. Girls love freckles, and don't you forget it."

For some reason, Levi had always responded to Bitsy's brusque manner—much like Yost did. "Okay," Levi said, obviously reassured that if he was unloved, at least he wasn't ugly.

As if he knew they were talking about him, Billy Idol reappeared from under the floor with a dead mouse in his teeth. Levi caught his breath and drew back as Billy Idol laid the mouse at Levi's feet as if offering him the first bite. "*Ach!*"

"Billy Idol," Bitsy scolded, "you know mice aren't allowed indoors." She picked up the dead mouse by the tail, which was more than Yost ever would have done, and dangled it in front of Billy Idol's face. "You can eat it outside. Go on now."

Billy Idol watched the swinging mouse for a few seconds before hissing angrily, snatching it in his teeth, and climbing down the hole again.

"You might not be able to guess, Levi, but Billy Idol is my favorite cat."

"He is?"

"*Jah*, because I don't have to coddle him."

A line appeared between Levi's brows. "What does *coddle* mean?"

"I don't have to treat him like a baby. He can take care of himself, and he makes things easier for me." She waved her hand in the direction of Farrah Fawcett, who hadn't moved from her comfortable spot in the basket since they'd arrived at the cabin. "Farrah Fawcett is high maintenance, as the *Englisch* say. She wouldn't catch a mouse even if it was trying to kill me."

Yost raised an eyebrow. Had a mouse ever tried to kill a human before?

"But sometimes I don't appreciate Billy like I should. He probably thinks I don't like him because I haven't given him a special place on the window seat or a fancy pillow to sleep on. He brings gifts of mice that no one thanks him for, even though he keeps the mice out of my beehives."

Levi widened his eyes. "Mice can get into the beehives?"

"*Jah.* They like the warmth in the winter, and in the summer, they're looking to steal the honey. Like I said, Billy Idol is my favorite cat." She took her thumb and index finger and squeezed one of Levi's earlobes. "Little brother, your parents haven't stopped loving you. They depend on you. They don't have to coddle you, so sometimes they forget how important you are to the family. Who would milk the cow if you didn't?"

Levi sniffled back more tears. "Well, Amos milks too."

Bitsy reached over and snapped one of Levi's suspenders. "And who makes sure Amos does it?"

"I guess I do." A slow smile formed on his lips. "So I'm like Billy Idol, and he's your favorite cat?"

Bitsy nodded. "It wouldn't hurt to walk right up to your *mamm* and say, 'Mamm, do you love me?' and then watch what she says. You know what she's going to say."

"I guess I do." Levi leaned back on his hands. "Can I have another piece of cake?"

"Have two," Bitsy said. "We still have more than half."

Billy Idol crawled back through the floor without his mouse and stationed himself against the far wall as if guarding the rest of them from attack.

Yost couldn't have put two words together if his life depended on it. His heart felt so full, it expanded into his throat. Bitsy Kiem could know the lyrics to every rap song ever written, and he would still love her with his whole soul. How could he have judged and dismissed this beautiful, kind, feisty woman? She wore earrings and bear beanies, but her heart was as good and kind as anyone he'd ever known, including Ruth. He was astonished and astounded and ashamed of himself and determined to make up for lost time. As astounding as it seemed, he loved Bitsy Kiem and he wanted to spend the rest of his life with her.

He crossed his legs and pretended to look at the cake while studying her out of the corner of his eye. She would make him very happy, and he could make her very happy too, if she would let him. She was already full of *gute* works. Surely she could be molded into a *gute,* dutiful, proper Amish *fraa.* He loved her. He had no doubt he could convince her to give up her wild hair colors and her fancy earrings. He could find passages in the Bible to admonish her for her worldly ways and convince her by gentle persuasion that if she wanted salvation, she needed to live by the *Ordnung.*

He locked his gaze on her blue hair. The light shade accented her lively eyes. She loved her hair and her earrings and her tattoos, but he could show her a better way, and she would thank him for loving her enough to change her. It would be hard, but he loved her too much to even consider giving her up.

Levi finished his second piece of cake and rubbed his sticky hands down his trousers. "Can Billy Idol and I go out and climb that tree?" he said, pointing out the window to a sprawling basswood tree with low, sturdy branches.

Bitsy looked to Yost.

Yost nodded, "Don't go so high you can't get down."

Levi leaped to his feet and summoned Billy Idol. Billy Idol hissed and scowled, but he followed Levi out the door, followed by Sigourney Weaver and Leonard Nimoy. Farrah Fawcett had no interest in climbing trees.

His love burned like a fire that threatened to consume him. The sooner Bitsy was his wife, the better. Under the pretense of wanting another piece of cake, he scooted closer to her. What should he say? Where should he start? He was passionately in love. Was he even capable of sounding sensible? "*Denki*," he managed to blurt out after several seconds of deep thought.

"For what?"

"For understanding Levi. I don't care what Paul Glick says about your family. You are more Christian than most of us."

Bitsy snorted. "Don't mention Paul Glick. The thought of him always puts me in a bad mood. And never compare how Christian someone is with someone else. You can never know what's in someone's heart. Jesus is the only righteous judge."

He nodded. "I'll try to leave Paul Glick out of all future conversations. But even if it's wrong to compare, I think we have failed in our duty to train Levi up in the nurture and admonition of the Lord."

Bitsy curled one side of her mouth, and Yost's gut clenched. The temptation to kiss her almost overpowered him. "You've trained him fine. Mary has eight little ones. My cats are going to make me lose my mind, and there are only four of them. And they're cats. It is not Mary's fault or Reuben's or anyone else's. Sometimes young ones lose their way. Besides, my parents only had two children and being paid too much attention was worse than being ignored."

"I still feel bad that Levi has been unhappy."

She gave his hand a stiff pat, and he nearly jumped out of his skin. "Every boy should have a *dawdi* like you, Yost Weaver. Most men couldn't be bothered, especially the *Englischers*."

Yost gave her a cautious smile. Did that mean she liked him?

Of course she liked him. She might be grumpy and opinionated, but she didn't seem to mind when he came over, and she had never pointed her shotgun at him.

And she'd made him Bee Sting Cake. Surely he could mold her and then convince her to marry him.

He dared to reach out his hand and finger one of her earrings. It tinkled softly. "Are you ever afraid this is going to catch on something and rip your ear off? I think it would be dangerous to wear them."

"Earlobes are wonderful strong, even with heavy earrings."

"Are those earrings heavy? Does it make your ears hurt to carry that much weight?"

She sort of half frowned and squinted in his direction. "Why do you care about my earrings, Yost? Is it because they go against the *Ordnung?*" She didn't seem mad, or even mildly irritated, which was her usual state of mind.

"I'm curious. Amish women don't wear earrings."

Her mouth relaxed into a smile, and she touched her earring post. "This is the first pair of earrings I ever bought."

"They must be your favorite."

She glanced at him as if he was intruding on the conversation she was having with herself. "I bought them the day I got to Green Bay thirty-five years ago."

Yost's heart drooped like a sack of potatoes over an old man's shoulder. Thirty-five years. That was a lifetime ago, but maybe not to Bitsy. A few weeks ago, she'd told him it was too late to ask for forgiveness. Had she been holding on to it all these years?

She slid the earring out of her ear and dangled it between her fingers. "I did it to spite my parents, even though they would never see me in them. I did it to show Yost Weaver that I was a big girl and didn't need a boy's help for anything."

"Oh."

"It was wrong of me to be so spiteful, but I was eighteen and that has to be my excuse. That's why I wear them sometimes when you come over. You should get to see them since I bought them with you in mind."

Yost couldn't swallow. "We . . . we were young, Bitsy," he said, as if that justified his actions, but it sounded like a hollow reason, even to him.

She smirked. It was a hollow excuse to her too. "It was my eighteenth birthday. Remember?"

He nodded.

"I didn't want my *dat* to call the police to arrest me for running away. I held on until I was a legal adult."

"I'm sorry that your *dat* was unkind," he mumbled.

Bitsy swung her earring back and forth slowly, like a fan. "It made it easier to leave."

"It was the reason you left."

"My sister tried to help, but after she married and it was just me and my *mamm* and *dat,* I had to leave."

"I know," Yost said. He may have forgotten for thirty-five years, but he knew how hard home had been for Bitsy. She wasn't inclined to conform to the rules, and her *dat* hated her stubborn independence.

Yost and Bitsy had been unlikely friends. He was straightlaced and level-headed, not daring to step one toe outside of the *Ordnung.* She was rebellious and tended to act before she thought things through. She seemed to purposefully do things to anger her *fater,* and his righteous retribution was swift and harsh. Yost had been drawn to her spontaneity, the way she lived every day as if it were the most exciting time of her life, and of course, her *gute* heart, which had only grown bigger in thirty-five years.

"I went to Green Bay because I had a friend there to give me a room and a job."

"I remember," Yost said, trying not to squirm. He knew what she was going to say.

She rolled her eyes in his direction. "Do you vaguely remember that you were supposed to come with me?"

She tried to act like she didn't really care, but the pain buried deep behind her eyes took his breath away. He'd hurt her, and he'd known it for thirty-five years. He'd simply talked himself out of feeling guilty.

"I'm . . . I'm sorry, Bitsy. We were both in *rumsch-pringe,* but I knew if I ran away to Green Bay, I'd break my *mamm's* heart. When the time came, I couldn't do it. It must have been terrifying for you, getting on that bus and going to Green Bay all by yourself."

She shook her head. "You don't know anything, Yost Weaver. I've done a lot harder things than riding the bus by myself. I sneaked out of the house that night, but you never showed up at the crossroads like we'd agreed."

He studied his boots. "I figured you'd go without me."

She grunted her displeasure. "I waited an hour in the rain and missed the first bus. I walked to the station—in the rain, mind you—and caught the next bus in the morning. I didn't need you, but I trusted you. You could have at least come and told me face-to-face that you weren't going to get on that bus. I would have understood, but for you to leave me high and dry—or wet—was pretty cowardly."

"I suppose it was."

She gave him the look she usually reserved for Levi when he acted too big for his britches. "The two most important men in my life had let me down by the time I'd turned eighteen. How long do you think it took me before I could trust a man again? Except for *Gotte,* of course." She laid the earring in her lap, stretched her legs out in front of her, and leaned back on her hands. "Come to think of it, I don't know that I do."

Yost widened his eyes. "You don't trust any man?"

She cracked a reluctant smile. "Okay. I'll admit that's a lot to lay at your door. It's not all your fault, or even mostly your fault, but for goodness' sake,

Yost, if you had shown up that night, I wouldn't have had to carry around this nasty grudge that has festered for thirty-five years."

"It's not right to hold a grudge," he said, at a loss for any words of comfort.

She sent a frown in his direction. "If you haven't noticed, I have a little problem with forgiveness."

He swallowed hard. "Did I break your heart?"

She laughed so forcefully, she snorted. "Don't flatter yourself. You're too cautious for my taste. I didn't love you, but I trusted you."

She couldn't have known how those words stung. It was true. They hadn't loved each other then, but for sure and certain he loved her now. Yost wanted to sink into the floor. It had only taken him three or four months to talk himself out of feeling guilty for leaving Bitsy waiting for him. He'd justified his actions by telling himself that Bitsy was the wicked one and that he'd been wise to just leave her by the side of the road so she wouldn't have a chance to drag him to hell with her. After he'd talked himself out of any responsibility for his own actions on that night, he had barely given Bitsy a second thought for thirty-five years.

Now she was all he could think about.

Suddenly, that thirty-five-year-old decision became the worst one of his life.

"Bitsy, I don't know what to say except I'm sorry. I was young, and as the time got closer, I knew I couldn't go through with it. I couldn't leave my family. I didn't want to leave the church. Green Bay was too far away and too big. I was afraid I'd get robbed or beat up or murdered."

Bitsy cocked an eyebrow. "Murdered?"

"I'd heard horror stories about the big city. I didn't show up at our meeting place because I was afraid you'd either cry or yell at me."

She pursed her lips to stifle a smile. "I would have yelled at you."

He pinned her with a serious gaze that compelled her to pay attention. "I'm sorry, Bitsy. I should have been a better friend. I tried to justify myself, but I was wrong. Please forgive me."

To his delight, Bitsy turned her smile loose. It lit up the old hunter's cabin like springtime. "I've waited thirty-five years to hear you say that."

"I should have apologized a long time ago."

"Not the apology. I've waited thirty-five years for you to admit you were wrong."

He chuckled as relief swept over him. "Was it worth waiting for?"

"I suppose. I would have liked an apology that day, but then I wouldn't have been mad enough to spend my food money on these earrings, so it was probably a blessing that you waited so long." She picked up the earring from her lap and handed it to him. "Since I bought this with you in mind, I think you should keep it, just to remind yourself about what you said."

"That I was wrong?"

She closed her eyes and took a deep, satisfied breath. "*Jah*. That you were wrong. I'll never tire of hearing that."

Yost smiled and closed his fingers around the earring, pushing aside his doubts that a godly Amish man shouldn't own an earring. He could take it home and stuff it in the back of his underwear drawer.

He drew his brows together. His underwear and

Bitsy's earring should never come in contact with each other. It didn't seem proper. He'd put it in the cookie jar.

Yost would have liked to sit in the rickety hunter's cabin until it blew over, gazing at one-earringed Bitsy and listening to the low, inviting silkiness of her voice, but Levi needed to get home for dinner and Yost needed to get home and make a plan.

They put out the fire and roughly swept the cake crumbs from the floor. The mice would eat the rest. There would always be mice, no matter how many Billy Idol killed. Yost took up the basket with Farrah Fawcett, and Bitsy carried the cake container. They went outside and watched as Levi and the three cats climbed down from their tree. The cats seemed to be happy to return to the warmth of the basket, and now that he knew his parents loved him, Levi seemed eager to get home to see them.

Yost's heart started hopping the minute he climbed into the sleigh. Would Bitsy notice if he took Levi home first? Probably. Did it matter? He hoped not. His heart could have been one of those bouncy balls, ricocheting around his chest, pounding on his ribs. He thought he might be sick, but now that the idea was in his head, there was no way of prying it loose. Bitsy wasn't mad at him. She probably liked him, and he was in love enough to make a fool of himself. But, what would the bishop say? Yost didn't have the time or the desire to stop to ask him. It would be worth the risk, even if he had to repent later.

He drove the sleigh to Levi's house first. Levi and Bitsy made a plan for more candle making the next day so Levi's *mamm* could have her own candle. Once they said goodbye to Levi, Yost scooted as close to

Bitsy as he dared without making her suspicious. He snapped the reins and got Rocky moving.

When they arrived at Bitsy's house, he carried the basket of cats inside and set it on the floor next to the window seat. Then he stood up straight, shuffling his feet and looking at the floor trying to think of something to do with his empty hands. He would have liked to waste no time taking Bitsy in his arms and kissing her, but he'd never kissed a girl who hadn't been expecting it. How did a person go about doing it when it was a total surprise?

Bitsy set the cake container on the butcher-block island, regarded Yost with a critical eye, and folded her arms across her chest. "Okay, then. I'd say you've overstayed your welcome. *Denki* for the sleigh ride. We will see you tomorrow."

He felt like a fourth grader, chasing girls around the playground hoping to catch and kiss one. His pulse vibrated against his ears as a wave of nausea ebbed and flowed in his stomach. Love could be very unpleasant. His feet felt like a pair of anvils as he took four steps toward her. "I . . . well, Bitsy."

She narrowed her eyes and pressed her full pink lips together. She suspected something. He glanced behind him. Her shotgun stood by the door, ready to put a hole in his head if he did this wrong—well, two hundred holes in his head. Buckshot was nothing to be casual about. Oh, *sis yuscht!* Sweat trickled down the back of his neck. He'd taken kissing for granted for too many years, and now it was as if he'd never kissed anyone in his life.

Couldn't he just come right out and ask her?

Nae. Nae.

Nae!

That would be a disaster.

She'd already invited him to leave. Maybe he could stall for time until he figured out what to do. "Could I use your bathroom?" he said.

If anything, her posture stiffened. "Okay."

Nae. The bathroom was a terrible excuse. He needed to quit hemming and hawing and act. Now. Certain she could hear his heart drumming against his ribs, he sidled closer and slid his arms around her waist. If he went slowly enough, maybe she'd have time to get used to the idea before he actually did it. That seemed a reasonable plan.

She leaned back and away from him and lifted her brows as if she was exasperated beyond endurance. Was that a *gute* thing? Maybe she was annoyed he hadn't kissed her sooner. Maybe she wanted him to ask. Maybe she was worried about what the bishop would say. That didn't seem likely, but he could never be sure with Bitsy.

It didn't matter. He wanted to kiss her so bad, his lips were likely to slide off his face. The time was now.

He leaned in and puckered, half closing his eyes in a signal for her to get ready. When his lips were inches from their goal, she wedged her hand between his lips and hers.

"Don't kiss me," she said, as if he'd insulted her intelligence—as if he'd spilled beeswax on the rug.

Oy, anyhow. He let go of her and took one step back, clamping his lips shut as if the thought of kissing her hadn't even crossed his mind. "Why . . . why not?"

"I don't want you to."

And that was it. His hopes deflated like a leaky

bladder, and his heart thudded to the bottom of his chest. There was no one as blunt as Bitsy, and he'd never been put in his place quite so thoroughly before. "*Ach.* Okay. I'm sorry."

Bitsy expelled a long breath and looked up at the ceiling. "Dear Lord, I know Yost has been out of commission for a long time, but couldn't you have given him a tiny bit of romantic imagination?" She propped her hands on her hips and regarded him with a critical eye. "First of all, you don't talk about the bathroom right before you plan on kissing someone. That completely destroys the mood."

"Oh. Okay," he said, squeezing the words out of his throat.

"Second, you need to invite me out on the porch to look at the moon and tell me I'm beautiful, or at least pretend you think I'm beautiful. A woman likes to think a man is attracted to her for more than the money she's got stuffed in her Bible."

Yost frowned. "It's not even dark yet. How can I—"

"And don't apologize for trying to kiss someone. It makes you seem wishy-washy."

"I'm not wishy-washy."

"Then why don't you just kiss me instead of trying to do a tap dance? Do you like me?"

Yost was beginning to wonder if he did. He took off his hat and scrubbed his fingers through his hair. "For goodness' sake, Bitsy Kiem, I do like you, though heaven alone knows why."

"Then kiss me like you mean it. Or at least try."

Of course he meant it!

His heart seemed to come back from the dead, leaping and galloping like a young stallion in the pasture. He seized Bitsy's hand and pulled her outside to the porch. "There's no moon," he said, making the irritation evident in his voice, "and there isn't enough money in four Bibles that could tempt me if I found you unpleasant. You are more than pretty, Bitsy Kiem. You are beautiful and godly and too stubborn for my own sanity, but I'm dying to kiss you because, as strange as it seems, I think I love you."

For probably the first time in thirty-five years, he'd surprised her. She opened her mouth but no words came out—just a small puff of air—probably all that was left of her smug confidence.

He seized his opportunity. Wrapping his arms firmly around her, he lowered his head and kissed her . . . teeth. *Ach, du lieva.* Was he ever going to get it right? He relaxed his hold on her.

Bitsy shrugged and grinned sheepishly. "You're a stickler for the rules, Yost. I didn't think you'd really do it. You should probably try again."

That was plenty of encouragement. He drew her close again and brought his lips down on hers. A thousand fireworks exploded in his head as their lips touched. Despite her hard exterior, Bitsy was as soft and as warm as one of her cinnamon rolls right from the oven. And just as sweet. His whole body pulsed with warmth as she wrapped her arms around his neck and pulled him closer. Could he have guessed what ecstasy it was to have Bitsy Kiem, the woman who found fault with everything, to actually be inviting his kisses?

He drew away, and she sighed, a dreamy, self-satisfied smile on her face. "Was that okay?"

She lost her smile, huffed out a breath, and shook her head. "You never ask if a kiss was okay, Yost. You'll know if it wasn't because I'll never let you kiss me again."

"But was it okay? I'd rather not guess."

She tapped her chin with her finger and looked up at the sky—too light to see the moon. "I've had worse."

How many men had she kissed? He didn't think he wanted to know the answer. "So would you let me kiss you again sometime?"

She got that mischievous look in her eye as a slow smile grew on her lips. "I said I've had worse. But I don't think I've ever had any better."

Yost's pulse resumed a breakneck pace as he chuckled and pulled her close again. "You enjoy making me squirm, don't you?"

"It's my favorite pastime. I live to comfort the afflicted and afflict the comfortable. And you, Yost, are too comfortable in your notions of how things should be. The *Englisch* call it a comfort zone, and you've been living there entirely too long."

He had no idea what she was talking about, and he didn't care. He just wanted another kiss. "I simply adore you, Bitsy Kiem."

"I think you could grow on me," she said, still that mildly exasperated curve to her lips.

He leaned in and kissed her again, this time making sure he didn't get her teeth. Despite all the fuss she had made, the kiss was gentle and sweet, and he could have stayed locked to her lips for an hour, even though that seemed very impractical.

The kiss wasn't nearly long enough, but Bitsy sort of nudged away from him, leaving him breathless and more than a little *ferhoodled*. "Now you've really overstayed your welcome." She tilted her head and looked to be resisting the urge to smile. "But you can come back tomorrow, if you like. During school."

He nearly swallowed his tongue. She wanted him

to come back without Levi? Would they need a chaperone? He'd never discussed rules of dating for widowers with the bishop before, and he'd never been one to live dangerously. Oy anyhow, letting himself fall in love with Bitsy was dangerous enough.

All he knew was that spending uninterrupted time with Bitsy would be more exciting than standing up in the sleigh and waving his arms around—with probably the same result. Behaving irresponsibly always had consequences. No doubt spending time alone would lead to no good, but all he could think about was the rush of happiness he felt when he kissed her and the joy he felt in just being with her.

Everything would be all right. All Bitsy needed was a loving hand to help her become the godly Amish woman he knew she could become. He couldn't very well guide her steps if he never spent any time with her. This was all part of the plan, though he'd only just realized it.

"Don't look so concerned," Bitsy said. "The Amish used to do bed courtship. I can't imagine the bishop would object to you coming over to fix my refrigerator."

"Is it broken?"

"*Nae,* but I can make arrangements." She pumped her eyebrows up and down and made him chuckle. Then she shook her head and squinted in his direction. "If the bishop can't trust two adults to behave themselves, I don't know that he can trust anybody."

"But we did just kiss. Twice."

She gave him the look she sometimes gave Farrah Fawcett when she refused dry cat food. "Stuff and nonsense. A little kissing never hurt anybody. And I don't know about you, but I feel twenty years younger than I did ten minutes ago."

"*Ach, vell.* That is true."

He stood staring at her for a few more seconds before she sighed, snapped one of his suspenders, and opened her front door. "Goodbye, Yost Weaver. We'll see you at noon for supper. Bring your own Bible if you want to have an argument. I can't risk losing any money."

With a no-nonsense frown on her face, she stepped inside the house and promptly shut the door.

Ach, he'd bring his Bible for sure and certain. Bitsy had no chance against his superior knowledge of the Scriptures. He would convince her of the error of her ways. Yost wanted a spring wedding, and he'd settle for no one but Bitsy Kiem as his wife.

A reformed and improved Bitsy Kiem.

They'd be engaged before New Year's.

Chapter 5

Bitsy caught herself humming "Love Shack" by the B-52s and growled loudly. If there was one thing she couldn't abide, it was unbounded cheerfulness, even in herself. Cheerful people were annoying, as a general rule, and she wanted no part of it, no matter how happy she was or how much Yost Weaver seemed to creep into her brain and stay there. She couldn't shake him, no matter how many times she sang "Total Eclipse of the Heart" to herself. Maybe she should try "All By Myself." Celine Dion always made her cry.

It wouldn't have mattered. She'd cleaned the litter box, scrubbed two toilets, wiped the grease out of the bottom of her oven, and she still felt like doing the moonwalk around her kitchen. Maybe she should paint her fingernails black, shave one side of her head, and slouch. Those girls with black lipstick, nose rings, and bad haircuts seemed so miserable.

It had been almost two weeks since the first time Yost had kissed her, and he'd been to her house nearly every day since. How could she help but be insufferably sunny?

To make herself feel better, Bitsy picked Farrah Fawcett up from her comfortable window seat, set her on the floor, and tried to get her to chase an adorable cat toy that was shaped like a mouse. Farrah Fawcett couldn't have been more insulted. She glared at Bitsy as if she'd just thrown away all the good cat food. Farrah Fawcett turned up her nose at anything that seemed like play or exercise.

Bitsy found the whole princess act irritating, but it did the trick. After three minutes of trying to get Farrah Fawcett to chase the toy, Bitsy felt comfortably grumpy once again.

The problem was that Yost Weaver was never far from her thoughts. She grinned in spite of herself at the thought of Yost working up the courage to kiss her. Amish men were notoriously sure of themselves. Their wives were never supposed to contradict them, their children were expected to give unquestioning obedience. At least that was Bitsy's view of most Amish men. Her nephews-in-law, while annoying and altogether too eager, weren't such men. They were *gute* and honest and loving, and didn't fancy themselves superior to or smarter than their wives.

So maybe Bitsy needed to alter her generalized opinion about Amish men. And in truth, she already had. Just because Yost was set in his ways didn't mean he wasn't kind and thoughtful and . . . loving. *Ach, du lieva.*

Loving.

He loved her. He'd told her so himself.

And against her will, she sort of liked him too. A

dyed-in-the-wool Amish man. She never would have believed it if it weren't happening to her.

Yost was definitely aggravating in how set he was in his ways, but that stubbornness was also something she liked about him. He was steady and trustworthy, like a lighthouse in the fog or a mighty tree in a windstorm. He wasn't righteously indignant when she argued with him, and he even sometimes admitted that he was wrong. How could she not love that?

Despite his tightly buttoned-up notions, Yost was genuinely fun to spend time with. He teased her about the money she kept in her Bible and the candles she wasted by actually burning them. He was willing to try strange new foods like pot stickers and salmon tacos, and he always cleared his plate and announced whatever she'd cooked to be the best thing he'd ever tasted. They talked for hours about beehives and fruit trees, debated Amish doctrine, and argued about earrings and dress colors.

And maybe she was fine with not wearing her earrings anymore, and maybe it was fine that she didn't wear them because Yost was happier when she didn't. Was it bad to do something purely for someone else's happiness?

He kept saying things to hint that he wanted to take care of her. She could probably put up with a companion, but she did not want or need anyone to take care of her. But what about that? Did he want to marry her? Did she want to marry him?

Maybe she did.

Maybe it wouldn't be so bad to give up her earrings and her dancing and the little battery-operated CD player that she pulled out only in extreme emergencies, like after she went to visit her parents. Were those pieces of her *Englisch* life that maybe she didn't need anymore? It would make Yost happy to see those things go. He liked her better without them, and he was concerned about her salvation. She couldn't get mad at him for that.

Besides, she floated to the ceiling and back every time he kissed her—which unfortunately had been restricted to once a day, because he hadn't wanted to sin by overindulging. Once a day wasn't enough, but at least it gave Bitsy something to look forward to when she woke up in the morning. Who knew kissing Yost Weaver would be the most glorious part of every day?

Bitsy tucked an errant piece of hair under her *kapp* and caught herself smiling again. This was going to have to stop. She'd never get any work done if all she did was daydream all afternoon.

At precisely two o'clock, Lily, Poppy, and Rose, waltzed into the house. Bitsy loved it when her girls were prompt. Promptness was next to godliness as far as she was concerned. She nearly smiled then thought twice about it. It would be better for everyone if she weren't so chipper.

Bitsy immediately took Luke Junior from Poppy's arms and kissed him three times on each cheek. "*Ach,* he's like an ice cube."

"It's fifteen degrees out there," Poppy said, giving Bitsy a strong hug. "I bundled him up but good."

Lily and Rose got their own hugs as well. "You look very well, Lily," Bitsy said. Lily's baby was due on New Year's Eve. She looked more than a little uncomfortable.

Lily placed her hands on her abdomen. "*Ach,* she does somersaults every night just as I'm trying to fall asleep."

Bitsy nudged the coat off Luke Junior's shoulders. "Maybe she'll be a dancer when she grows up."

"Or a hockey player," Poppy said. Everyone but Bitsy laughed at the thought of that. She'd been cheery enough for one day.

Bitsy's girls took off their coats and rolled up their sleeves. "What should we make first?" Rose asked.

Bitsy sighed. "I hope the community appreciates what a charitable woman I am. We've got to make a cake for the *singeon* at Millers, a casserole for Levi Weaver's family, bread for *gmay,* and I told Yost I'd make some cookies for the school Christmas program."

Bitsy did not miss the look that Lily gave Poppy. "You told Yost?"

"It's not anything to get your knickers in a knot about. Mary is busy with her little ones, and Levi has the biggest part. Yost loves my Christmas sugar cookies."

Poppy propped her hands on her hips and studied Bitsy's face. "B, Yost has been over here almost every day for the last two weeks."

Bitsy narrowed her eyes. "You don't know that."

A slow smile formed on Poppy's lips. "I live just down the road, B. I spy on you all the time."

"And Josiah says Yost passes our farm every day in his buggy," Rose said, looking delighted and guilty at the same time, if that was possible.

Bitsy decided to be contrary. "Just because he passes your farm doesn't mean he comes to my house. There's plenty of things between his house and mine."

Lily giggled. "But nothing as interesting as you."

Oy, anyhow. Her girls were nosy.

Poppy eyed her with a smarty-pants look on her face. "B, you like him. You like him a lot."

She thought she probably loved him, but her snoopy nieces weren't going to pry that out of her. "I suppose I do, even though he can't keep a beat to save his life and he's going gray at the temples and he chews his fingernails."

Rose and Lily squealed, and in a burst of insanity, jumped up and down and clapped their hands.

Bitsy looked up at the ceiling. "Dear Lord, it's *gute* you gave me the patience of Job, because these girls are sorely testing it. There's no need to overreact."

"He's wonderful nice," Rose said. "He gives Josiah advice about farming, and he fixed our thresher when it broke down. He's very handy yet."

Unlike Rose's husband, Josiah. Rose hadn't noticed the shortage of duct tape on the couch, and Bitsy didn't want to hurt her feelings by bringing it up.

Lily brushed her hand along the butcher-block island. "He's a wonderful *gute dawdi* to his grandchildren. At least that's what his daughter Hannah tells me."

"He could take care of you, *Aendi* Bitsy," Rose said. "You wouldn't have to worry about working the farm by yourself."

"B doesn't need someone to take care of her," Poppy said, almost under her breath.

Rose tilted her head to one side. "*Nae*, but it might be nice, all the same."

Jah. It might be nice. Pulling honey nearly put her in her grave every year. She was fifty-three years old. They might as well start planning her funeral. Maybe it would be nice to give away her beehives and spend her last few *gute* years with Yost Weaver. She could throw away her earrings, sit around all day, and eat cake. At least getting fat wasn't a sin.

Ach. It probably was.

She didn't like the way her girls were staring at her, as if they were just waiting to be let in on a secret they already knew. After handing Luke Junior to Poppy, she turned her back on all three of them. She reached into the cupboard and pulled out the cat food. The cats needed their bowl topped off.

"*Cum* and eat, Snowball," she said, shaking the cat food into the already-full bowl.

"Who is Snowball?" Rose said.

Bitsy looked up. The cat food had been a very bad idea. Now her girls looked at her as if she was the bearded lady at the circus, and her chin couldn't have been that bad. She plucked it regularly. "Yost had a wonderful *gute* idea. Farrah Fawcett and Billy Idol are *Englisch* stars, and naming my cats after them only makes me long for the *Englisch* world."

Much as she loved Sigourney Weaver in *Alien*, Bitsy was fifty-three years old. A grown woman should have no problem letting go of such silly things.

She cleared her throat and picked up the cat formerly known as Leonard Nimoy. "This is Carrot. The white, snobby one is Snowball. Sigourney Weaver is now Fluffy, and Billy Idol is Mittens."

Rose formed her lips into an O and laced her fingers together in front of her. Her knuckles turned white. "Those are very pretty names, *Aendi* Bitsy. Did Yost help you pick them out?"

"*Jah.* I liked Pumpkin but he thought Carrot sounded more like a cat."

"Oh. They're very nice," Rose repeated, as if trying to convince herself. A painful smile formed on her lips. "Josiah named his dog Honey. Carrot is a food too."

The lines piled up on Poppy's forehead. "B, your hair is gray."

It irritated her that Poppy was so observant. "I've been gray since thirty-five."

"You always dye it red at Christmastime."

Bitsy instinctively put a hand to the nape of her neck. "I thought I'd try plain gray this year. Yost likes it better this way."

All three girls eyed her as if she had a piece of spinach hanging from her nose.

"You never try plain," Lily murmured.

Rose seemed on the verge of tears. "It's . . . very pretty like that."

Bitsy took Luke Junior back from his mother and squeezed her arms tightly around him. "What's the matter with everybody? You act like I died this morning. Don't start dividing my furniture."

Lily pasted a smile on her face. "Of course you didn't die."

Bitsy narrowed her eyes. "That is about the strangest thing you've ever said, little sister."

"So Yost won't let you dye your hair or wear earrings either?" Poppy said.

"Won't let me? He doesn't have a say whether I dye my hair or not."

Rose frowned one of her I'm-trying-to-be-kind frowns. Bitsy didn't like it, and she didn't even know why. "But you said he likes it when you don't."

Poppy scrunched her lips. "Is he bossy about it?"

"Bossy?" Bitsy took a deep breath. Annoyance felt like a pot of asparagus stew bubbling inside her stomach. Was she annoyed at her nieces or herself? Had she let the color fade from her hair only to make Yost happy? And was there anything wrong with that?

Yost wasn't bossy. He had told her he loved her while her hair was purple. Did he love her better now that it wasn't?

"Yost isn't bossy, and we have fun together. Last night he took me ice skating and then to McDonald's. And if I didn't wear my earrings it was because I didn't want my ears to get ripped off on the ice."

"You must like him if you let him take you to Mc-Donald's," Lily said.

"Their fries are pretty good. And I slid down the clown slide."

Lily giggled. "It sounds like the perfect date."

Bitsy smiled. It was a *gute* date. A *wunderbarr* date. She'd made Yost laugh, and he'd irritated her several times. "I got stuck on the slide, and Yost pretended he didn't know me."

Rose's eyes got as wide as caverns. "You got stuck?"

"One of the kids in line behind me gave me a shove to dislodge me. The manager asked us to leave after that. He was quite rude so I prayed that the *gute* Lord would send him a pimple."

"But B," Poppy said, "you love coloring your hair."

What was Poppy's sudden concern for her hair? If Yost didn't care that she colored it, why should Poppy? "I like it this way too," Bitsy said, annoyed at how unconvincing she sounded.

Well, no matter how she sounded, she *was* convinced. Gray hair was nothing to be ashamed of. Plenty of famous people had gray hair—Kenny Rogers, George Washington, Cruella de Vil.

Rose leaned over and gave her a kiss on the cheek. "If he makes you happy, that's all that matters."

Poppy didn't seem apt to agree. "It matters very much if she loses herself in the process."

Bitsy tried hard to keep the impatience from showing on her face. For sure and certain, Poppy had some silly notions. A passerby might have thought Bitsy was dating a vampire or a werewolf. "I'm not going to lose myself. I have my address memorized. And it's not me who needs a lecture. Luke ate every last cookie in the jar last time he was here. Has he no shame?"

Poppy shed her somber mood and laughed. "Luke loves your oatmeal raisin cookies, B. He can't help himself."

"He's going to get very fat someday."

"Not when he works so hard." Poppy's grin took over her whole face. "Even his muscles have muscles. *Ach,* he's so handsome."

"I won't argue with that," Bitsy said. "Luke Junior looks just like him, and Luke Junior is the handsomest baby in the world, at least until Lily's comes along."

Lily laughed. "There will be no shortage of beautiful babies in this family."

Rose longed for a baby, but she smiled a beautiful, genuine smile. "Of course."

Bitsy looked up at the ceiling and said a silent prayer. The *gute* Lord was taking his sweet time, but Bitsy could be wonderful tenacious. Surely *Gotte* would send Rose a baby just to shut Bitsy up.

Bitsy and her girls spent the afternoon laughing and talking and baking. They made sugar cookies shaped like Christmas stars while Rose fretted about what latest gossip Paul Glick was spreading about their family, and they all decided he wouldn't settle down until he found himself a wife. Unfortunately, the girls in Bienenstock were exceptionally sensible, and there wasn't a girl with any sense who would have him.

Lily made a broccoli cheese casserole for Levi's family while Poppy kneaded bread and Rose and Bitsy made a pineapple-coconut cake, Rose's specialty. They dyed the coconut red and green so that it would look extra Christmas-y for the *singeon* on Sunday night. They shared a light dinner of canned peaches and tuna fish sandwiches before the girls headed home.

Poppy left first so she could feed Luke Junior and put him down for the night. Lily and Rose strolled across the flagstones arm in arm. It wasn't a very Amish way to feel, but Bitsy was proud of her girls. They were *gute,* kind, and so much fun to have around. She liked to think it was because when they were growing up, she'd always dyed her hair some cheerful color and wore earrings that tinkled merrily. Who could be sad in the presence of a pair of tinkling earrings?

Her frown sank deeper into her face. Yost could. He liked her better without the earrings or tattoos or hair dye. But how did she want herself to be? She was happy when she wore her earrings, but even happier when Yost came to visit. Could she have the one and still hold on to the other?

Yost came whistling up the lane not ten minutes later, his hands stuffed in his pockets, his easy gait a sign of his wonderful happy mood. "I talked with the bishop," he said, leaping up the porch steps and giving Bitsy a swift kiss on the cheek. Those quick ones weren't as good as the long ones, but they still set her heart racing like a hound after a raccoon.

"What did the bishop have to say for himself?"

Yost's smile could have set a dry field on fire. "He says we can see each other as often as we want, not wait two weeks between dates like *die youngie*."

Bitsy smirked. "He knows if we waited two weeks between, we'd die before we had a chance to make any plans." She cleared her throat and pressed her lips together. They sometimes came close to talking about getting married, but never came right out and said it. Bitsy didn't want to come right out and say anything. She might like Yost a lot—she might even be in love with him—but marriage meant baptism and *Gellasenheit* and possibly no tattoos ever again. She hadn't worn a tattoo since the first night Yost had kissed her. Could she abstain for the rest of her life? Did she love him that much?

Yost lost his smile. "But the bishop has advised me that sliding down slides at McDonald's isn't fitting. I told him we wouldn't do it again."

In some sort of rebellion against the bishop, Bitsy grabbed Yost's big hand and pulled him into the house. She got on her tiptoes, threw her arms around his neck, and kissed him thoroughly. His surprise registered in the way he hesitated, his arms dangling at his side like two sausages. But it didn't take him long to get over himself, slide his arms around her waist, and pull her close. She loved the warmth that seemed to envelop her when they kissed and enjoyed the thought of making the bishop just a slight bit annoyed.

"That was unexpected," Yost said, when she finally released him.

"Sometimes, I have to do what I have to do."

"But nice too," he said. A grin played at his lips before fading to nothing. "But I don't think we should kiss like that again. It opens the door to temptation."

Bitsy felt slightly irritated for no reason whatsoever and couldn't resist maybe irritating him just a little. "What's wrong with that?"

He didn't take the bait. Chuckling, he took her by the shoulders and walked backward while pulling her forward. He guided her to the windowsill where she'd set one of the beeswax candles she and Levi had made. They'd both agreed not to burn it. It was such a pretty Christmas decoration, and they didn't want to ruin it. "It's the same reason you don't burn this candle. We wouldn't want to spoil something so beautiful."

She wanted to argue with him but didn't have the heart. The bishop had given them some *gute* news, and she'd be a party pooper if she tried to pop Yost's balloon. Instead she took him to the refrigerator and showed him the handle, which was missing a screw. He grinned, pulled a screwdriver from the drawer, and went to work.

"It smells delicious in here," he said. "You and the nieces must have baked up a storm."

She pulled the container of frosted and glittered sugar cookies from the cupboard. "These are for the school program tomorrow night, and don't even think about sampling them."

He glanced up from his screwdriver, took a look in the bowl, and smiled. "They look like you pulled them out of heaven. Probably taste like that too."

"Well, if they don't taste good, you can sneak them onto the eats table, and no one will have to know who made them. That might be a *gute* idea anyway. People tend to get indigestion when my name comes up."

Yost set the screwdriver on the counter, wrapped

his hands around Bitsy's upper arms, and looked her square in the eye. "Don't ever put yourself down like that. I have lost track of how many *gute* deeds you have done for my family, let alone what you do for everyone else in the community. Mary is so busy she doesn't even have time to blink more than twice a day, but Levi will have treats to take to the school program because of you. I couldn't have made them or bought something at Glick's Market. You were my only hope."

"Why not Glick's Market? They sometimes have cookies or Martha's famous homemade rolls." Bitsy was proud of herself for not rolling her eyes when she said it. When Lily was dating Paul, she only got a homemade roll when she paid for it.

"I thought you knew. I don't go to Glick's Market anymore."

"Why ever not? The sandwiches at the gas station will make you sick. That's a mistake I'll never make again."

He rubbed his hand up and down her arm. His touch was comfortable and familiar. "Paul Glick and his family have slandered you and your nieces over and over again. I won't give my business to someone who talks that way about the woman I love."

It wasn't so much what he said but the way he said it, with his chin lifted and fire blazing in his eyes, that made Bitsy's legs weak and her heart melt into a puddle at his feet. How long had it been since any man besides her nephews-in-law had stood up for her? Her *fater* certainly never had. The bishop, the ministers, the deacon? They seemed happy when she came to church, but they always eyed her with suspicion, prone to believe whatever gossip Paul or anyone else repeated about her.

No one dared, or even wanted, to defend a rebellious Amish woman with pink hair. Until Yost. Her body felt as warm as chicken noodle soup on a cold December day.

How could she not love Yost Weaver?

Of course she loved him, and the thought made her slightly dizzy.

For once in her life, she was speechless. She couldn't have said anything without bursting into tears, and as far as she knew, she had never burst into tears in her life. She wasn't about to start now.

She clamped her mouth shut, even though she should have had the decency to say *denki*.

Yost reached out and nudged his thumb down her cheek. "Flour," he said. "Two days ago Paul and his *dat* were in the harness shop, and Paul was telling some outrageous story that you paid an *Englischer* to pour something stinky on his shirt at your nieces' wedding. I nearly peeled out of my skin I was so angry. But *Gotte* has said that he who is angry with his brother is in danger of hellfire, so I didn't say anything. But when they left, I told Ira that there was no truth to it."

Bitsy's lips froze to her teeth. "That's not entirely true."

A line buried itself deep between Yost's brows. "What's not entirely true? The story or my denying it?"

She took his hand and led him to the sofa. Things always seemed less dire on the sofa. "Luke caught wind that Paul was going to try to ruin the wedding. We had to do something. I couldn't shoot him because I don't believe in guns. So we asked one of our *Englisch* friends to spill our bottle of valerian root on him. He stunk so bad he had to leave, and the wedding went on peacefully without him."

Yost sat very still for several seconds, then took Bitsy's face in his hands and kissed her until she thought she might suffocate. He finally came up for air and laughed. "You are a genius, Bitsy. Paul Glick makes himself unpleasant wherever he goes. I'd say he got his just deserts."

"I'm glad you think so. The deacon chastised me for over an hour. It was almost like being in church. But then he forgave me, and I gave him the rest of the valerian root because he has trouble sleeping at night."

Yost threw back his head and laughed even harder. "I'm wonderful happy you didn't shoot Paul, because I refuse to date someone in prison, no matter how much I like her."

Bitsy finally smiled. "Prison orange is not my color."

Yost wrapped his fingers around an errant lock of Bitsy's hair. "I like the salt-and-pepper gray. It's so pretty on you."

Someone knocked on the door, and Yost scooted away from Bitsy. After he'd been so kind about Paul, she didn't know why that small movement bothered her so much. Bitsy opened the door, and her *gute* day was ruined. Her *dat* stood on the porch, leaning on his cane and peering into her house as if he might find something wicked going on right before his eyes. His frown hung off his face like drooping Christmas lights on an *Englischer's* house.

Bitsy could have counted on one hand the times her *dat* had come to her house in all the years she'd lived there. He probably thought just being there was some sort of sin.

Dat didn't need an invitation to come in, which was good because all Bitsy could do was stare at him.

Why was he here? He hobbled over the threshold and brightened considerably when he caught sight of Yost sitting on the sofa. "Yost Weaver," he said, holding out his hand. Yost jumped up and grabbed Dat's hand before he fell forward. "I'd heard rumors," Dat said.

"*Cum*, Sol," Yost said. "Sit here."

Yost gave up his place on the sofa, but if he expected Bitsy to sit next to her *dat*, he didn't know her as well as she hoped. She pulled a chair from the table and slid it into the sitting room. Yost glanced in her direction then sat next to Dat.

Dat leaned forward, propping his hand on his cane, probably hoping to get close to Bitsy so he could take a *gute* whiff. He liked to make sure Bitsy didn't smell like perfume. She probably smelled like coconut, which, as far as she knew, hadn't yet been declared a sin by the bishop. "Elizabeth, I have noticed some wonderful-*gute* improvements in your life. You still fall far short of the glory of *Gotte*, but you have stopped coloring your hair and wearing those prideful tattoos. I am well pleased."

Bitsy had discovered years ago that if she could make herself indifferent to Dat's insults, they didn't hurt quite so bad. But indifference didn't seem to be working today. It galled her that her *dat* could still make her feel so small, like that sixteen-year-old girl who never did anything right. The girl who craved her *fater*'s love like the desert craved moisture. At eighteen, she had gotten on that bus before she dried up and blew away on the wind.

After she returned to Bienenstock with her nieces, she did her best to avoid her parents, and on the rare times they saw each other, Bitsy found she could bear their criticism better when she was obstinate—or sassy, as her friends at the dental office used to say. Her *dat* hated sassy, and so she found she loved it. The only thing she enjoyed more than her *dat's* approval was his disapproval.

"Susie Borntreger colors her hair," Bitsy said, propping her elbow on her knee, cupping her chin in her hand, and gazing at Dat as if she were sharing some great secret.

Yost nodded. "It's true. I checked at *gmay* last week."

Dat was the master of selective listening. He picked up his cane and shook it in Bitsy's direction, but he looked at Yost. "I did my best to train her up in the way she should go, and she turned her back on me and *Gotte*. I gave up hope for her soul. But I can see that you have changed her, Yost, and helped her remember her duty. I am grateful."

Yost frowned, shook his head, and lowered his eyes in an impressive show of humility. It made Bitsy's teeth ache. "I can't take any honor on myself. I only told Bitsy I like her hair better gray. She is the one who has made all the changes, and I admire her for trying to improve herself. She's tired of standing out."

Yost might as well have sprouted horns for as shocked as Bitsy was. She was tired of standing out? Where had Yost come up with that notion?

He looked at her with such affection in his eyes, she momentarily forgot to be irritated. Had his love made him blind? Or just *dumm*? Had her fascination with him made her devoted or just weak?

One thing was for sure. She couldn't have been more irritated. "Dear Heavenly Father," she said, right out loud, "please give me patience. I need it right now."

Dat glared at her, while Yost widened his eyes, pressed his lips together, and inclined his head in

Dat's direction, hinting that she shouldn't pray out loud while her *dat* was in the room—as if she didn't know that already.

"*Now,* Lord," she growled. "I really need it now, or I might be forced to ask for a nasty heat rash."

Dat pounded his cane on the floor. "I can see there is still some work to be done. Bitsy was always a headstrong girl, never seeking humility or righteousness."

Yost seemed to grow calmer even as Dat became more agitated. He laid a hand on Dat's knee. "Now, Sol. We can never go back to the past, but it's time to set things right. If Bitsy had been shown love instead of disapproval as a child, maybe she wouldn't have left home. Can you consider that maybe, possibly in a small way, you are responsible for her leaving?"

Of course Dat couldn't ever consider such a thing.

Warring emotions pulled Bitsy this way and that like a piece of taffy. Anger at her father was never far from the surface, but she was grateful—deeply grateful—to Yost for trying to make her *dat* see the consequences of his unyielding temper. But it also chafed that he talked about her as if she weren't in the room.

She felt the irritation like sandpaper against her skin. Yost seemed to think he'd changed her and that those changes made her a better, more desirable woman. He loved her—at least she thought he loved her—but he also wanted a conventional Amish *fraa,* and it was apparent that he was hoping he could somehow manage to have both.

Her heart sank so far, she'd have to crawl under the house to find it. This was all her own fault. She had let herself get so caught up in being in love that she had lost part of herself—the part that wouldn't conform just to make someone else happy. The part that told her that she was enough—that *Gotte* had created her and loved her for who she was, not in spite of it.

One thing was for certain. She had to get rid of both Yost and Dat immediately. She couldn't hear herself think while Dat glared at her and Yost gazed lovingly. She thought of grabbing her shotgun and pointing it in Dat's direction, but that would only make her look ridiculous, and she would never actually use it on him.

"I brought her up *Gotte's* way," Dat protested. "Spare the rod, and you spoil the child."

Her gut clenched. She was sick of both of them. Would they leave if she threw up?

She'd have to scare them away.

Without using the gun.

"But what does that get you?" Yost said. "You might have obedient and fearful children, but they won't love you, and when they grow up, they'll only want to leave."

Bitsy stood up and walked out of the room. Dat and Yost were so busy debating child-rearing theories they didn't notice her leave. She jogged up the stairs and into her room, where she took off her dress and donned her long pink nightgown and her green fuzzy slippers with the googly eyeballs on the toes. She took off her *kapp* and let her braid fall over her shoulder. Dat wouldn't like the uncovered head, but he would be pleased that her hair was a lovely mixture of strands of gray, white, and black.

She marched down the stairs and stood by her chair. All conversation ceased as Dat stared at her hair, and Yost stared at her slippers. *Jah*. They were terrified. "I'm wonderful tired from a long day of falling short of the glory of *Gotte*. It's time for you to go."

Yost couldn't have jumped to his feet faster. He took Dat by the elbow and helped him stand. "Of course," he said, glancing at her doubtfully. "You must be tired from all that baking."

"Wonderful tired," she said. Of all of it. "Don't forget your cookies and the casserole for Levi's family."

Yost flinched as if the thought of cookies had surprised him. He seemed uneasy but unsure as to why. She'd give him a why, if she decided to let him in the house ever again. That thought sent a twinge of pain zinging right through her heart. "Of course," Yost said. "I can't forget those." He grabbed the containers from the counter. "*Denki* again, Bitsy. This means so much to all of us."

Just go, Yost.

There was too much to stew about without Yost's piercing blue eyes muddying her thoughts. Things would be so much easier if she didn't like him. *Ach, du lieva*, the whole thing was too annoying.

Dat was too shocked or maybe too indignant to say anything. Yost followed him out the door and winked and smiled at her before closing it behind him. Wink? How dare he wink? She should have used the shotgun. No one winked when they had a shotgun pointed at them.

Unless they were stupid.

Jah, Yost would have winked with or without the shotgun. She'd be overjoyed never to see him again. Mostly.

She leaned her shotgun against the wall and took her beehive-shaped candle off the windowsill. What was the use of saving it? A candle was meant to be burned. She sat on the floor next to the window seat and lit the candle. The cats played at her feet while she watched it burn. No flame had ever been lovelier.

She sat there, looking into the flame and rethinking her life, and renamed all her cats.

Chapter 6

Yost could have floated to Bitsy's house. Last night after Bitsy had suddenly gotten so tired, Sol had invited Yost to his house, where Sol had given his whole-hearted approval to the marriage. Sol had even listened patiently when Yost had admonished him to be a better, more loving *fater* and to stop finding fault with his lovable, feisty, completely *wunderbarr* daughter.

With Yost's help, Bitsy and Sol could mend fences. They had been holding grudges too long.

Bitsy was going to make him dinner tonight before they went to Levi's school Christmas program. The program was a big event, and the scholars prepared for weeks. Levi and his siblings were nervous, his parents were nervous, and Yost was a wreck. Levi needed something to go well for him.

Yost bounded up Bitsy's porch steps and knocked on her door. All he wanted to do was take Bitsy in his arms and kiss her. He couldn't help himself. Sol approved, Bitsy's hair was a normal color again, and the bishop had said they could see each other every day of the week. It was going to be a very Merry Christmas.

He drew his brows together. What was that sound coming from inside the house? It sounded like a table saw cutting into a piece of sheet metal. Was Bitsy in some sort of trouble? With his heart pounding against his chest, he threw open the door. Bitsy sat on the sofa reading a book and her shoulders were moving in time to the loud and obnoxious "music" coming out of a small CD player next to her.

But it wasn't the music that knocked the wind out of him. Beneath Bitsy's *kapp,* her hair was bright, fire-engine, Christmas-wrapping-paper red. It hurt his eyes to look at it. What had she done?

"Bitsy?" he said, loud enough for her to hear him over the music.

She flinched and looked up. That's when he saw not one but three temporary tattoos on her neck. She might as well have thrown a rock at him. She caught her breath and gave him the stink eye. "Yost Weaver, don't you know how to knock?"

"I knocked but the music was too loud," he said, barely containing the annoyance that simmered inside him.

The beeswax candle that used to be on her windowsill sat on the counter. It looked as if it had been burning for hours. The beehive was halfway gone.

She reached over and turned off the CD player. Blessed silence. "What did you say? I couldn't hear you over the music."

He wasn't even sure where to begin, so he started with the most trivial thing first. "I . . . what . . . you lit the candle."

"Candles were meant to be used, Yost. They were meant to brighten the night and share their light—

which sounds like the start of a very *gute* poem. The candle was not meant to sit on a shelf and behave."

He shouldn't have asked about the candle. It was all nonsense. "Bitsy, what is going on here? I thought you . . ."

She closed her book and set it on the sofa, giving him a look of patient forbearance mixed with her familiar annoyance. "I suppose I won't get to read any more of this trashy novel today."

"I . . . what happened to your hair?"

"*Ach*, the girls reminded me yesterday that I always dye my hair red for Christmas. It's a tradition, but I think I overdid it a little."

"A little? Bitsy, it's outrageous."

She smiled, actually smiled, as if his astonishment was a *gute* thing. "*Denki*. I'm glad you like it. I think I'll rinse it out a little before the program tonight. I don't want the scholars to forget their lines because they're looking at my hair."

"But I thought we agreed that your hair looked better plain."

She furrowed her brow. "Hmm. We did agree about that, didn't we? *Ach, vell,* I decided I like it better dyed."

He sort of stumbled toward her. "Bitsy, I thought you weren't going to wear tattoos or dye your hair anymore."

"Have a care, Yost, or you'll step on El Diablo."

Yost looked down. Mittens was right at his feet. The cat arched his back and hissed at Yost. "El Diablo?"

"I decided to rename my cats. You have to admit that the names we came up with were a little boring." She pointed to Snowball, formerly Farrah Fawcett, who lounged on the windowsill. "That is Marie

Antoinette. The orange one is Cyndi Lauper, and the other one is Lady Macbeth. And of course, El Diablo."

Bitsy seemed so calm, so cheerfully grumpy, but she didn't fool him. Something was horribly wrong. Their gazes met, and her eyes flashed with something intense and deep that Yost hadn't seen before. Her expression held a mixture of determination, courage, and exquisite pain. The raw emotion took his breath away.

He set his coat and hat on the table and strode to the sofa, being careful not to step on any cats. Sitting down next to her, he took her hand tenderly in his. "Bitsy, what is wrong?"

"Nothing's wrong. Marie Antionette is a *gute* name for that cat."

He placed his hand on the side of her face, leaned in, and kissed her tenderly. She didn't resist, but she didn't exactly warm up to him either. "Bitsy, I love you with all my heart. Tell me why you are hurting."

She squared her shoulders and folded her arms. "Do you love me? Even with four tattoos?"

Four? Yost had only seen three. He didn't dare guess where number four was. "I do. But I thought we agreed that you would stop all that."

Bitsy snorted. "You got me to go along with you, and I almost fell for it. I'll admit I have no one to blame but myself. I should be able to see manipulation from a mile away. But I love you, and it clouded my judgment."

If he hadn't been so confused, Yost would have shouted for joy. "You love me?"

She nodded. "Much as I'm opposed to it. But I

won't let you make me over into your image of a perfect Amish *fraa*. Either you take me as I am, or walk out that door and leave me be."

Yost didn't feel like floating anymore. "But, Bitsy, you'd be so much happier living a plain and simple life. Aren't you tired of people avoiding you because of your hair and earrings, afraid you'll be a bad influence on their children?"

"Like you were afraid with Levi?"

"*Vell, jah,* I suppose."

Bitsy lifted her chin. "The whole *gmayna* loves to make themselves miserable worrying about my sins. I will not let them make *me* miserable too. They have no right to tell me how I can behave."

"This isn't who you really are, Bitsy. You were born to be a godly, faithful Amish woman."

"I was born to be Bitsy Kiem, even though I wish my parents had named me Hyacinth. *Gotte* doesn't love me any less because I color my hair."

Yost stood up and paced back and forth in front of the sofa, scrubbing his fingers through his hair. "But what about your eternal reward? Will you go to hell over earrings and a tattoo?"

"You think I'm going to hell?"

Yost wanted to shake some sense into her, but he needed to start talking sense first. "Of course not. I just think . . . I know you'd be happier living the Plain life. The true way to *Gotte*."

Bitsy frowned and seemed to fold into herself. "The worst time of my life was when I was forced to live the Plain life."

Yost stopped short and studied Bitsy's face. It was a mask of pain and anger. "Everything you do is to spite your *fater,* isn't it?"

She curled one side of her mouth and played with a

lock of bright red hair at the nape of her neck. "Making my *fater* uncomfortable is as good a reason as any to color my hair."

"That's childish."

Her eyes flashed like lightning. "Childish? You heard him gloat yesterday about how pleased he is with my improvements—or I should say, *your* improvements. He would shave his beard before he gave me credit for anything *gute*. If being who I am makes him unhappy, then for sure and certain that is his problem and not mine. My *dat* was too rigid, too stingy to love me. I don't feel obligated to do anything or be anyone for him."

Yost's sigh came from deep within his throat. Bitsy's wounds went clear to the center of her heart. He joined her on the sofa and wrapped both arms tenderly around her shoulders. "Sol was a harsh *fater,* and it hurts my heart to think of what your life must have been like. You are his daughter, and he treated you like an enemy."

"*Nae.* Jesus says to love your enemies. Dat treated me worse."

"But Bitsy, you can't hold on to this forever. It's time to forgive your *fater.*"

Bitsy erupted from the sofa, marched to the door, and grabbed her shotgun, holding it vertical, her fingers white around the barrel. "I won't be preached to, Yost Weaver. You left me alone on that road thirty-five years ago."

"I said I'm sorry."

"And I forgive you, but your choice forced me to make some choices of my own. It shaped how I felt about the world and the Amish. I had to get strong, mighty quick. Anger at you and my *dat* is what gave me the strength to turn my back on all of you. Only love for my sister and nieces could have compelled me to return to the community. I'm not childish. I'm angry, and that's what's kept me going all these years." She pointed at the door with the butt of her shotgun. "I'm sure you'd rather not be seen at Bitsy Kiem's house. It's best to leave now before anyone catches you here." Did her voice tremble slightly?

"But I love you," he blurted out. "The bishop thinks it's a wonderful *gute* idea. I've even talked it over with your *dat,* and he approves too."

It was the wrong thing to say, and he knew it the minute it tumbled from his lips. "My *dat* approves?" She laughed so hard she snorted, but there was no happiness in it. "How nice for you."

"I'll gladly marry you if you mend your ways."

"You're so kind to do the jobs no one else will do."

"That's not what I meant," he said.

"My ways aren't broken so I'm not inclined to mend them. I wouldn't marry you if you were Tom Cruise with five more inches of height. Besides, we can't get married. I haven't been baptized and if living a life of austerity and misery with you is the reward for joining the church, I think I'll pass."

Yost's mouth fell open. "Wha . . . what do you mean? Of course you've been baptized."

She seemed to enjoy his utter confusion. "*Nae,* I haven't. Surely you've heard the rumors from Paul Glick."

He couldn't catch his breath. "I . . . I have, but I thought he was making it up to tear down your family."

"I'm surprised the bishop didn't warn you."

Yost furrowed his brow and gaped at Bitsy. "He probably thought I knew. Why didn't you tell me?"

"I thought we could cross that bridge when we came to it." She lowered her eyes as she lowered the gun. The stock made a dull thud against the wood floor. "I considered getting baptized for you." That thought hung heavy in the silence between them. Yost's heart swelled even as it was breaking. "Love can make you do irrational things," she said. "I'm glad I got some sanity before it was too late. If you want to join me in the *Englisch* world, I'll consider a proposal, but until then, you need to go home."

Yost could think of nothing to say. She had all but lied to him. She refused to compromise on anything. He should have followed his first instinct. It was better if Bitsy Kiem was out of his life. He stomped across the room, picked up his coat and hat, and stormed out the door without putting them on. The wind met him at the threshold and chilled him to the bone, but he refused to pause long enough to do anything about it.

Bitsy was nothing to him now. As far as he was concerned, she didn't even exist. And the big hole in his heart was proof.

Chapter 7

Yost smiled widely and clapped and clapped at the end of the school Christmas program, but if someone had asked him what his favorite part was, he wouldn't have had anything to say. He had barely noticed when the children stood up to say their lines. He didn't remember what songs were sung or Scriptures recited. He didn't know if Levi had gotten his part right, even though he and Bitsy had practiced it with him a dozen times.

All he did the whole program was try not to think about Bitsy Kiem sitting three rows in front of him, looking as fierce and beautiful as an avenging angel. At first, he'd been mad that she'd had the nerve to show up to the school Christmas program with that slightly less bright red hair. But then he couldn't help but be grateful that she had come for Levi's sake. Levi had invited her, and she had told him that wild horses couldn't have kept her away.

After the applause died down, parents, siblings, and grandparents congregated at the eats table. Bitsy's yellow stars were there, but Yost refused to eat them on principle. Why had he ever wanted to marry Bitsy? She was pretty and feisty and more breathtaking than a roller coaster, but she was also stubborn and rebellious, and she could hold a grudge as if it was attached to her body. How could he love someone who couldn't forgive and refused to improve herself?

He snatched a snickerdoodle from the plate closest to him and took a hearty bite. It was as dry as cardboard and just as flavorful. He chewed slowly while trying not to gaze longingly at Bitsy's cookies. They were disappearing faster than snow on a warm spring day. Maybe he should try at least one before they were all gone.

Too late. Benny Yutzy scooped up the last three in his chubby little hands and ran into the coat closet to eat them. Yost almost chased him but thought better of it. What would his neighbors think if he seized cookies from one of the scholars?

Yost positioned himself in the corner as his gaze involuntarily followed Bitsy everywhere. She squatted down to talk to Ada Beiler, John Beiler's daughter, who was confined to a wheelchair and whose mental disabilities kept her out of school. Bitsy oohed and aahed over Suvie Nelson's baby and helped little Dean Zook reach a cookie from the platter, snatching an extra one for him when his *mamm* wasn't looking.

Bitsy's presence filled the entire schoolhouse. She was everywhere, silently calling to him. She ignored him completely, but he couldn't look away.

Abraham Yutzy, Benny's *dawdi*, ambled over to Yost's corner. "Wonderful *gute* program," he said.

Yost was sure it had been wonderful *gute*, even if he hadn't been paying attention. "Wonderful *gute*."

"Your grandson Levi has a nice, firm voice. He'll

be a minister someday with that strong delivery." Abraham took a bite of his cookie. "I hear you and Bitsy Kiem are dating."

Yost's gut twisted around itself. They weren't dating anymore, and he never, ever, ever wanted to date her again. It felt *gute* to be rid of her. "*Nae.* We're not."

Abraham formed his lips into an O and nodded. "*Ach,* Yost, I am relieved to hear it. Edna told me she saw your buggy at Bitsy's farm, but I couldn't believe there was anything between you. I told her a godly man like you would never get mixed up with Bitsy Kiem. She'd drag you down to hell as sure as you're born."

Yost couldn't do anything but nod for the lump stuck in his throat. For sure and certain he was grateful he hadn't let Bitsy trick him into marrying her. Life with her would have been nothing but Bee Sting Cake, blue hair, and laughter all the time. Who needed that? Who needed broken stoves and duct tape, absurd cat names and Scripture debates? Who needed money stuck in Bibles and green fuzzy slippers and shotguns and praying aloud?

The weight on his chest was so heavy he couldn't breathe. He knew the answer to that question.

Abraham moved away to be with his grandchildren, and Levi ran up and gave Yost a hug.

"You remembered your part and didn't falter once. You looked so confident," Yost said. That had probably happened.

Levi nodded. "Bitsy told me to imagine people in their underwear, and I wasn't even nervous."

Yost tried to be sufficiently indignant that Bitsy had said the word "underwear" to his grandson, but he couldn't stifle a smile. Bitsy Kiem would say anything to help a nervous little boy perform well in his Christmas program.

Levi beamed like a string of *Englisch* Christmas lights. "Did you see, Dawdi? Bitsy came. I asked her to come, and she came. She asked if I would be embarrassed if she had red hair and tattoos, and I told her it would be okay with me. Dat said we should stand up for our friends and not be ashamed of them."

The lump in Yost's throat grew bigger, either because of the dry cookie or the lesson his twelve-year-old grandson had just taught him. "That is *gute* advice."

Levi reached up and placed his hand on Yost's shoulder as if he was an adult and Yost was a child. "You like her, don't you, Dawdi?"

He wanted to scream out a denial, but he wouldn't ever lie to his grandson. "*Jah,* I like her."

Levi bloomed into a grin. "I knew you did. You stare at her all the time without hardly even blinking."

Yost sighed and ruffled Levi's hair. "Bitsy and I don't suit well, no matter how much I like her."

Levi scrunched his lips together and made a face. "It doesn't matter what someone looks like or if they wear funny shoes or weird beanies. It matters what's in our heart, Dawdi. Bitsy's heart is full of big plans. And probably thousands of recipes. But do you know what's mostly in Bitsy's heart, Dawdi?"

"What?"

"Love. She's got so much love, and everyone can see it because it spills out all the time. Go talk to her. Maybe you'll find out you suit better than you think." Levi drained his cup of punch. "I need another drink."

Yost barely noticed Levi walk away. His attention was focused on the other side of the room where the woman with thousands of recipes and lots of love in her heart stood talking to Susie Borntreger, no doubt about one of Susie's physical ailments. She had a lot of them and loved to give people frequent updates.

He couldn't pretend that his life would be fine without Bitsy. He couldn't even pretend his life would be bearable. He was so mad at her he could have spit, but he was also so in love with her that he couldn't see straight.

He wanted Bitsy to be his wife, no matter the sacrifice.

His chest tightened. He knew what he had to do, but didn't know if he had the courage to do it.

He would find the courage.

He loved her. He had no choice.

Chapter 8

Bitsy pulled the stollen out of the oven, and then started wondering why she'd made it. Nobody liked stollen except the few stalwart Germans who swore Christmas wasn't Christmas without the dense bread filled with dried fruit and raisins. Bitsy had made stollen every year since she and her nieces moved to Bienenstock, and everybody ate a piece to honor the tradition even though Poppy held her nose while she ate it. Christmas was a time of new beginnings. Maybe Bitsy would start a new tradition next year, like chicken enchiladas or sushi.

She stirred her small helping of chili bubbling in the pot. Tomorrow was Christmas Eve and the nieces and their families would come for a big party. The Amish didn't really celebrate Christmas Eve, but Bitsy had always celebrated it as an *Englischer* and didn't see any sin in having another get-together with the family.

Of course, there were some people in the community who were eager to see sin everywhere, and those people would probably be offended by a Christmas

Eve party. But Bitsy couldn't spare an extra minute to think about them or be sad that they were never going to come to her house again. If they thought she was that sinful, she was happy they stayed away. She didn't need the judgment or the heartache.

Didn't need the heartache one little bit.

Gute thing she was too busy to brood about it.

Her beeswax candle had burned down to nothing but a puddle of wax on her counter. She'd scrape it off tomorrow, but for tonight, she liked looking at the puddle and remembering how beautiful the candle had been when it was burning. It had wasted to nothing doing just what it had been created for. She rejoiced in the memory of the light. Never again would she let a candle go unburned.

Someone knocked on the door, three times in perfect rhythm. She rolled her eyes. She still needed to roll out the cookie dough and bake the cookies tonight so they'd be ready to frost for the party. She had no time for interruptions. With an oven mitt on each hand, she pushed aside the curtains to see who was at her door. It was full dark outside, and all she could make out was a strange *Englisch* man with short-cropped hair, blue jeans, and bright white athletic shoes. He was probably a hoodlum looking to rob the poor unsuspecting Amish lady. Still in her oven mitts, she picked up her shotgun, pointed it at about the height his head would be, and opened the door.

"Oh, *sis yuscht*," the hoodlum muttered, slowly raising both hands over his head. "I know you're mad, but could you please put down the gun?"

Bitsy gasped. She'd heard that voice before. It belonged to . . . "Yost Weaver?"

The *Englischer*, who was not an *Englischer* at all, took a step into the light.

It was Yost, but she kept her gun at the ready. In the two days since she had seen him, he'd obviously gone crazy. His brown hair was short and wavy, and a thick strand fell across his forehead as if it wasn't quite sure what it was doing on his head. His horseshoe beard was gone, revealing a small scar on his chin and two red spots where he'd obviously nicked himself. He still wore his Amish coat, but the T-shirt underneath had a picture of a skull with a lightning bolt through it. "Grateful Dead" was written across the top in block letters. His jeans were too tight— poor thing, he looked quite uncomfortable—and those white shoes had to be brand new and had to have cost him at least fifty dollars.

But the most shocking thing about Yost Weaver was that he was wearing Bitsy's dangly earring in one ear. Well, he wasn't exactly wearing it. It hung from his earlobe attached by a piece of duct tape.

Jah. He'd gone stark, raving mad.

Crazy or not, he was still the handsomest man she'd ever laid eyes on. If her heart hadn't already been broken, it would be in pieces on the ground by now.

"Yost," she said, keeping her voice pleasant and low. She didn't want to scare him—even though he had a gun pointed at his head. "Do you need help finding your way home?"

He looked absolutely miserable standing out there and not just because his jeans were too tight. "Can I come in? It's freezing out here."

"What do you want, besides a better haircut?"

"I want you, Bitsy, if you'll have me."

She narrowed her eyes and frowned, even as her heart started beating like a Deen Castronovo drum solo. "All right. You can come in, but only if you take off the earring. It's ridiculous."

A hopeful light glinted in his eyes as he nodded then peeled the duct tape from his earlobe. The earring came with it. "I thought maybe you preferred men with earrings."

"Lenny Kravitz can get away with an earring. You, Yost, absolutely cannot. Don't ever do it again."

"*Ach.* Okay."

She stepped back, lowered her gun, and stepped aside so Yost could come into the house. He wiped his brilliant white shoes on the mat and shut the door as she peeled off her oven mitts. Standing on her rug, Yost looked at her like a puppy who'd lost his boy.

"There's a phone shack just down the road," Bitsy said. "Should I call an ambulance?"

"What for?"

"Because you shaved your beard. You're obviously delirious."

He peeled off his coat and draped it over a chair. That Grateful Dead T-shirt had sparkly threads sewn right into the fabric. "Bitsy, I love you. I love you so much that I ache when I'm not with you. I love you with everything in my heart, and I'm willing to quit the church to marry you."

Bitsy stopped breathing. Her heart stopped beating. Time stopped moving. Yost was willing to give up the church for her? Willing to give up everything he had known his whole life? Could he really love her that much? The thought stunned her, and she almost fell to her knees. If she didn't do something immediately, she was going to burst into tears.

She wrapped her arms around him and kissed his dejected face. Kissed his cheeks, his bare chin, his frowning lips. He kissed back with all the desperation of a condemned man. "Yost," she whispered. "I'm not worth eternal damnation."

"You're worth Earth, heaven, and perdition, Bitsy Kiem, and that's the truth. I'm leaving the church. I want to marry you."

"I can't let you do it."

He slid his arms around her waist. "It's my choice, not yours."

"You'll be shunned. You'll be separated from your children and grandchildren," Bitsy said.

"Will you marry me?" He looked so utterly miserable, a casual observer might have thought he had asked her to shoot him.

She grunted her disapproval, took his hands, and led him to the sofa. He sat reluctantly, as if he thought she might try to talk him out of it. Or maybe it was the tight jeans.

"Please, Bitsy," he said again. "Marry me?"

She knelt down in front of him and propped her arms on his knees. "Not with that haircut, I can't. And you're much better looking with a beard."

He rolled his eyes. "Now you tell me."

She took his hand and kissed every knuckle. Oh, how she loved him! Oh, how she loved that he was willing to trade his whole life for her. "The T-shirt was a nice gesture, but I hate the Grateful Dead. I was more a Journey girl."

One side of his mouth curled up. "The guy at the store said you'd like it."

"How old was he, like seventy?" She took his other hand and kissed those knuckles too. "Yost, I love that you would do this for me, but I can't let you. You'd be miserable within months."

"But I'm miserable without you."

"As you should be. But I'm closer to being Amish than you are to being *Englisch* by a long shot. You don't even know how to buy a *gute* pair of shoes. After my nieces were married, I talked to the bishop about getting baptized—even though I like to dye my hair and wear earrings. Believe it or not, the elders are happy when someone wants to join. The bishop was willing to overlook my defects for the sake of my soul."

"Why didn't you tell me this the other night?"

"Because I was hopping mad at you, Yost Weaver. I didn't want to give you so much as a sliver of hope."

"You succeeded."

"I'm not sorry I did it. You're too big for your britches." She pulled on the hem of his jeans. "Right now more than ever."

A smile grew slowly on his face, followed by a low chuckle. "The man at the store said 'chicks dig tight jeans.' "

She puckered her lips to keep herself from smiling. "I can certainly appreciate a pair of tight jeans, but not if you end up crippled." She made a big show of smiling. "Much as I try to avoid making my *fater* happy, I'm willing to be baptized to save your soul."

His breath came out in spurts and he seemed to grow weak just sitting there. "*Denki*, Bitsy. *Denki*." He pinched the bridge of his nose, and his eyes teared up. "*Denki*, Bitsy. I love you so much."

Bitsy blinked back a little moisture from her eyes. There was no reason to get mushy. "I love you too,

Yost Weaver. In spite of yourself. But I want you to know that I won't change anything about myself after we're married, not even the earrings."

He gazed at her and smoothed his thumb down her cheek. "I wouldn't want you to, and I should have realized that all along."

She couldn't resist getting under his skin just a little. "And of course, there are some things I can't change, like that tattoo that's never going to come off."

His eyes nearly popped out of his head. "You have a real tattoo?"

She pumped her eyebrows up and down. "Only my husband will ever know for sure and certain."

He couldn't seem to catch his breath. "I'm horrified and fascinated at the same time." He looked up at the ceiling. "Lord, lead me not into temptation."

"Yost," Bitsy squealed, "you just said your first out-loud prayer! How *wunderbarr*."

He smiled sheepishly. "It was an emergency."

She slid next to him on the sofa and lifted his arm and put it around her. "*Frehlicher Grischtdaag*, Yost. Merry Christmas."

The way she was looking at him made his heart swell until he couldn't breathe for the happiness. "*Frehlicher Grischtdaag*, Bitsy." It would be the best Christmas ever.

Bitsy kissed him on the cheek. "I'm so happy, I could do a dance right here in the sitting room."

Yost shook his head. "Let's not get carried away. I'm still getting used to the idea of a secret tattoo."

Bitsy slid her Bible from the bookshelf and thumbed through the pages. She found the passage she was looking for and practically shoved the book in Yost's face.

"Right there," she said. "David danced naked before the Lord. It's in the Bible. The bishop has to approve."

Yost groaned and buried his face in his hands. "*Ach, du lieva.* Don't even think about it, Bitsy. Don't even think about it."

The Christmas Candle

LISA JONES BAKER

*To John and Marcia Baker, the two
who love me unconditionally*

Acknowledgments

Huge thanks to my family and friends who have supported my writing endeavors over the past two decades. A special thank-you to my Amish go-to girl who diligently reviews every story I write, and to the folks in Arthur, Illinois, who fascinate and inspire me. Last but not least, much gratitude to the late Maxine Poff of the Weldon United Methodist Church, who realized my love for hot rolls from my 4H days to adulthood, and who offered me every tip in the book for making a winning batch!

Chapter 1

As Lydia glimpsed the small pothole in front of her, the soft purring of an engine startled her. She looked up. A guy hung his head out of an opened window and rested his arm where the glass met the sill.

"Are you okay?"

The deep, low timbre of a man's concerned voice got her attention. With great care, she stood, balanced herself, and brushed the rocks from her palms as she faced a tall, dark-haired, burly-looking male who had stepped from his vehicle. Immediately, she recognized him from the fair.

With a kind smile, he waved an inviting hand. "Come on. My truck's nice and warm. I'll give you a lift."

She hesitated, but only for a moment. It wasn't exactly proper for a single Amish girl to be alone with a single man, but pain combined with the fact that her house was some distance away caused her to seriously consider his kind offer.

She wondered how she'd make it home with the loose candles and broken box. Besides, the fierce stabbing in her right ankle wouldn't allow her to put much weight on the sore foot.

Several moments later, she responded with an eager nod. "I'd appreciate that very much."

He extended his arm in a greeting. "John King."

She gently shook his hand. "Lydia Schultz." She hesitated a moment to absorb the name that was all-too-familiar to her. "From King's Bakery in town, *jah?*"

When their gazes locked, his eyes did a jovial dance. The only thing she could possibly do was to smile back at him.

"That's me. In fact, I recognize you from the fair. My sister purchased one of your candles."

"And Mamma came early to buy a dozen of your cinnamon rolls." Despite the cold December temperature, heat warmed her cheeks. She wasn't sure why. She reasoned that it was because of her unfortunate predicament. "It's no secret that your pastries are famous around here."

He gave a humble roll of his eyes. "We aim to please." He paused to pull his scarf tighter around his neck. "So you're on your way home?"

Suddenly realizing that they were standing outside in the cold wind, she focused on what needed doing and nodded in the direction of the two-story house that seemed unusually far away.

"*Jah.*" She pointed. "That's where I live."

As his gaze followed hers, Lydia ran her fingers over the front of her coat to wipe off the loose gravel and forced a smile as she began collecting her candles. But the container had torn, and carrying her goods would be impossible.

A stabbing sensation above her foot made her

wince. "Ouch." With one swift motion, she bent to rub her ankle and closed her eyes until the sharp pain subsided.

"Here. Come on." John helped her to his Chevy pickup, where he opened the passenger door and assisted her up to the bucket seat. Despite the fact that his touch wasn't proper, she reasoned that it was common courtesy and gratefully welcomed his efforts. Inside of the small cab, the heat coming from the vents in front of her prompted her to breathe in delight.

He closed her door halfway and stopped. "Make sure your foot's all the way in."

Lydia moved her right leg closer to her left, and John closed the door with a gentle motion. "Get comfortable while I collect your candles."

He pointed to the handle. "And roll the window up. That way, it will stay nice and warm for you, Lydia." He darted her a reassuring wink before turning.

"Thanks."

He dipped his head. "My pleasure."

She adjusted herself in her seat and breathed in the delicious-smelling aroma of cinnamon rolls and grinned while glimpsing the white boxes stacked in-between the driver and passenger sides. Without looking, she was fairly sure of what was in the closed containers.

The smell gave it away. But it would be rude to peek. That definitely wouldn't be something Mamma would approve of. So instead, she focused on John.

He retrieved the candles, one by one, and placed them in a box he pulled from a compartment in the back of his pickup. He moved lithely and without effort. She took in his deep brown winter jacket that came down to his hips and the hat that easily covered his ears.

As she sat in his cab, a car passed them. The driver waved, and she returned the gesture before refocusing on the man who'd come to her aid. As she studied him, she drew her brows together. He wasn't thin by any means; at the same time, he wasn't heavy, either.

His build was strong, rugged. In fact, she could easily picture him working in a field more so than inside a bakery. Of course, she didn't know much about him. He might very well have another job.

When he started back to the Chevy, she quickly turned in the opposite direction so he wouldn't catch her watching him. She hadn't meant to stare, but something about him intrigued her.

It could be the sparkle in his eyes, his smile, his deep, reassuring voice, or even the way he'd immediately made her feel at ease. Maybe it was all of those qualities. She wasn't sure.

A short time later, he joined her.

Cold air quickly filled the small interior. Without wasting time, he pulled his door closed and removed his gloves before fastening his seat belt and putting the vehicle into drive. As Lydia watched John check for traffic, she once again felt her ankle throb. But she gritted her teeth.

Her situation could have been much worse. She could have been without a ride.

So she considered herself fortunate. Besides, she'd soon be home to apply ice on the injured area. John slowly moved back onto the country blacktop. As he accelerated, they sat in silence until he eyed her foot. "How's that ankle?"

She looked down at her shoe before lifting her chin to meet his gaze. "I think I twisted it. But it'll be okay. Thank goodness you came by just at the right time."

As they proceeded down the long, winding country road, Lydia grimaced. Loose gravel crunched under the tires. An occasional pebble flew out to the side. As they picked up speed, the wind whistled.

Part of her was in agony. At the same time, a strange, inexplicable contentment filled her. Her shoulders relaxed, and she enjoyed the soft feel of the fabric bucket seat. She wasn't sure why, but she truly enjoyed the friendly company of this man, even though they'd just met.

As she breathed in the delicious aroma of cinnamon rolls, she smiled a little. He happened to catch the corners of her lips lift into a grin.

"You must not hurt too much." He cleared his throat. "Something's making you awfully happy over there."

She smiled. "I was just enjoying the scent of cinnamon. It smells so . . . *gut!*"

He grinned in amusement as he flipped open the box on top of the stack with his right hand and nodded to the pastries. "Go ahead, Lydia. Help yourself."

She turned her attention to the delicious-looking desserts and drew in a small hopeful breath.

"They're extras. There should be some napkins inside of the glove box."

She leaned forward to open the compartment in front of her to retrieve a serviette. There was a slight click as she closed the latch. She turned to the rolls and took in the neatly arranged array loaded with white icing and with great care, scooped a treat with a single napkin.

She took a bite and closed her eyes in delight. When she opened her lids, she swallowed, nodding approval. "John, this is the best yet!"

He laughed. "Glad you think so, Lydia. The truth is, the batches we made for the fair turned out exceptional. It's not exactly a perfect science, unfortunately. You know, sometimes the yeast rises better than others. When it comes to dough, there are all sorts of factors. But before you take another bite . . ." He darted her a scolding glance.

Holding the roll in front of her, she eyed him with skepticism.

He grinned. "Don't ruin your appetite."

Lydia smiled a little. She considered his comment, but didn't respond. Because even if the roll did spoil her dinner, she certainly wasn't about to say no to the pastry. Especially this one.

And she sensed that he knew it. Because the frosted goods inside of this very box . . . well, she considered this treat "personalized." It had been given to her directly from the baker himself.

She licked sweet icing off her fingers and talked in between bites. "I would *love* this recipe. Every time I eat one of these, I'm convinced it's the best I've ever tasted." She smiled a little.

"I guess that means that we improve with every batch we make," he said in an amused tone.

"I'm serious about getting your recipe. Please?" She lifted an uncertain brow and hesitated, lowering the pitch of her voice a notch. "I know others who'd die for it, too." She tore off a bite and chewed it. After she swallowed, she considered her statements and went on.

"Strangely, no one has a clue to what's in them. A lot of folks make rolls. But this recipe . . . you add something that no one else does." A silent plea edged her voice. "What's the secret?"

He shook his head and slowed at the T intersection. After looking both ways, he accelerated and adjusted in his seat. "Good try, Lydia. Truth be known, this recipe has been handed down in our family for generations. By word of mouth, only."

She took in his comment. "You mean it's not even in writing?"

He gave a firm shake of his head.

Lydia took another bite. After she swallowed, she pressed. "Really?"

"It's true. My great-great-grandmother was always thinking of ways to improve her dishes. She baked 'round the clock. And when it came to the rolls . . ." He offered a dismissive shrug of his shoulders. "She was determined to keep it a secret and vowed to never record the ingredients."

He chuckled. "That's probably why no one has copied it. I've tasted other pastries that came close . . . but our recipe has remained anonymous and unique, fortunately."

"Your grandmother must have been a great lady to create this recipe. She's made a lot of people awfully happy!"

They shared a laugh.

"I could live on these."

As she leaned back in her seat, she acknowledged that the pain in her ankle had greatly subsided. She was sure that conversing with John had taken her mind off her injury. As she considered her new friend, she smiled a little. She enjoyed the soft purring of the truck's engine, automatically taking in the familiar scenery in front of her.

Of course, she knew it by heart. On both sides loomed empty corn and bean fields. The stark bareness was such a sharp contrast to only a few months ago when it had been difficult to see around tall brown cornstalks.

Puffs of smoke rose from chimneys in distant houses, lingering before disappearing into the air like steam from a teakettle. Large, fluffy clouds loomed in the stark gray sky. The sun hid behind the clouds.

Although bright sunny days made her heart beat to a happy pace, the dismal picture didn't at all stymie Lydia's excitement of the blessed season that was commencing. She recalled what her father had mentioned at breakfast and sat up a little straighter. "Daddy said the first snowfall might come tonight."

John nodded. "That's the forecast. It's what I'm hoping for, too." Several heartbeats later, he went on in a thoughtful tone. "There's nothing as beautiful and tranquil as the first snowfall of the year. The snow's so white."

He breathed in and continued. "Maybe it's my imagination, but don't you think there's something especially wonderful and comforting about it?" He glanced at her before returning his attention to the road.

She scrunched her shoulders and wiped her fingers on the napkin. Wondering where to put it, she started to stick it in her pocket. "There's a trash bag in between us, if you don't mind checking under the boxes."

She was quick to find a small plastic bag and pull it from underneath the stack. She stuffed the used napkin inside and placed the bag on the floor. So John was tidy.

Of course, that would make sense if he spent most of his time in a kitchen. And she guessed he was organized, too. She supposed he had to be to run a successful business.

The wind picked up speed as Lydia considered the beginning of the Christmas season. She pulled her hands over her chest. "I love winter nights."

"Yeah?"

"Uh-huh. In fact, I enjoy sitting by my kerosene heater in front of my bedroom window after dinner and writing Christmas cards. I start the first of the month, with a couple a day, so there's enough time to send to everyone. And I make my own cards."

"Ya do?"

She nodded. "Handmade greetings are so much fun. Mamma and I . . . We decorate the stairwell rail with them. So I hope everyone sends early this year so there's more time to admire them."

Lydia paused, dreaming of the coming holiday. "I especially love when it snows on Christmas Eve. I like to drift back in time and try to picture Mary and Joseph with the three Wise Men and their camels."

She drew her arms over her chest in great awe. "What happened is so amazing." Suddenly realizing that she was doing most of the talking, she silently chastised herself.

Lydia was sure one of her downfalls was that she loved to chat. But Mamma had always told her not to monopolize the conversation. And she'd always stressed not to tell everything you're thinking. That some things should be kept private.

But what Lydia had said . . . wasn't it something

everyone thought about? She turned her head enough to catch the thoughtful expression that crossed his face from her peripheral vision.

He didn't respond. But he didn't need to. It was as if there was a mutual understanding and contentment between them. He hadn't said so. Neither had she. But the expressions on his face and his demeanor told her that it was there.

She enjoyed their conversation, and an ache pinched her chest when they neared her home. She stiffened at the realization that their ride was coming to an end. Because after she and John parted, it was most likely that she'd never enjoy this man's company again.

After all, she was Amish. He was Mennonite. Although he hadn't told her, she knew it from what she'd heard about his family. She squeezed her eyes closed. When she opened her lids, salty tears stung her eyes.

Although both faiths were Christian, she was fully aware that she was expected to marry an eligible Amish man. Of course, she and John weren't in a relationship, but the Amish stressed sticking pretty much within their own community.

It wasn't because they weren't sociable. It was due to the fact that they wanted to avoid temptations from the English world. That meant she wouldn't have the opportunity to spend time with him. Still, Lydia yearned to savor their brief time together.

He darted her a wry smile and changed the subject. "So how long have you been coming to our shop?"

Still enjoying the mouthwatering scent in his truck, she responded with a quick nod. "For years. Every time Mamma and I go to town. We've tried other rolls. You know, stuff from the grocery store. But King's are the best. Hands down."

She grinned. "I always ask for extra icing. The girl who usually waits on me is delightful."

"Hannah?"

Lydia shrugged. "I'm not sure. She's got a huge smile, lots of freckles, and reddish-brown hair."

John chuckled. "That's Hannah. She's the youngest of my siblings." He tapped his palm a couple of times against the steering column and dragged his gaze to Lydia. "In fact . . . I can see the two of you being great friends."

"Oh?"

He nodded. "Yeah. Most definitely you would be joined at the hip. You've both got bright, bubbly personalities. Even the same laugh."

Lydia blushed a bit. "Thanks for that, John. I take that as a compliment."

"You're welcome."

He lifted his shoulders in a gentle shrug. "There are advantages to having a family business. There's no need to look elsewhere for help. And it's not like we're a chain. And that's the way we'd like things to stay."

She considered what he'd just said and pressed her pointer finger to her lips. "That may be true. But you must have a large clientele. Mamma and I always stop when we're in town. And when we do, your shop's buzzin' with customers. In fact, I can't recall when we started first in line."

She drew her hands over her lap. "But it's so worth the wait. Mamma and I . . . we savor the pastries during our ride home in the buggy. I guess you could say they're our rewards for shopping. Mamma always tells me to make the roll last because we won't have another one till we go back to town."

She thought a moment. "I've been in King's Bakery on many occasions, but I've never seen you."

"That's not surprising. I'm usually in the back doing behind-the-scenes things. Book work. Inventory. Ordering supplies. Making sure the kitchen's well stocked."

"Of course. It's funny; I've never really considered all of the different tasks that go into being a successful bakery, but now that you've brought it up, there's obviously much more to running your shop than meets the eye."

"Hannah and Pete usually man the front counter. It works because they like interacting with our customers." He winked.

"Everyone in the family plays their own role. So we won't run out of cinnamon rolls. Because after talking with you . . ." He cleared an emotional knot from his throat. "I'm starting to see what it would do to our customers if we did."

She laughed. Suddenly recalling their annual charity drive, Lydia sat up a little straighter and moved her palms to her thighs. "And by the way, I think it's great that you make rolls for the needy every Christmas. What a generous contribution to those who wouldn't otherwise get to enjoy treats. You've got to know that your pastries are the talk at church. And in town. Christmas Eve, *jah?* Because that's when a lot of the folks have their family dinners."

As she awaited a response, she turned toward him with an appreciative smile. But to her surprise, he didn't respond. And when he glanced at her, she noted how his brows drew together in skepticism.

That he strummed his fingers against the steering column to an uneven, nervous beat.

His odd reaction prompted the corners of her lips to do a quick dip. She wasn't sure what she'd said to change the upbeat mood. But somehow, she'd managed to strike an unhappy chord. She definitely wanted to fix whatever was wrong. Mamma had always said that nothing was impossible.

When he finally spoke, concern edged his voice. "Everyone's expectations of the drive are so high, Lydia."

"Of course! Because you and your family have something that gifts the needy. And that's surely satisfaction to you and your family."

With a quick flip of his hand, he turned the heat switch up a notch. Warmer air caressed Lydia's hands and she bent her fingers in delight. "Sometimes, we need to face reality."

"What do you mean?"

"I hope we can pull it off this year. I'm saying strong prayers for God to help me."

His comment prompted her to press her lips together in a straight line. As she held her palms in front of the vents, she wondered why on earth this strong, friendly man next to her would worry about anything, let alone something he and his family had accomplished so many times.

Of course, she'd just met him, so she didn't know much about him, personally, but Mamma always told her that her instincts about people were unusually perceptive. And her intuition shouted that the dark-haired man in the driver's seat would be successful at anything he undertook.

"You're concerned." After a brief pause, she lowered her pitch to barely more than a whisper. "About the Christmas Eve drive that you and your family have done year after year?"

He let out a sigh and rested both hands on the bottom of the steering wheel while he slowed the truck. "Don't get me wrong, Lydia. I don't mean to sound ridiculous. Normally, I'm the optimistic sort, but realistically . . ."

He shoved out a sigh. "Producing so many orders of cinnamon rolls won't be easy. Like I said, we're a small business. We only have so many ovens. And the ingredients will cost much more than in years past. The sad truth is . . . If my calculations are even close, coming through for everyone . . . it might not be possible."

She considered his statement, not comprehending his concern. "But it's not anything new. . . ."

He smiled a little and waved a dismissive hand. "I know. Don't misunderstand; I certainly have no right to complain. And I'm not. God has presented this particular opportunity to serve to my family and me."

He lowered the pitch of his voice to a more serious tone. "I consider it a privilege to help. It goes without saying that something of this nature requires months of preparation so we'll have all the items necessary plus more. We plan for extra just in case something goes awry. You know, every batch doesn't come out perfect. Some, we discard. But the number of requests this year . . ." He inhaled a breath and pushed it out.

He grinned skeptically at her. "We're excited for the opportunity to help our neighbors, for sure. Especially during such a blessed time of year that's all about giving. That's the reasoning behind what started our drive years ago."

"Of course. Then what's the problem?"

As Lydia awaited a response, she drew her hands together on her lap. A long pause ensued while she clutched her fingers together tightly and wondered if she'd been nosy. Her neck tensed.

She supposed that she had. She should have given him the opportunity to continue without asking questions.

Finally, he gave an uncertain shake of his head and lowered the pitch of his voice to a serious tone. "It sounds simple. But here's the thing, Lydia." He lifted a hand before letting it drop back on the steering column.

"In the past, making and delivering the rolls has been within our reach. But this time, it's a whole different game. Do you know that we have over double the number of people on our list as in past years?"

A surprised breath escaped her. "Oh . . ." Now she understood. It was about supply and demand. And the demand was too high.

He gave a slight nod. "There are two ways to look at it. Lots of people requesting our services could be looked at as a blessing, I guess. It's always an opportunity to be of service for those in need."

While she waited for him to go on, she took in the small clock on his dash that showed it was dinnertime. This morning, Mamma had made dough for noodles. At six a.m., the smell of baked chicken had floated deliciously throughout the house.

Lydia looked forward to chicken and dumplings. At the same time, she didn't want her conversation with John to end. She turned to him with interest.

"To be totally honest, Lydia, I'm concerned that our small outfit won't be able to provide for every request. And that would be awful." Reconsidering his words, he continued. "I didn't mean to dump this on you. Can this stay between us?"

She offered a quick nod, feeling privileged that he'd confided in her. The drive which he talked about was important to a lot of folks. And she was in on somewhat confidential information now. "Of course."

"I haven't discussed this outside the family, but when you asked, it just came out. I've known for some time what we're up against. But I've been holding it inside, hoping a solution will come to me."

"So you haven't figured out how to do it."

He gave a strong shake of his head. "No, I haven't. And the more I think on it, the more frustrated I get." The pitch of his voice lightened. "If you want the truth, sharing this with you picks up my spirits. It actually feels good to get it off my chest."

"I'll bet it does. There's no need for you to carry such a burden alone."

"I've been bearing this worry on my shoulders the past few weeks. I'm praying for guidance to complete the task God has given us. Thank you for listening."

"I'm glad I'm here to be your sounding board." A long silence went by while Lydia contemplated the severity of what he'd just told her.

His obvious sincerity and his concerned expression tugged at her emotions until she felt a part of his situation. She acknowledged that she truly was involved in the crisis now. Because he'd confided in her. Didn't that mean she had to help him?

She believed it did. It was no secret that the needy in the nearby communities counted on King's Bakery to provide delicious edibles for their Christmases.

Lydia knew for a fact that the rolls were the desserts for many holiday dinners. People counted on them. And in the past, there had never been reason to doubt that they would materialize. At least, that's how it seemed.

Over the years, she'd heard so much about the great joy the King family contributed, she'd never really given serious thought to the hard work required to provide for so many. Let alone the cost. And John had confessed he'd begun planning over a month ago.

He shoved out a hopeful breath. "We'll come through for everyone. We have to."

"I'll think of a way to help you, John. Mamma has always told me that I'm a good problem solver."

"Then what would you do?"

She considered the potent question, then raised her palms to the ceiling of the truck in a helpless gesture. "I'm not sure. But it'll come to me. Things always work out." She smiled a little. "In fact, I'm not much for planning. I love surprises."

He raised an inquisitive brow. "Not me. I don't like change. And a drive of this nature doesn't allow me to just let things go and see how things work out. It requires planning. Lots of it."

"I understand." She hesitated before her voice lifted with enthusiasm. "But aren't you a little excited about it?" Before he could get a word in, she went on. "You've got to be. Because you'll make everyone on your list so happy!"

Her words came out in a convincing manner. Yet she saw his point. Because making the charity a success would involve more of everything and everyone than they normally counted on.

She was only one person. So even if she personally volunteered, would her efforts guarantee that the drive would be successful? She frowned.

As she tried for a solution, she noticed the needle on the speedometer was on thirty-five. John must have expected input from her. Because he'd slowed his truck significantly.

After a slight pause, he went on. "How 'bout you, Lydia? Are you excited about Christmas?"

An oncoming vehicle approached them, and John slowed to pull over to the side to give the other driver room to get by. As he did so, she considered his question. It quickly prompted a disappointed sigh. After the other car went by, John returned to the middle of the narrow blacktop and stepped gently on the accelerator.

From her peripheral vision, she was quick to note his brow lift with curiosity. Shifting in her seat for a more comfortable position, she crossed her legs at the ankles. "I'm afraid you're not the only one facing a dilemma."

"You mean you've got a predicament, too?"

She offered a slow nod while contemplating whether sharing hers was proper. She quickly decided that it was since she'd listened to John's. Even if they'd just met, that he'd confided in her had already stepped up their trust in each other. In her opinion, anyway.

Eager to talk about her worry, she bent her chin to her knees and started in a low tone. "*Jah*, I sort of have my own thing I'm battling."

She rolled her eyes. "We're so different. I mean, in dealing with our problems. You don't like change. I love surprises. And you've been holding your worries inside while I've been telling practically everyone I've come into contact with about mine. I'm afraid I'm one of those people who shares my worries with everyone."

He grinned. "Do you think there's something wrong with that?"

She moved her right shoulder in a shrug. "I'm not sure. I know that's not necessarily good. In fact, ever since I can remember, Mamma has told me that I need to stop being so verbal. That people won't want to have a conversation with me if I bombard them with my issues. And that in a conversation, there needs to be a certain balance, whatever that means."

She stopped a moment for a breath. "But, John, it's just the way I am. And I'm one of those people who enjoys unburdening to others."

He nodded, understanding. She smiled in response. "It's my nature to offload my worries, I guess. But this year, staying quiet is a challenge. And it's all because . . ."

When he glanced her way, she sat up straighter in her seat and decided to put it out there. She moved her palms to both sides of her hips and pressed them into the soft fabric of the bucket seat.

Regardless whether she discussed it or if she didn't, her dilemma existed. Not sharing it certainly wouldn't make things better; that she was sure of. On the other hand, talking about it wouldn't make it worse.

Maybe John would offer a response that could help her to at least deal with what was on her mind. Pulling in a breath, she lifted her chin and straightened her shoulders. "Every year, my older sister and I decide on a Christmas blessing and try to make it come true."

He turned and lifted an inquisitive brow. "That's

wonderful, Lydia. What on earth could be wrong with that?"

Before she could cut in, he continued in a voice edged with sudden excitement. "It sounds like a self-less goal. In fact, that's very generous of you." After a slight hesitation on his part, he lowered the pitch of his voice to uncertainty. "But I don't understand . . . What's the issue?"

She gave a soft lift of her shoulders. "I shouldn't complain. It's just that this year going through with it will be more difficult." She cleared the knot from her throat.

"Over the years, Anna and I had so much fun coming up with our goal to make something nice happen for someone by Christmas Eve. And when it did, we'd light our homemade candle together in the living room window. That very one candle that we don't touch until our goal's accomplished."

When he turned toward her, his eyes reflected lack of understanding. She decided to make her point. "But this year . . . you see, things are different." She lowered her gaze to her lap. Her hands were clutched so tightly together, her knuckles turned white. Finally, she unlaced her fingers and pushed out a sigh.

"I'll be doing it alone." She softened the pitch of her voice. "Anna got married a couple of months ago and moved to Ohio."

After a lengthy pause, he offered a sympathetic nod. "Ah ha. I get it. You're missin' your big sis. You've always decided your Christmas wishes together, and well . . . this year will be a huge adjustment because you'll be doing what you've done for years with her alone."

For some strange reason, the genuine understanding in his voice and the soft expression in his eyes prompted her to relax a bit. Sighing relief, she rested the back of her head against the seat and closed her eyes a moment.

She'd confessed her worry. The tenseness in her shoulders quickly disappeared. When the words had come out, they hadn't sounded nearly as severe as they'd seemed. She opened her lids and smiled a little.

As Lydia digested what she'd just told him, she silently acknowledged the huge significance of her confession. "John, all of my life, I've depended on Anna to help me with things. Things that I thought were important, anyway. Like friendship. Support. Advice."

"That seems natural. I mean, to lean on an older sibling. I wouldn't know . . . I mean, I'm the eldest of twelve. But now that you mention it, my brothers and sisters count on me to help with their decisions all the time."

"When I think about it, maybe I sound naïve."

"Not at all. But you must have expected your older sister to eventually get married."

Lydia nodded. "Of course. She courted Jacob Yoder, and Anna confided in me that she couldn't wait to be a wife and a mamma. But . . ."

She hesitated before finishing. If she'd known her sister would marry, then what was the problem? "Of course, I knew she'd marry. But for some reason, I didn't actually realize the huge void that she'd leave in our house. Our home . . . it's so quiet now. And there's no one to help with chores but me."

She swallowed an emotional knot when John glanced at her. Something about his expression encouraged her to continue to open up.

Before she could go on, he cut in. "You miss having someone to talk to."

Lydia nodded in agreement. "It's much more than that, John. I miss the laughter. Her presence. Even hearing her sneeze when she picks up cats that stray into our yard." The thought prompted a laugh.

"My sister loves animals but has bad allergies when she gets near them."

She breathed in. "I don't believe I'm saying this, but I even miss her chastising me to pin my hair under my *kapp*." With one quick motion, she pointed to her head. Of course, several loose strands had escaped her covering, and she quickly tucked them back underneath.

"But you've got your mother to talk to."

"*Jah*. That's different. Anna and I joked around. But the conversations I have with Mamma . . ."

She paused to decide why they differed from her chats with Anna. Finally, she knew. "When Mamma and I talk, our conversations are usually tied to what needs doing. Things going on in the church. Marriages. Babies."

Lydia's throat constricted with emotion. She tried to swallow the knot, but it remained. "Anna and I . . ."

"You did girl talk."

Lydia smiled a little at the way he said it. "Girl talk. That's it. We hit on more personal topics like how many kids we want. How many rooms we'd have in our houses. Even things like how we'd keep up sewing clothes for our children if we had a large family."

When he glanced at her, the color in his cheeks deepened a bit. "How many kids are we talking?"

Her own cheeks heated up until she was sure they were on fire. When he lifted a curious brow, she replied in a hushed tone that was so shy, it was barely a whisper. "At least ten."

The corners of his lips lifted into a big grin. He looked straight ahead, but she glimpsed his expression from her peripheral vision. Her verbal admission prompted her to giggle with excitement.

Thoughts of a large clan helped to nix her worry about the Christmas goal with which she struggled.

Her mind stayed on the brood she yearned for more than anything. "I know it sounds like a lot, but I love children! And noise and laughter . . . Every house needs them to be happy. I can't wait to have little ones chasing each other in a nice big home with lots of bedrooms."

"I'd bet you'll be a good mom."

Her jaw dropped. Not because she wasn't sure she'd be a good mamma. But because it surprised her that he'd told her she would be. "You really think so?"

He gave a firm nod. "Absolutely. I can hear your love for children in your voice. And love is the most important prerequisite for being a mom, don't ya think?"

She considered his question before offering a quick, decisive nod.

As Lydia's home neared, an uncomfortable knot pinched her chest. And she knew why. She wanted more time with the kind man next to her. In fact, to her own astonishment, she wanted to talk about a lot of things with him.

She liked watching his eyes twinkle. And she enjoyed the soft timbre of his low voice. And, of course, his responses.

"This one, right?" He motioned to the white two-story that had been built by Lydia's great-grandfather.

"*Jah.*"

The understanding pitch of John's voice suddenly filled with a tone that was a sweet combination of concern and sensitivity.

Automatically, she folded her arms over her lap.

"I'm sorry about your sister's move, Lydia. In fact, I can't imagine the adjustment you must be going through. I know you miss her, but try to see the positive in her move."

Lydia lifted a skeptical brow, unsure if there was anything good about losing her sister.

"What life throws at us isn't always what we would choose." He sat up a little straighter in his seat. "But you're glad your sister's happy, right?" He paused. "Besides, you said yourself that you like change."

Lydia nodded. "Of course. But is it wrong to wish she lived closer?"

"No. Not at all. We always want to be around our loved ones. But when you see each other, just think how special that time together will be."

Salty moisture stung Lydia's eyes, and she quickly ran her finger over the tears before they could trickle down her cheek. How she wished Anna and Jacob would move back to Arthur. How she yearned to hold the little ones Lydia was sure they'd have.

She quickly turned in her seat, regarding John with a combination of great hope that he would say something to help her feel better. "What?"

He glanced her way and grinned sympathetically. Automatically, she lowered her gaze to the black mat on the floor and suddenly realized that she'd totally forgotten about her fall. In fact, at that very moment, her ankle felt fine.

Her conversation with John King certainly had helped ease the pain. That realization stunned her, and she drew in a small breath that was surprise combined with relief.

"Christmastime is an emotional season. For everyone, Lydia. The feelings you're experiencing? You're not alone. In fact, I'm going through the same thing."

She lifted an inquisitive brow for him to continue.

"On a different level, though. Last year, my uncle Mervin went to the Lord."

"I'm so sorry . . ."

"Thank you. But like it or not, losing our loved ones is part of life. Just like births."

Lydia admitted his correctness. But she still wished her sister hadn't moved away.

"Uncle Mervin . . ." John paused a moment before continuing. "He was the fun behind our cinnamon roll drive. It's hard to explain, but he made it so exciting. Before the month of December, he always pumped up the drive, building on the excitement until we couldn't wait for it to happen."

"Oh."

"We've done the event for years. And you want to know who started it?"

"Mervin?"

Before Lydia could respond, John offered a big nod. "Yup." John chuckled. "He was one of those people who wanted to save the world."

Lydia's heart warmed at the fondness in John's voice as he spoke of his uncle. And she knew others who were made from the same mold. She thought immediately of Old Sam Beachy, who was famous for his special hope chests.

"It was his idea to offer what we can to our community. He always stressed using our talents in a way that helped others. And for us?" He stopped to catch his breath. "That was to bake pastries."

"He must have been a wonderful person, I mean, to start the drive." She lowered her gaze to the floor before lifting her chin to meet his eyes. "But I understand what you're saying, John. Doing the drive without him must be hard for you."

"That's an understatement. Because I miss him every step of the way. But you know what?"

She lifted a curious brow.

"Since I was little, I always knew that we're planted on this earth for a short time. Fortunately, what my uncle did for my Lord and Savior was to be a good example for me. To teach me the true meaning of service. And you know what?"

She gave him a nod to continue.

"I've thought a lot about that concept. And I've sort of come up with my own theory."

"*Jah?*"

He wagged a dismissive hand. "Oh, it's not a big deal. Let's just drop it."

"No! Now you've got me curious. You have to tell me!"

"Well . . . What I've decided is that just because someone's not physically with you doesn't mean they can't still play a role in your life. Does that make sense?"

Lydia frowned uncertainly while she contemplated his point and finally offered a slight nod of agreement. "You've got a point, John." Several heartbeats later, she went on. "I won't disagree."

"Because it's true. Even without him here in person, I can feel his presence. For instance, I hear it in a person's voice when he thanks me for something. Or see it in someone's eyes. It's a good feeling. And everything he taught me?"

John gave a small lift of his shoulders. "It's not

wasted just because he's not here. No, no. In many ways, he passed his goodness on to me, and I have his ideas to help me through life. He was an incredible, positive influence. He always took charge of the drive. He arranged the delivery list; you know, decided the most efficient routes."

"I'm sorry, John. You must miss him something terrible."

John nodded. "This season only makes it harder."

"I know what you mean. Because the same holds true for me. I really miss Anna. John, when she got married, I was so caught up in helping plan the wedding that I never realized how empty the house would feel when she left."

He nodded.

"After that, loneliness hit me. And it was then that I realized she was gone. That she'd never be in our house again. I mean, not living there."

"But she visits, right? Holidays?"

"Sure. But it's not the same. Every time they come, they have to see friends and family. In fact, they're so busy, it seems like they're hardly home."

"I can imagine."

"Can you?"

He arched a brow.

"I mean, there are twelve of you. Plus your parents."

"Doesn't matter. It's funny: even though we're a large brood, each one of us plays a special role. And even when one of us isn't around . . ." He shrugged. "I feel it."

He paused to shake his head regretfully. "With only you left in the house . . ." A long pause ensued until he went on. "That would be unbearable."

"It is, John. I thought it was bad until Christmas was right around the corner. And now . . ."

She rolled her eyes in disbelief. "Just getting through this month, let alone establishing a goal and seeing it through, will be a bigger challenge than I've ever encountered." The pitch of her voice lowered to a tone that was a combination of desperation and sadness. "I don't know how I'm going to do it."

Chapter 2

John frowned with concern. The pitch of Lydia's voice was a combination of dismay and regret. She honestly was struggling with getting through Christmas. No one should have to do that. After all, wasn't this the most joyous time of year?

As he eyed her from the side, one thing became clear to him as he strummed nervous fingers against the steering column. He had to do something to help this beautiful girl. And she was lovely. Inside and out.

When she spoke, her eyes lit up with a combination of eagerness and enthusiasm. The soft, excited tone of her voice made him enjoy listening to everything she said. But this kindhearted person beside him . . . she needed his help. And fast.

And the more he listened to her, the more determined he became to ease her troubled mind. But how could he make things better? Bringing her sister back to Illinois certainly was possible. But likely?

He shook his head. Of course, he couldn't ask Anna and Jacob to return. And even if he did, they most likely wouldn't. A move across state lines was drastic, especially within the tightly knit Amish community that still got around by horse and buggy.

And if Anna had migrated all the way to Ohio, he was convinced there was a strong reason for it. Apparently, this was one time that change wasn't welcome to the girl who'd confessed she loved surprises.

And solving Lydia's dilemma wasn't possible, but choosing the right words might make her feel better. He thought hard, trying to decide what to say that would lessen the severity of her situation. His deceased uncle's face popped into his mind. *What would you tell her, Uncle Mervin? You were a great decision maker.*

Finally, the words came to John. Now, all he had to do was to try them on her and see if they worked. With a subtle movement, he rested his head against the headrest, slowing to stall for time.

"Lydia, I understand your situation so well. And I'm trying to think of how to help you." He steadied the pitch of his voice to a more apologetic tone. "Believe me, I wish I had the perfect answer, but unfortunately, I don't."

He turned to meet the regretful expression on her face. He had to do his best for Lydia. He wasn't sure why; what he did know was that he had to try. "Most likely, your situation won't change."

From his peripheral vision, he noted her frown. "Unfortunately, one of the things we do most here on earth is to try to accept things that are out of our control."

"But what do you do, John? I know it's not a perfect world, but how would you deal with my situation? To be honest, this is one time when change doesn't make me happy."

He drummed his fingers on the steering wheel. "When I'm faced with any dilemma, the first thing I do is to pray for guidance. Only God knows what will be resolved and what won't. So we're obviously happier if we can accept reality, right?"

She offered a slow nod of agreement.

"Are you praying about it?"

"Every night. And unlike bringing your uncle back, with Anna, there is a way to fix things. But to do that, God would have to move her and her husband back here. And then his family would be the ones who missed them. You see, Jacob's family is in Ohio. So is his business."

As he absorbed the significance of her words, he watched the helpless lift of her shoulders. And he fully understood what she was up against.

"So to be honest, I don't see a move back to Illinois in the future."

"Maybe not. Think about it, though. If his family's out of state, and hers in Illinois, they can't live in both places. His business is in Ohio. So Ohio won out. But Lydia, don't be discouraged. Your sister's move is recent. It'll take time to accept and figure out how to deal with her being away."

He turned into the Schultz drive. As the smoke from the fire pit morphed into the cold, brisk air, she looked directly in front of her.

She glimpsed flames in their living room fireplace. Saw the horses standing still in the fenced-in pasture. But the familiar scene in front of her soon became nothing more than a blur as she absorbed what her new friend had told her.

Suddenly, she was a bit ashamed that she'd poured out her sadness to someone she'd just met. He'd been

generous enough to offer her a ride. She should have
spent their brief time together trying to help him
with his dilemma. Instead, she'd selfishly poured out
her own problems.

She turned and softened her voice. "I'm sorry,
John. I apologize."

His dark brows narrowed. "For what?"

"I didn't mean to complain."

John barely heard her. Because something nagged
at him. And it wasn't that Lydia had had her say. It was
because he was about to tell this girl good-bye.

While loose gravel crunch crunched under the
wheels, John bounced in his seat. The unevenness of
the ride was a sharp contrast to the smoothness of
the blacktop.

"We're here."

Lydia's soft, reassuring voice seemed to float over
to him. The moment the turn signal stopped its light
clicking sound, his chest tightened with uncertainty.
As the Schultz home loomed in front of them, he realized that he probably wouldn't have the opportunity to enjoy Lydia's company again.

He frowned and attempted to find a way to deal
with it. As his gaze landed on the second hand that
circled the small clock inside of the dash, he wondered how his life could have taken such a drastic
turn within the past hour.

Even though he'd just met her, for some reason,
that particular thought brought on an unsettling knot
inside of his chest. But what was he feeling? And why?
What he was certain of was that meeting Lydia had
stirred something inside of him that less than an
hour ago, he'd never known existed. And the moment
he would leave her drive, he was sure he wouldn't forget her.

As he tried to make sense of it all, he sat very still, delaying turning off his truck. A woman inside the home waved a friendly hand to them from the front window. John responded and admitted what was inevitable. It was time to let Lydia go.

With huge regret, he pushed his gear stick into park. A silence that was an eerie combination of comfort and regret lingered between them while the wind met the truck and the soft flow of heat oozed from the vents in front of them. John swallowed an emotional knot that blocked his throat.

I'm in a predicament I've never encountered. His fingers stiffened on the steering column. He was quick to note that Lydia didn't budge, either. Did she feel the same way? Did she hate that this would be their first and last time together?

He didn't want to say good-bye to her. And to his dismay, he yearned to preserve their time together. Wanted to explain how he felt. But what did he feel?

He certainly couldn't tell her if he wasn't even sure himself. While he considered his state of helplessness, he acknowledged that their time together had to end.

And to make matters worse, he couldn't tell her what was on his mind. That he didn't want to leave. That he wanted to see her again. And again. In this situation, his thoughts and voicing them were totally inappropriate. After all, the beautiful girl next to him was Amish. He was Mennonite.

Not only that, but although out of the several Mennonite churches in the area his was the most liberal, and even though he and Lydia both practiced Christianity and believed in the same God, the rules they lived by were as different as night and day.

Admitting defeat, he turned the key. Immediately, the warmth coming from the vents disappeared, and the temperature inside the cab dropped a couple of notches.

John turned. Lydia did, too. Their gazes locked in what seemed to be a mutual understanding. As John took in the white flecks that danced in her deep blue eyes, an unprecedented shiver that was a combination of happiness and contentment darted up his spine and landed at the nape of his neck.

But he didn't shrug to rid the comforting, unfamiliar sensation. Whatever Lydia made him feel prompted the corners of his lips to lift.

Say something. As a light whistle of wind created a noise that reminded John of steam coming from a teakettle, he admitted to himself that his life was pretty much the same routine every day.

Of course, issues with his siblings came up out of the blue that needed to be dealt with, but all in all, he was pretty good at predicting what would happen.

And that's the way John preferred it. Unlike the girl next to him, he liked things to stay the same. But until now, he'd never really appreciated his uneventful life. He faced a situation with Lydia that he wanted to be different.

He acknowledged that not seeing her again would be something he needed to reconcile with. Because he would have to find a way to accept the void she'd leave in his life. It disturbed him that the girl beside him forced something unrecognizable inside of him. He frowned.

He knew this area well and had glimpsed the

Schultz house on numerous occasions in passing. Finally, Lydia unfastened her seat belt. The light metal click prompted John to do the same. She motioned with her hand to a small one-story building with a window on both sides of a simple-looking wooden door.

Lydia lifted her chin. "That's Mamma's store, John. Ever since I can remember, she's had her own business. And I help make home-made things for customers, too. You know, jams; raspberry is the most popular. And she sews beautiful table linens and pillow covers on her old Singer sewing machine she keeps in our living room."

"Does she get much business?"

Lydia offered a quick, enthusiastic nod. "*Jah*. Especially around the holidays. You see, Mamma loves to cook, and she also makes extra money by having a buffet at our house twice a month. People say no one can match her homemade chicken and dumplings. They find out about it through brochures at the Welcome Center. It keeps us all busy."

"Sounds like your mother's a talented lady."

Lydia lowered her gaze to the floor and nodded. When she lifted her chin, she smiled. He noticed the light pink shade that colored her cheeks. "Daddy's busy, too. He farms and makes cabinets."

John glimpsed the wooden fence that extended from the large red barn. Two goats ran loose in the side yard. A horse trotted, head held high, through the bare pasture inside of the fence. Large windows at the front of the house revealed bright orange flames in the fireplace.

Finally, John got out and stepped to Lydia's side.

As he squeezed the handle, her door opened. He steadied her and helped her to the ground. "Let's go inside. Then I'll get the candles."

The expression on Lydia's face reflected eager hope. "Come meet my parents. Would you join us for dinner?"

As John entered the Schultz home behind Lydia, she offered a brief introduction to her father. John quickly shook hands with the stocky man of medium height who greeted them at the front door. "John King."

A set of light tan brows narrowed in skepticism.

John quickly explained his presence. "Your daughter needed a lift, and I happened to be there to help."

"Eli Shultz."

Lydia stepped in. "Daddy, I fell and twisted my ankle walking home."

She lifted her sore foot and pointed to the injured area. When her father didn't respond, she raised the pitch of her voice. "Please don't worry. I'm okay."

She darted John a glance and smiled. "Thanks to John. He picked up my candles that spilled and gave me a lift. I'm grateful for the ride and asked him to stay for dinner."

As John inhaled the scent of chicken broth that filled the kitchen, his stomach growled. He realized he hadn't eaten since breakfast.

"I'm Miriam." A petite lady wearing an apron and white *kapp* quickly stepped forward to welcome John. But her attention shifted to Lydia, who took a seat at the dining room table. As John chitchatted with Lydia's gruff-voiced father, he glimpsed Lydia removing her shoe and her mother making an ice pack. It was easy to hear their conversation.

"We've got to get some ice on that right away."

"Mamma, it's much better now. At first, it really hurt."

Automatically, Eli and John joined the ladies. "You've got a mighty nice lump there," her father cut in as he peered down at the knot below her ankle. "I reckon your *maem* will get you fixed up in no time at all."

He turned his attention back to John. "Let's take that coat off and get you comfortable. Are you from that bakery in town?"

John nodded with a courteous smile. As his gaze locked with Eli's, the fire popped. At the same time, John caught the sound of something boiling on the stove. From the smell, he knew it was chicken broth.

Eli waved toward a small hall bathroom. "Go ahead and wash up. Dinner's about ready."

A mélange of delicious aromas filled the area around the kitchen table. Mamma's ice patch numbed Lydia's ankle as her father said the blessing. "Amen."

When Lydia opened her eyes, she propped her swollen ankle on the rolled-up towel Mamma had made so the ice patch wouldn't budge. Raising her gaze to the long oak table, Lydia smiled a little as she accepted the chicken and dumplings, helped herself, and carefully passed the heavy white dish to her father.

As she regarded the plate in front of her, she laughed inside. As usual, there was very little chicken and lots of noodles. But it was okay. Her mother always made extra pasta so Lydia could indulge without guilt of unbalancing the contents.

But right now, Lydia's focus was on the kind, gentle man across from her. Their gazes locked for a couple of seconds. A warmth filled her chest while their eyes connected in a mutual understanding.

His reaction was a warm smile. She returned the expression as silverware clicked lightly against china. Her dad poured cream into his coffee and stirred it. Mamma buttered a homemade roll and added raspberry jelly.

Before taking a bite, Mamma directed her attention to Lydia. "Is your ankle better?"

Her father cut in. "Judging by that large knot, you did a fine job of twisting it."

Concern edged Mamma's soft voice. "The ice surely helps. Before bed, I'll rub some apple vinegar on the swelling."

Lydia nodded. "Thanks, Mamma. It will be fine." Lydia was sure Mamma had already thought of every homeopathic remedy available. And Mamma always did the right things. With her oils and herbs, no one in the family stayed sick for long. But Lydia didn't want to think or talk about her injury right now. She considered this dinner with John bonus time. And she wanted to enjoy every moment she had with him.

As Lydia peppered the chicken broth, her mother and father chitchatted about seeing Anna and Jacob for the holiday. They were coming to visit; it's just that the time hadn't been confirmed yet.

Lydia was sure Anna had a lot of decisions to make with her husband's large family of seven brothers, their wives, and children along with the Schultz relatives. And she and her husband would make sure that everyone was seen over the holiday.

Lydia glanced up at John as he finished his last dumpling. He, too, belonged to a large clan. And she was sure he kept busy over the holidays visiting his family.

All along, she'd been aware of his bakery, yet she'd never had any personal interaction with him. He looked up to catch her watching him. Hot blood rushed to her cheeks, and she merely offered an embarrassed smile.

But the moment he grinned back, Lydia's heart did a joyous somersault. Her response stunned her, and she wasn't sure what to think. She'd never experienced such a reaction to a man, but she didn't question her excitement. She reasoned that such a response to someone who'd come to her aid was all too logical.

His much-appreciated act of kindness had spared her a very long walk home with a swollen ankle. And the warm cabin of his truck had been a welcomed contrast to the chilling wind. She was grateful her family could offer him dinner, and that he'd stayed.

She considered herself fortunate. Realizing that her thoughts had interrupted her from barely tasting her favorite dish, she focused on Mamma's culinary efforts.

The dumplings finally helped her to relax and to even better appreciate John King. Lydia's father led the conversation, making sure, as usual, that everyone knew that Mamma's chicken and dumplings were his favorite meal.

"So you were at the Christmas Fair today?"

John nodded. "I was. Our family donated cinnamon rolls." He paused to take a drink of water. Ice cubes clinked against his glass as he returned it to the white coaster.

"Yes," Mamma cut in. "I was there early to get a dozen rolls."

After taking a sip of coffee and returning the mug to the wooden tabletop, Lydia's dad swallowed and offered a satisfied nod. "Word has it that the fair was a hit."

Lydia chimed in. "Daddy, it was so much fun to work with our neighbors for something every one of us might need in the future. Who knows when we'll use a nursing home?"

Mamma set her glass of ice water down and swallowed. "I can't wait to hear all about it. That new wing will surely help a lot of folks."

She turned to John. "As you're probably aware, the Amish don't send family members to nursing homes unless there's no other option. And we're learning that sometimes, it's necessary."

Lydia piped in. "Like last year. When Mamma broke her hip. We wanted to take care of her here at the house, but the doctor recommended four weeks in the nursing home. He believed she'd heal faster there."

She rolled her eyes. "It took a long time to convince us to have her stay there, but we're glad we finally heeded his recommendation."

Mamma cut in. "You see, I needed therapy every day. And they started it right after the operation. Staying in the nursing home made it much easier on all of us for that reason."

When John raised an interested brow, Lydia went on to explain. "At first, I thought it would be bad of us to do it that way. I mean, Mamma's taken care of us when we're down. And I thought we should do the same for her. But when you think about it, staying at the nursing home really made sense. And looking back, we're glad we did it."

Eli interrupted in a gruff tone. "Before the operation, we didn't realize how difficult it would be for Miriam to get around afterward. So many things were hard that we hadn't even considered. Like stepping down the front stairs."

He gave a frustrated shake of his head. "It didn't take long to figure out that if she'd stayed here, we would have had to get her into a vehicle every day, which wasn't easy. Not to mention, we'd need to hire a driver to take us to therapy, then hire another driver to bring her back. And of course, getting inside of the car was the most challenging task of all. Even with Lydia, Anna, and me all helping. And it was painful for Miriam. To be honest, staying there worked."

A long silence passed while silverware clicked lightly against china plates. As Lydia helped herself to more dumplings, her mamma passed extra rolls around the table in a light wicker basket that had been handed down from Lydia's grandmother.

"I'll be honest, John, I didn't leave easily. Knowing I wouldn't be home to make dinner every night was harder on me than I'd anticipated. And while I was away, I worried round the clock about the three of them having enough to eat. Even if they did spend a lot of time at the nursing home offering me support. But looking back, those four weeks went by quickly."

She made a snap with her fingers and lifted her

palms to the ceiling in a dismissive gesture. "And
when I finally came home, I'd made huge progress.
Before I knew it, I was back in my own bed. Oh, I still
needed help stepping into the buggy, of course."

She grinned from ear to ear. "That was even more
of a challenge than stepping into the car. But over
all, getting around was so much easier. And we did
things that made life easier. Like putting a handle to
the right of the door."

She motioned with her hand. "Eli added a few
enhancements."

John smiled a little. "That's a touching story. So
this Christmas Fair held a personal meaning for you
and your family."

Lydia nodded. "*Jah.* It will help others. At the same
time, it's important to us." She paused for a shrug. "Because of Mamma. And a few others from our church
spent time recuperating after procedures. We've totally
changed our perception, John. What we learned is that
nursing homes are a godsend when you need them.
We'll never underestimate their worth."

"That's right."

As Lydia downed the chicken and dumplings, she
eyed John from her peripheral vision while savoring
the taste of the broth.

"Mrs. Schultz, your rolls are delicious."

Her smile widened. Small wrinkles crinkled underneath her eyes. "I take that as a huge compliment
coming from King's Bakery!"

He waved a dismissive hand. "I'm serious. And I
think I might just have to ask for your recipe. Now I
know who to come to when I need expertise." He
winked.

Lydia piped in. "We'll make you a deal. Mamma's
recipe for your grandmother's cinnamon roll secret."

John merely grinned while Lydia explained to her folks.

As she listened to John converse with her parents, she tried to remind herself that this was their first meeting. They discussed weather and crops as if they'd been talking about those subjects forever.

Amazingly, it seemed as if the man who helped to run King's Bakery was part of her family. And to her astonishment, it didn't seem to matter that John was Mennonite or that they were Amish. They sounded like friends sitting down to talk after a hard day's work. That very thought brought a satisfied trickle of joy up Lydia's arms.

She barely tasted her food as she continued to take in the comforting scene around her. She went on to consider the day and her new friend. While her folks asked him questions about his business and his siblings, Lydia gave great thought to the man who appeared quite comfortable with her and her parents.

The more she listened to him interact with her parents, the more certain she became that there must be a lot more to the eldest of twelve than met the eye. He spoke with ease about the price of corn and beans.

To her surprise, he knew quite a bit about woodworking. And they touched on the new vet in their area, Dr. Zimmerman, when Lydia learned that the King family milked their own cows for the butter they used at the bakery.

And his genuine interest in what her mother and father said warmed her heart. She enjoyed the gentle lift of John's voice. His expressive eyes showed concern.

Her heart fluttered. And there was something about his smile that prompted her to return his warm expression. From the moment she'd met him, she'd been convinced that he could be her very best friend. Next to Anna, of course.

A beautiful light shade of green flecked in his hazel eyes when he grinned. The joy that emanated from him when he spoke or gestured was surely happiness from the Lord. Lydia couldn't help but think about how wonderful it would be to spend more time with him.

She was fully aware that although Mennonites worshiped the same God as the Amish, their style of living differed. In their area, there were several Mennonite churches, and all held to slightly different standards.

Suddenly, she heard her mother say her name, and Lydia caught everyone regarding her. She grimaced when she realized she'd barely heard a word. At that moment, reality hit her, and she straightened her shoulders and beamed.

It donned on her that even without Anna, Christmas season was off to a great start. And it was because of her unusual meeting with John King. Lydia became aware as she met his gaze, that something inside of her told her that this wasn't the last she'd see of him.

That evening, Lydia breathed in the woodsy scent of greenery and the vanilla fragrance from her homemade candles and smiled satisfaction. As she cleared the table and scraped dirty dishes from the table, she thought back on the afternoon to the ride home in

John's truck to the wonderful dinner conversation to the regretful expression on his face as he'd waved good-bye to her outside in the cold.

Letting out a sigh, she stopped to glance out the small window above the kitchen sink. Propping her elbows on the countertop, she rested her chin on her palms and bent her knees while she stared at the barn in their backyard.

She glimpsed the black buggy underneath the small shed roof. A goat meandered back and forth from the shed to the house. But she barely saw what was right in front of her.

Instead, she imagined the front of King's Bakery and grinned. Of course, it was impossible to see where John worked because it was several miles away. Still, she visualized it, imagining John in the back, stocking shelves as the pleasant scent of cinnamon filled the air.

She could almost see the big black letters of King's Bakery on the shop's window. And she could hear the bell sound as she opened the door to go inside. She gazed outside and eyed the gravel drive that led to the blacktop.

When a dull ache in her ankle made her close her eyes, she lifted her foot and turned it a bit to take some weight off, hugging her palms to her hips while a sigh of satisfaction escaped her.

She put her hand over her mouth as lights from a vehicle briefly illuminated the road in the distance. Without thinking, she migrated to the living room and lowered her gaze to the single red candle in the window sill. As she stared with emotion at the home-made decoration, her thoughts drifted to Anna.

How am I going to think of a Christmas blessing with-

out you? How can I see this change in my life as a positive thing?

She swallowed the hard knot that obstructed her throat.

Automatically, what she'd discussed with John floated through her mind until she finally took a seat in the nearest rocker and propped her foot on the stool next to it.

As she sat back in the chair, the light throbbing in her ankle came and passed while she inhaled the pleasant vanilla scent of the white homemade candles that burned nearby. Thankfully, her pain wasn't nearly as bad as what she'd expected it to be when she'd fallen.

White candles lined the windowsills. Soft orange flames offered the Christmas spirit until she considered the goal she needed to decide. She frowned.

Only one wasn't burning. The wick in the center of the red candle. The decoration that had been especially selected by her and Anna last year to represent this year's Christmas blessing.

It would, hopefully, burn on Christmas Eve when that very blessing finally came to fruition. *But what's the blessing?*

Lydia pressed her pointer finger to her lips while she contemplated the potent question. As the moon lit up the sky in between scattered stars, she considered John's opinion that even though a loved one wasn't physically present, they were still with you, really, because of how you've shared a relationship and how they've affected your life. Like the situation with his beloved uncle.

She thought a moment. Of course, death certainly wasn't uncommon, but Lydia felt sorry that John had lost someone he'd been so close to. John's loss spawned

guilt that Lydia had complained about her sister
being away when John would have to wait till eternity
to see his uncle. Stretching her legs, Lydia's thoughts
drifted to Anna. A smile tugged the corners of Lydia's
lips upward.

Think positive. Her dilemma with her sister wasn't
nearly as dire as John's situation with his uncle. After
all, she would still be able to unite with Anna on occasions. Holidays. Weddings.

Suddenly, something even more disturbing un-
expectedly floated into Lydia's thoughts, and she
stiffened. What would she give Anna for Christmas?

Lydia closed her lids a moment, seriously pondering another dilemma. When she opened her eyes,
the question lingered on her mind.

With one swift motion, she stood and stepped
quickly back to the table where she ran a clean dish
rag over the top. It was difficult to focus on her task at
hand as the potent question stabbed at her until she
stopped what she was doing and eventually made her
way to the side of the room that offered a view of the
yard.

She gazed off into the distance, seeing nothing.
Darkness had set in. But the eerie howling of the wind
meeting the cracks in the house was easily heard.
Every once in a while, a limb from the pines would
meet the dwelling in a sound that reminded her of a
bale of hay meeting the barn floor after Daddy
shoved it over the edge of the loft.

She yearned to offer her sister something extra
special this year. A gift that Anna would think of as
special. Lydia swallowed an emotional knot from her
throat, struggling to decide her options.

Finally, she rested her palms on her hips and gazed

out at the stars. Trying to decide on a present, she smiled a little as she recalled the gift Anna had given her last Christmas.

The beautifully wrapped box had contained two balls of yarn of gorgeous shades of blue. The colors had reminded Lydia of the sky. There was a light hue that resembled the sky on a cloudless day. And another darker shade, that resembled how it looked right before a storm.

Anna had interpreted the simple gift in two different ways. It had been a joke, sort of, because Anna was fully aware that Lydia had never acquired enough patience to sit down and knit.

At the same time, the yarn had been a token of encouragement. Lydia was fully aware that Anna had always loved making warm things. She especially enjoyed soft scarves and hats.

Anna yearned for Lydia to experience the same joy, fully aware that getting Lydia to knit something was unlikely. It was no secret that Lydia's strength was in her cooking, and Anna's strongpoint lay in sewing and knitting.

Lydia pressed her lips together in a straight line. She still didn't know what to buy for her sister, but she focused her full concentration on coming up with an answer.

Finally, she gave up and returned her attention back to John. As she contemplated his reassuring manner, she stretched her legs so both heels rested on the hardwood floor. His positive outlook on how things worked warmed her inside. She drew in an appreciative breath, blew it out, and the tenseness in her neck went away.

A calm, easy sensation swept up her arms and settled comfortably in her shoulders. At that moment, she recognized something that had just happened because of John King. That Anna was gone for the Christmas season hadn't spoiled the blessed season at all.

Even without Anna, Lydia would decide a wonderful Christmas goal and like always, she would do her best to make that goal materialize. In fact, as she focused on what to make happen, this year's Christmas dream came to her.

Her pulse picked up to a more enthusiastic speed as she leaned forward. The goal was so obvious, why hadn't she thought of it earlier?

That evening, John shoved his hands into his pockets as he traversed his family's large backyard to the barn. He closed his eyes a moment as the strong, cold wind hit his face.

The building blocked a large part of the gust. Inside of the barn, he unbuttoned the top of his coat to allow for more arm movement as he reached for the oversized rake hanging on the wall and continued to corral dirty straw from the cattle area into a large heap.

While he worked, wind whistled through the cracks of the old structure. Although the building was far from warm, its four solid walls served to protect from the cold. As the metal prongs made a light scraping against the concrete floor, he breathed in the all-too familiar scent of straw and cattle and sighed satisfaction.

Silently, he credited his father for their large herd. John paused to utter a quick, thankful prayer for his healthy large brood of siblings and the two loving people who'd raised them in a loving Christian home.

As he compared them to Lydia's parents, he stopped and took in the docile animals around him. He smiled a little while as the dinner conversation with her folks flitted through his head.

Strangely, despite that her family was far smaller than his own, he'd felt quite at ease at their table.

Deep in thought, he continued his work, eventually loading fresh clean straw into the stalls and spreading it evenly across the floor.

Halfway done with his task, he stopped again to rest, watching the cattle get comfortable in their fresh bedding. Without warning, Lydia Schultz's beautiful, kind face popped into his mind and stayed there.

While he considered his evening with her, a strong, unfamiliar emotion tugged at his heart. He didn't recognize the gentle, reassuring sensation. Even so, it wouldn't leave him alone. For some reason, it sprinted up his arms and settled in his shoulders while he added to the straw.

To his surprise, his thoughts wouldn't leave the Amish girl he'd just met. He didn't know her well, but what he was sure of was that thinking about her made him grin. And he didn't doubt why. She was such a generous, sharing spirit.

As one of the horses entered the barn with a loud whinny, he wondered how Lydia would fit in with his eleven brothers and sisters. With his parents. Storm, the favorite horse to the little ones in his family, approached John and begged for attention.

Laughing, John accommodated, running an affectionate, reassuring hand over the long cream-colored face. While he did so, the wind grew stronger. The creaking of the structure became louder. Every once in a while, a limb from the tall oaks made a dull sound against the building.

And Lydia Schultz's smile and enthusiasm filled his head until he shook it in surrender. *Why can't I get her off my mind? And how does she live without siblings? I'm sure I couldn't survive without my brothers, sisters, and nieces and nephews. I love a noisy, love-filled home. In fact, I can't recall a time without laughing, crying, or talking. And over all of my years, I have no idea how my mother managed to keep everyone's laundry done. Or food on the table. Even with the help of my sisters.*

His mother washed every Tuesday and Friday morning. She was, without a doubt, the most organized person he knew. Of course, she had to be. The best cook, too. Automatically, he wondered if Lydia's parents had yearned for more offspring. As the great strength of the wind tried to heave open the large doors, he acknowledged that he couldn't wait to start a family of his own.

Boys, girls, gender didn't matter. What counted most was being together in a loving, Christian home. Automatically, his thoughts centered around Lydia. As Storm sucked up water from one of the troughs, the sound broke through John's thoughts, and he chuckled. "Remind me to teach you some manners, pal."

While the friendly horse gave a swift shake of his head, water drops hit John in the face. But he didn't focus on the beads hitting his face. Instead, he considered Lydia and how very little he knew about her.

Amazingly, it seemed as if he'd known her his whole life. How could that be? He tried common sense. *Perhaps it's her friendly, caring nature. Or maybe it's the enthusiastic sparkle in her eyes when she speaks. There's something in her tone and her obvious sincerity that makes me want to listen to her all day long.*

The mere thought of her prompted his heart to pick up to a happy pace. He drew a deep breath and blew it out in frustration. Why on earth was she on his mind so often? He silently chastised himself. He had keen instincts and Lydia seemed the epitome of everything good and wholesome.

Obviously, her parents were fine people. Most of all, so was the girl. He loved everything she appeared to be: good and truthful. Of course, she was of the Plain Faith, which meant that there was even more reason to admire her.

The Amish are hardworking folks. Loyal to their church. Their word's good. But I'm Mennonite. He frowned. *Because of that, I've got to stymie my interest in her. Because I'm sure she plans to join the Amish Church. And I'm already a devout Mennonite.*

He rested his palms on the rake and tapped the toe of his black boot to a nervous, uneasy beat. *Besides, we're total opposites. She enjoys spontaneity. I like the same schedule every day. I hold my worries inside. She talks about hers. There are many reasons why I've got to quiet my feelings for this girl. And fast.*

Lydia separated the eggs, placing the whites into one bowl and the yolks into another. She wiped her hands after dropping the shells into the lined garbage bag.

"You do make the best sponge cakes," Mamma said as she stepped inside the kitchen.

"Thanks, Mamma."

"The little ones you'll have someday will appreciate your culinary skills. You've definitely got a baker's talent."

"Mamma, I've been thinking a lot about what to get Anna for Christmas. You got any ideas?"

Mamma stepped beside her and rested an affectionate hand on Lydia's shoulder. "Let's see, now. She loves to knit and sew. Maybe you could buy her some material?"

Lydia offered a simple shrug of her shoulders while she considered Mamma's idea. As she mixed half of the sugar into the whites, she turned just long enough to catch the amused rise of her mother's brow. "What?"

"What do you mean, what?"

"You've got that look on your face. That expression that tells me when you're thinking something you're not saying. Tell me what's on your mind."

"I was just thinking." Her mother began to pull the silverware from the drawer and polish each individual fork. "Anna always longed for you to knit. Didn't she give you some yarn last Christmas?"

Lydia nodded, not diverting her attention from her task at hand. "You know that I'm the cook and Anna's the seamstress. I wouldn't even attempt to begin to be half as good as her in that area."

Lydia stopped a moment to consider what she'd just said. She frowned. Because she was contradicting her very own outlook on change. She welcomed it!

As she began mixing again, an idea started flitting through her mind until she straightened her shoulders and turned quickly toward her mother. "That's it, Mamma! I'll knit Anna a gift with the yarn she gave me last Christmas!"

Mamma joined her with a smile. "That's my Lydia. Always up for a challenge. I think that's a wonderful idea."

While Lydia beamed at knitting something for her sister, she was convinced that whatever she did with the yarn would truly be special for Anna. Something made from the beautiful hues of blue would definitely stand out from anything else that Lydia could buy. And even though Lydia didn't have the slightest idea what she'd make, she was, without a doubt, most certain that whatever it was would bring her sister great joy.

That evening, Lydia glimpsed the balls of yarn on her bed and shoved out a determined breath. With skepticism, she eyed the two silver knitting needles that she'd borrowed from Mamma.

I confessed to John that I enjoy change. There's no better time to really prove it than the present. She'd never yearned to knit. Now, she was going to do it. For her sister.

Attempting to focus on what needed done, she began her project, unraveling some of the strand. She knew how to knit. Anna had taught her. Now, like it or not, it was time to put what she'd learned to use.

As the needles clicked, she made herself comfortable against the headboard, leaning back and bending her knees so that the yarn rested in between her legs.

An hour later, what she'd accomplished prompted her to draw in a breath that was a combination of surprise and joy. As she continued her work, she allowed her thoughts to wander to when her sister would be home.

Lydia smiled a little. As the kerosene heater warmed the room, the burning candles surrounded her, providing enough light for Lydia to knit. The anxiety she'd experienced at the start of her project slowly evaporated and she found herself dreaming of Christmas with her sister.

While the smell of cinnamon candles floated deliciously through the room, she wondered how many dumplings Mamma would make. There would be lots of people. Tons of food. Gifts. Laughter. Lydia imagined opening her gifts. Even better, she envisioned handing hers to each member of her family.

She studied what she'd done so far and smiled a little. The most difficult part of knitting had been deciding to do it. Now she actually enjoyed picturing the expression of great joy and appreciation on Anna's face when she held Lydia's gift in front of her.

Lydia wanted this particular work to be a special surprise. Something that would show Anna just how much she really loved her. And Lydia would save this particular present until all others had been opened.

She smiled while she dreamed of the cinnamon roll drive Christmas Eve and her family gathering Christmas Day. *And I thought this year was going to be the worst Christmas ever. It will be the best. A blue knit scarf is the perfect gift for my sister!*

A couple of days later, John looked toward the entrance of the bakery. As it opened, Lydia stepped inside. The bell sounded. A huge gust of cold air accompanied her.

Automatically, he laid down his metal tray of pastries and stepped to close the door for her. After returning her friendly greeting, he motioned to a circular table next to the fireplace. As she moved to the chair, he pulled it out for her and gently pushed it closer to the table after she'd seated herself.

While they looked at each other, that all-too-familiar excitement that he experienced when he was around her zoomed up his arms. He quickly found his manners and glanced at the area behind the counter. "Lydia, this is Hannah, one of my sisters. Hannah, Lydia Schultz."

His sister's eyes reflected immediate recollection when she glanced back and forth between them. "The girl you gave a lift home the other day?"

Lydia waved a friendly hand. "That's me."

John made his way back to his task at hand. "Hannah, would you give Lydia one of our fresh cinnamon rolls and a drink while I finish up?" Before Hannah could say anything, he added, "Whatever she wants is on the house."

While he scooped hot rolls from a baking pan and placed them under the front counter, he took in the light conversation that went on between Hannah and Lydia.

"How's your ankle?"

Lydia's voice bubbled with happiness. "Much better; thanks for asking. I lost my footing while trying to balance my box of homemade candles when I was walking home from the Christmas Fair and . . ."

She pointed to the floor with her finger. "There I was on the road. Boom!"

Both girls laughed. John wasn't sure why, but deduced it must be the way Lydia had said *boom*. Her voice dipped as if she'd taken a sudden dive.

The dialogue between the girls kept moving while he made several trips back and forth to the kitchen. He tried to focus his efforts on the rolls as he transferred each individual pastry from the metal sheets on wheels to the plastic covered area visible to customers.

"The Christmas spirit is certainly in the air!" Lydia shoved out a happy sigh. "I just love all of the greenery in the shops. And the scented candles."

She closed her eyes a moment and breathed in. "There's something about the ambience that makes everyone happy."

The light bell above the door sounded as two women entered. While Hannah attended to them, Lydia stood. "I'll get out of your way," she said in an apologetic tone. "You're busy. Thanks for the delicious treats!"

Before she could leave, John stepped quickly to her table. "I'm ready for a break. Want to chat over another lemonade?"

"But you're busy . . ."

He waved a dismissive hand. "I'm glad to sit down a minute."

Lydia began pouring out with excitement the project she'd started for her sister and the background behind it.

"I admire you, Lydia."

Lydia parted her lips in surprise.

"I really do. You love challenges. And you're diving right into something you've never been interested in. That takes a special person to try something new."

"It will be the most precious gift I could ever give her."

"And what about the Christmas blessing you were trying to figure out?"

Before she could say anything, he leaned forward and smiled with interest. "Did you decide on one?"

Lydia's gaze met John's. "As a matter of fact, I did."

While he placed a coaster under his coffee, she imagined working in this shop all day, surrounded by the enticing smell of home-baked pastries. She wondered if she'd be able to resist the strong temptation to sample each dessert.

From her peripheral vision, she took in the vast array underneath the plastic. There were baked yeast rolls. Croissants. Sugar cookies with pastel-colored icing. Whole loaves of bread. Rye. Wheat. White.

In the background, she could hear a light sound of the oven vents. The soothing sound of Christmas music played over the speaker. And she glimpsed loaves of bread through the transparent part of the doors.

"I've been giving your situation a lot of thought, trying to think of what role I can play in helping you."

She drew in an excited breath and met his gaze as she pushed it out. "And I've come up with the perfect idea. For both of us."

"What?"

She leaned forward to emphasize her point. "Don't you see? I've decided my Christmas goal. And you've given it to me."

His brows narrowed. She couldn't believe he didn't get what she was saying, so she stated her aim as they held each other's gazes. "My goal is to help you with your cinnamon roll drive."

John's eyes lit up. Lydia noted a halo that danced around the pupils.

"I don't know what to say."

She leaned forward. "Say that it's a great idea, and that you'll let me be a part of it."

A long silence ensued while Lydia watched John sip from a paper cup that touted the words *King's Bakery*. When he didn't respond, she started a new subject. Perhaps he needed to get used to the idea of her playing a role in the drive. After all, for years, it had been a family project.

She smiled a little, knowing that he'd let her help with the drive. Her instincts were usually right on. And they were telling her that she'd get to contribute in some way.

"I wasn't kidding the other day when I told you that your rolls couldn't be matched. And by the way, thanks again for the ride." She glanced at the rolls under the plastic covering. "And for the roll."

"You're welcome. As far as giving you a lift, I'm glad to have helped." He grinned with his lips sealed. "But don't you think you have things turned around?"

She raised a curious brow.

"I'm really the one who should be thanking you."

Her mouth opened as she studied him with curiosity.

"Your mother's dinner was more than payback."

They shared a laugh.

The tone of his voice suddenly bordered on serious. "Lydia, I want you to know that when I told you my concerns about this year's drive, I wasn't complaining. It's important to me that you know that."

"Of course, I'm aware of that."

"And I think it's sweet that you'd like to help." He paused to lift his shoulders in a gentle shrug. "I can't believe that helping with our family drive will be your blessing this year."

He paused and lowered the pitch of his voice. "What can I say?" Before she could respond, he replied to his own question in an emotional pitch that was barely more than a whisper.

"I'm flattered."

Sitting up straight, she squared her shoulders in determination. Lifting her chin with a newfound excitement, she pushed herself up to her feet and locked gazes with his. "Then what are we waiting for? Let's start planning!"

Chapter 3

The following afternoon, Lydia sat opposite of John in the sitting area of King's Bakery. Eager to plan the coming drive, she regarded him with enthusiasm as she pressed her palms on her hips and smiled with a combination of eagerness and confidence.

Holding a pen between two fingers, she smiled a little. "Ready to get down to business?"

John nodded. As she cleared her throat, Lydia winked at Hannah. She also offered a friendly wave to John's brother, Peter, to whom she'd just recently been introduced.

John's lips curved in amusement. "Okay, Miss Schultz. Where to start?"

Lydia crossed her legs at the ankles and leaned forward. "I've been thinking a lot."

The light in his eyes brightened a notch. "And what did you decide?"

She smiled a little. Not at what he'd asked her. But at the silly roll of his eyes as he'd questioned her. "First of all, John, with this long list, you can't expect to do it all alone. What are your thoughts . . . on asking for donations?"

His brows drew together in a frown. In response, she uncrossed her legs. "I'm not talking about monetary donations. But don't you think contributions of flour and powdered sugar would help? And butter's so costly. Maybe the local stores and restaurants could pitch in?"

After dropping his gaze to the table, he scooted his chair back and crossed his arms over his lap. Several heartbeats later, he narrowed his dark brows and strummed his fingers against the glass tabletop.

As she took in his hands, she noticed a callus on his thumb. Of course, his hands wouldn't be pretty. He not only worked in the bakery, but he'd mentioned in an earlier conversation that he handled most of the farm work for their family as well.

When he stopped tapping, he straightened and looked at her. "I've never really considered donations."

She lifted a defensive hand. "Your bakery would still get the credit for the drive."

He grinned at the same time he shook his head. "I don't care about that."

Lydia let out a deep sigh of realization.

"Of course not. I'm sorry . . . I didn't mean to imply . . ."

He waved a dismissive hand. "Forget it. Actually, the idea of others pitching in ingredients makes a lot of sense." A few moments later, he smiled a little. "I like it." He paused. "Have you considered how to go about doing this?"

"I could pass around a sheet at church. We wouldn't need much of an introduction. Everyone's familiar with the drive. And our church . . ." She gave a casual lift of her shoulders. A breath of satisfaction followed. "I'm sure that they'd love nothing more than to be a part of this."

"And I could do the same with my church." They regarded each other thoughtfully. As Lydia took in his expression, the strangest, yet most satisfying sensation filled her until she folded her hands over her chest.

As they regarded each other, "It Came Upon a Midnight Clear" floated tranquilly through the shop. But something had just happened that forced her to swallow with emotion. It was a sudden, unexpected realization. A silent admission of why she really wanted this drive to be a success. That very acknowledgment nearly took her breath away.

The success of this year's cinnamon roll drive was important for the people on the list. But deep down inside, Lydia realized that she wanted it to work for the kind, gentle man opposite her.

She laid one hand on her lap and put the other hand on top. Her fingers shook. She almost laughed out loud. Because the feelings inside of her were to help someone she liked and respected. In fact, the Christmas blessing she wished for would benefit her as much as anyone.

Because helping John King and the two siblings behind the counter brought her great joy.

"I suppose doing some estimations wouldn't be a bad idea. Do you have any idea how much of these ingredients we'll need?"

He got up to grab a small hand calculator. When he returned, he used the device, recording numbers on the lined paper in front of him. While she waited for him to add, Lydia focused on whatever she could think of to ease his burden. Her mother constantly served on church committees. Lydia tried to imagine what advice she might offer. Her mamma had coordinated huge family weddings . . . Lydia straightened as she snapped her fingers.

John looked up from what he was doing.

"I thought of something else."

"What?"

She paused a moment. "Baking sheets. When Mamma does family weddings, she always has to borrow plates and dinnerware. And with this number of people needing the rolls, will we be able to bake all of them here in the shop? And are there enough baking sheets?"

The flecks on his eyes brightened at her last question. "Have you ever thought of becoming a businesswoman?"

She felt her cheeks warm. She looked down at her shoes to hide the color that she knew flooded her face. When she looked up, their gazes locked. Something about the way he regarded her caught her by surprise. For some reason, she couldn't look away.

She didn't know John well. Yet, something between them compelled her to yearn to work with him on the drive. To root for his success. And deep down inside, she wasn't sure that it was just for the needy.

He cleared his throat, and she startled. "Lydia, are you all right?"

"Oh!" She drew in a deep breath. "Sorry. I let my thoughts get away from me."

"We were talking about the number of cookie sheets."

"Of course." Trying to disguise her embarrassment, she recalled her last question. "Are there enough?"

"Let me do some more figuring."

As he focused on the numbers in front of him, Lydia turned to the tap on her shoulder.

"Would you mind giving me a hand for a minute?"

"Sure." Lydia stood to follow Hannah to the large opened cardboard boxes.

The freckled girl looked up at Lydia and smiled a little. "I'm so happy you're here with us!"

Lydia beamed. "It's a blessing knowing you and your brother. I can't wait to meet the rest of your family!"

As they organized paper bags of flour on the shelves, Hannah turned to Lydia. "Lydia, what's your favorite part about Christmas?"

As the old, familiar tune of "Joy to the World" played over the speaker, Lydia pushed a loose tendril of hair that had escaped her *kapp*. As she thought of a response, she ran her hands over the front of her apron and clasped her hands together in front of her.

Inside, her heart smiled. In many ways, her current environment was a sharp contrast to her home. She wasn't accustomed to hearing music; the Amish certainly loved hymns. At home, they sang them in Pennsylvania Dutch a cappella.

And she and Mamma often sang hymns while riding in the buggy. They spent a lot of time going from place to place, since many of their friends lived ten or so miles away.

Of course, there were no radios. So singing helped to pass the time. Not to mention, some of Lydia's favorite moments had taken place singing in the buggy with her sister and mamma.

On other occasions, they sang them in English.

In her own home, of course, there were no Christmas carols floating through the house via radio or television, but she rather enjoyed the music. The songs she knew by heart made the Christmas season come alive.

The bright sun coming in through one of the windows lightened John's dark brown hair a shade. The soft, beautiful hue reminded Lydia of leaves on their oak trees in the fall after they'd turned beautiful colors.

In her long dress and apron, she breathed in the pleasant, woodsy aroma of fresh pine branches and pushed out a deep breath. She looked at the stacked white boxes of different sizes behind the countertop. She couldn't actually see the tops, but knew that they said King's Bakery in gold.

Hannah wiped her hands together and smiled a little. "Thanks for your help, Lydia."

Lydia returned to her chair, and Hannah joined her and John. At the nearby table, Peter worked on a hand calculator. In front of her, Lydia tallied the list of flour and powdered sugar that she estimated members of her church would volunteer.

When she glanced up from the papers in front of her, John had slipped on reading glasses. As he jotted something down, she took advantage of the time he had his attention to the paper to observe him. Of course, she was fully aware of what he looked like. But the glasses provided different insight into the man who had offered a friendly ride in his car.

And she realized at that moment that there was much, much more to John King than met the eye. And she yearned to know every detail about the kind, generous Mennonite.

* * *

The following afternoon, Lydia glanced out of their living room's front window as she observed the candles lining the window sills. Since yesterday's visit at his bakery, her focus had been to help the Kings make their cinnamon roll drive a great success. In fact, she had given her Christmas goal so much thought, she couldn't bear the thought of her parents not allowing her to be a part of it.

And she knew, without a doubt, that she needed their approval. She hadn't talked to them about it yet, but planned to give them the heads-up so they could think on it before John got to the house later today. They'd discussed asking permission.

She looked out of the large window that provided a grand view of the front yard and the long stretch of drive leading to the blacktop road. She took in the familiar surroundings and smiled a little.

A buggy headed north. She could clearly see the horse, but was unable to make out who was inside of the black carriage.

Without warning, her sister popped into her mind and Lydia automatically lowered her gaze to the lone red candle in front of her.

It was the decoration she and Anna had made together last Christmas. Together, they'd decided to use it for this year's special Christmas dream.

That in itself made this particular candle extra special. Every December, before Anna had wed, they'd continued the homemade candle tradition. And each year, something unique and special would occur while they made them.

While they'd done this particular one, they'd gotten news that their eldest cousin had finally gotten pregnant. Of course, even though her family consisted only of her parents and sister, Lydia had a large number of relatives.

Her mother was one of eight sisters, and her father, the youngest of ten siblings. Between the Shultz and Troyer clans, it appeared that no one had had difficulty conceiving a child. Except for Leah.

In her late thirties, she was, by their family's standards, a bit old to give birth. But after years of trying for a family, her dream was finally coming true.

With an affectionate hand, Lydia touched the cinnamon-scented red wax. As she breathed in its aroma, she closed her eyes and pushed out a deep, satisfied breath. *Anna, I know you'd approve of my Christmas dream. I consider meeting John King a great blessing. Not only do I admire and respect him and his family for all they've done for our community over the years, but talking with him has helped me to decide this year's Christmas goal. And without you, Anna, coming up with that blessing has been all too difficult.*

She stopped what she was doing and stepped into the kitchen where Mamma was removing a pot roast from the oven. After careful consideration, Lydia decided to broach her mother with the subject.

"Mamma, remember John?"

Her mamma offered a quick nod and continued what she was doing. "Of course. What a nice young man. Their family is well thought of."

"Mamma, you know all about the cinnamon roll drive the King family does every year."

"Of course. We talked about it briefly when he had dinner with us."

After a brief pause, Lydia went on. "It's a family thing. Everyone pitches in."

While her mother wiped the countertop around

the oversized baking dish, she offered a nod of agreement.

"But this year, Mamma, it'll be harder for them to deliver rolls to everyone who needs them."

Her mother stopped what she was doing to rest her hand on her hip. "What do you mean?"

"Some of John's brothers and sisters are out of the house now and they won't be able to help. And according to John, the list of people on the need list is nearly twice as long as in past years."

A short silence ensued while Mamma organized the countertop, moving the roast into the center. The comforting, familiar smell filled the kitchen. Lydia's mouth watered.

In her opinion, no one made a pot roast as good as her mother. The beef was always tender. And Mamma added special spices to the meat to make it the most delicious meat Lydia had ever tasted.

"At King's Bakery yesterday, I talked with John and met some of his siblings."

Mamma grinned. "Those Kings sure have a large clan."

"*Jah.*" As Lydia considered the benefits of being part of such a family, she smiled a little. The idea appealed to her. "But Mamma, John's worried about this year's drive. As you know, every December Anna and I decide a blessing to make happen by Christmas Eve. And deciding what it is has been difficult."

Sympathy edged the concerned tone of Lydia's mother's voice. "I know how much you miss your sister and how hard it's been with her gone."

"But Mamma, the good news is I've finally decided this year's Christmas goal. And I'm so excited!"

A long silence ensued while Lydia determined how to ask permission to help with the event. Certainly, being part of such a wonderful charity wouldn't be wrong and her parents were always for helping others but for some reason, Lydia knew that getting a yes might be difficult because John was a single Mennonite man and she was a single Amish girl. That situation would certainly give her parents pause.

Lydia squared her shoulders and tried for her most confident tone. "Mamma, I'd like yours and Dad's permission to help John and his family with his Christmas drive."

To Lydia's surprise, her mother didn't respond and continued to organize. While Lydia awaited a reply, she pretended a sudden interest in the window and its sky blue curtains that Anna had sewn a few years ago.

Lydia had no interest in sewing. However, she loved learning new recipes.

People had always told her that she would make a great wife and mother. She raised a skeptical brow, wondering how being a good cook could make someone a great wife and mother. So many things contributed to being a good mamma that didn't involve food.

Lydia held her breath as Mamma's fingers nervously strummed against the countertop. Even the comforting aroma of the roast didn't calm Lydia as she acknowledged how very important it was to play a role in this drive.

Finally, Mamma waved a hand toward the dining room table. Lydia took a seat next to her at the oak table her father had made. After breathing in, Mamma expelled a deep sigh and locked gazes with Lydia.

"Lydia, I'm happy that you finally decided your Christmas goal and want to help John's family. The drive greatly contributes to our community. But helping him with it?"

She shrugged and lowered the pitch of her voice to a more uncertain tone. "I'm not sure what your father will say."

Lydia had never argued with her mother and father; at the same time, she knew it was vital to make her case to her parents. "Mamma, I want to make sure you know that John and I won't be working alone. There will be a lot of us. As you know, it's a family project, and John has eleven siblings. Still, it's going to be more difficult to come through for everyone on the list this year with part of his family gone. Not to mention the volume of flour, sugar, and butter he'll need to make the rolls. They're asking for volunteers."

Her mother said in a soft voice. "The Kings have always done the entire event by themselves. Maybe John needs to take donations to help with the cost."

Lydia considered her mother's opinion and quickly nodded agreement. "I've recommended that. Unfortunately, ingredients aren't the only issue. By the sounds of it, he'll also need extra hands baking the pastries and delivering them."

She hesitated to catch her breath. "Oh, Mamma, I want so much to make this special event successful. I can only imagine the happy expressions on everyone's faces when their rolls are delivered. Our family is fortunate. We always have plenty of food. But not everyone is as blessed as we are."

"I know that, Lydia. I'll discuss it with your father this evening." She wagged her finger. "No promises.

And don't be disappointed if he says no. Remember, you and the King boy are of dating age. And Mennonites are fine, respectable people. But their way of life is vastly different from ours. So the drive . . . it's not only about the rolls. It's also about you and John."

Lydia stretched and folded her hands over her lap. With a gentle lift of her palms she looked her mother in the eyes and used the most pleading expression she could muster. "I know, Mamma. But Christmas is the same no matter what church we go to. And the drive?" Lydia lowered her voice to barely more than a whisper. "It's the most important Christmas dream I've ever had."

Later that evening, Lydia's heart pumped to a fast pace as she listened to the purring of an engine in their drive. As she dried the last dinner dish and placed it into the cabinet, she said a silent prayer for her parents to allow her to be a part of the cinnamon roll charity.

She could hear her daddy washing his hands in the hall restroom. Her mother straightened paperwork on the dining room table. When three knocks sounded, Lydia's heart picked up to an excited, eager pace edged with anxiety.

Holding her breath, she opened the door and faced John King. The moment their gazes locked, she greeted him. As usual, her heart fluttered. She wasn't sure why his presence always affected her this way, but she was used to it. However, right now, there wasn't time to think about her reaction. At the same time, she acknowledged that this always happened when they were together.

"Hello, John. Please come in."

With a dip of his head, he thanked her. At the same time, her parents joined them. "What a pleasant surprise, John! Why, it's so good to see you." Lydia watched as he and her dad shook hands.

With a smile and a quick motion of her wrist, her mother motioned John to the living room, and Lydia and her dad followed. Before sitting down, Mamma asked, "What brings you here this evening?"

At the same time, they sat. Mamma and Daddy claimed their usual spots on the sofa, while John and Lydia took the two cushioned chairs opposite of them.

John leaned forward and rested his palms on his thighs. Locking gazes first with Lydia's mother, then with her father, he started. "Mr. and Mrs. Schultz, I've come to ask you a favor." He cleared a knot from his throat. "You're aware of our charity drive every Christmas Eve."

Mamma immediately nodded. "Of course. And John, I have to tell you that it's a wonderful thing for the community." Excitement edged her voice as she glanced at her husband before returning her attention to John. "Lydia tells me that this year, your list has more than doubled what it was in years past. What a lovely way to offer your services at the most important time of the year."

John's dark brows narrowed into a slight, thoughtful frown. Several heartbeats later, he gave a sad shake of his head before looking down at the floor. A few breaths later, he lifted his gaze and turned a bit to better face Lydia's parents. "That's the good news and the bad."

Lydia's father chimed in. "What's wrong?"

"It's what I came to talk to you about." He darted

Lydia a quick glance before returning his focus to the couple on the couch. "As grateful and honored as we are to serve our neighbors, the problem is that it's going to be difficult to deliver that large a number of baked goods to everyone who needs them, let alone to produce them. We're short-handed."

After a long silence ensued, he crossed his legs at the ankles and leaned back into the chaise. "But with the bad comes the good. Lydia has told me about the Christmas dreams she and her sister decide on every December. And this year, she would like that special goal to be to aid us in making the drive a success."

After breathing in, he squared his shoulders. "I've come to ask your permission for that to happen."

The room seemed unusually quiet. Lydia realized that if she dropped a safety pin onto the dark oak that shone with wood polish, she would be able to hear it meet the floor.

Finally, John broke the uncomfortable silence. "I respect whatever decision you might make. Just know that your daughter and I would be working with other volunteers, and I would ensure that Lydia would get safely to and from our bakery. My sisters and brothers are also recruiting friends."

Lydia held her breath. The frown on Daddy's face and the lack of response from her parents prompted a dull ache in Lydia's chest. *I might not get my dream.*

After a serious glance at each other, her parents stood at the same time. Her dad tapped the toe of his right shoe and shoved his hands deep into his pockets. After thoughtfully regarding his wife, he refocused his attention on John and Lydia.

Lifting his shoulders into a shrug, he smiled a little. "I see no reason why we shouldn't allow this. Why, we encourage our daughter to serve others, and at the same time I think this would be good for Lydia, especially with Anna out of the roost." Several moments later, he nodded. "You've got my blessing."

Later that evening, John pushed several bales off the loft. As soon as the straw landed on the barn's cement floor, John stepped down the wooden ladder and drew in a deep breath as he heaved the heavy bale of dried grain stalks over his shoulder.

Pieces stuck out from the twine and slipped out as he carried the fresh bedding to the animal stalls. John began raking what looked like golden straws into a pile. In very little time, he shoved dirty bedding near the back wall.

Grabbing the pocketknife from his trousers, he quickly sliced the twine holding the stalks together. A huge pile of loose straw spread into a large heap in front of him.

John breathed in the familiar scent and smiled with satisfaction. The smell of grain made him relax. He enjoyed working on the farm. Loved everything about the simple, rewarding country life.

Pressing his lips together in a thoughtful line, he began evening out the bedding while the most recent conversation with Mr. and Mrs. Schultz played through his mind.

For the moment, the mid-December wind had subsided, and the barn was pleasantly warm for this time of year. Without wasting time, he placed the rake against the metal front that separated the stalls from the open part of the structure.

With one smooth motion, he slid his jacket down

his arms and tossed it over one of the posts before reclaiming the rake and continuing to spread straw throughout the large area set aside for livestock.

From his peripheral vision, he glimpsed pigeons scouring the floor for food. He could hear Storm let out a loud whinny just outside of the opened door leading out to the pasture.

But his mind didn't linger on his surroundings.

While he worked, his thoughts drifted to the conversation he'd had just a couple hours ago with Lydia and her parents. After the straw was spread, he piled the dirty stuff into a metal dumpster and hung the rake back on the wall.

He considered Lydia's parents and their permission for their daughter to help him with his cinnamon roll drive. He swallowed an emotional lump and imagined her with his large clan.

Already, Peter and Hannah loved her. After she'd left the shop, they'd both sung her praises. Of course, he couldn't imagine the Amish girl not getting along with anyone. But a large family like his was certainly a huge contrast to only one sister.

As he listened to the cattle get comfortable in their new bedding, he wondered about Lydia and the rest of his large brood. *Will they get along?*

Lydia yawned as she looked down at her project. The moon was especially bright with stars sprinkled all around it. She was nearly finished with the scarf. To her amazement, the warm neck covering of gorgeous blue shades was going to be even more beautiful than she'd ever dreamed possible.

I'm so excited about this gift. I can't wait to see Anna's face when she opens the box.

She considered the cinnamon roll drive, and her heart pumped to an even more excited pace as she imagined all of the lives that would be brightened with the tasty desserts. As her needles clicked, she breathed in the pleasant aroma of freshly washed bedding.

She smiled a little at her work and also at the small remainder of yarn. She had the perfect sized box in mind for the gift. And Mamma had beautiful silver foil wrapping paper left over from a sale last year.

Lydia ran her fingers over the finished project and nodded satisfaction. She'd finished Anna's gift! Placing the needles on the stand next to her bed, she turned onto her side before jumping up to her feet.

She hollered as she rushed down the stairs, scarf in hand. "Mamma! Look!"

Her mother's jaw dropped as her gaze met Lydia's finished product. "It's absolutely gorgeous!"

"I can't wait till she opens it!"

Her mother grinned as their gazes locked in a mutual understanding. "I'm proud of you, Lydia. You tried something you've put off for years. Now, do you see why knitting relaxes me at night?"

Lydia nodded before lifting an amused brow. "I'm glad I did this for Anna. But Mamma, I'm sure you can understand that I much prefer cooking." She pushed out a decisive sigh before grinning. "Now, I know for sure that knitting isn't my cup of tea."

She gave a gentle lift of her shoulders before grinning at her role model. "I'm glad I completed this project. From now on, I'll leave knitting to you and Anna."

Chapter 4

December twenty-fourth came fast. Laughter and the joyous Christmas spirit floated through King's Bakery as volunteers prepared for making and delivering over two hundred dozens of rolls.

The light ringing of the bell on the entrance continuously sounded as volunteers entered, one by one. Each time the door opened, cold wind rushed in, making the temperature inside drop a couple of notches while the fire in the large fireplace tried to keep up with heat.

As Lydia checked the round clock on the wall for the time, she pulled in an excited, anxious breath in high hopes that her idea of the assembly line would result in everyone on the list receiving a box of famous King pastries by the end of the day.

The clapping of hands startled her. She glanced at John, who tried for everyone's attention. When he had it, he looked around the room and smiled. "I want to thank each and every one of you for being here."

Closing his eyes, he breathed in deeply and exhaled.

When he opened his lids, Lydia could see the light flecks that danced with great hope and excitement.

"First and foremost, let's give credit to the One who's behind this. The real reason for celebrating Christmas."

Looking to his left, then to his right, he joined hands with Lydia and Hannah. The instant contact with his fingers warmed Lydia's heart in reassurance. A strong sense of comfort transpired from his body to hers.

"Let's make a circle and ask God to help us get the rolls out to everyone who needs them." Excited voices morphed into one solid sound as they got into place to hold hands.

They bowed their heads in prayer. "Dear Lord, you've blessed us in many ways. Thank you for the birth of the Baby Jesus. And please be with us today as we set out to make and deliver more rolls than we ever have. Thank you, Lord, for all you've given us. And help us to serve you and only you. Amen."

"Amen!"

Lydia and the others took turns washing their hands in the small bathroom at the side of the shop and quickly stepped into the long queue that started at the back of the bakery and continued down both walls and into the front.

Each grabbed a pair of plastic gloves, and began preparing for their individual tasks. As "Silent Night" played softly over the speaker, Lydia thought of Anna and an affectionate ache tugged at her heart. But as soon as she began her job, great joy replaced the short spurt of pain.

Lydia turned to Hannah, who carefully adjusted the plastic over her hair. Hannah's voice bubbled with excitement. "Today's finally here! And we're going to make this our best drive ever!"

Lydia bent her knees in excitement and considered her Christmas goal and everyone's determination to make it come true. "I know! Can you believe it? We're finally getting down to business. Ten hours from now, we'll be out delivering delicious pastries to happy people who will eat them for Christmas!"

She paused to take in the significance of the joy their work would bring others. "I've been saying special prayers for us to come through for everyone!"

John's sister nodded agreement. "Me, too, Lydia. We've done everything we can do to make success happen. And God answers prayers!"

As they chitchatted about what they would eat tomorrow, Lydia added powdered sugar to the already-made butter and milk mixture in her oversized mixing bowl.

She quickly forgot her sister's absence and focused on keeping enough icing in the bowl for the rolls after they'd cooled and to pass them on to Hannah, whose job was to place each dozen into a separate box.

The final task belonged to two of John's teenage sisters, Martha and Esther. In Lydia's opinion, they had the most fun job to tie beautiful red and blue ribbons around the boxes with KING'S BAKERY on top and include a special Christmas Scripture to each recipient.

Only the oldest family members were allowed to partake in mixing the secret recipe. At the first station, John put the dough together before two brothers flattened the dough with rolling pins, placed butter, sugar, and cinnamon on top, and rolled each slice into an actual roll.

Two hours later, the team worked in full force. Today, the shop was closed to the public. As Lydia struggled to keep up mixing powdered sugar, milk, and soft butter, she thought of Anna and their previous Christmas dreams.

As she spread the soft-looking white mixture over the cooled treats, she imagined tomorrow, when their home would be bouncing with people, laughter, and little ones running around in bare feet.

But to Lydia's dismay, a sad admission caused the corners of her lips to turn down into a frown. Because she already loved the King family as if she was a part of their clan. And she was especially fond of John.

She'd become so accustomed to talking to him and watching his eyes light up when they conversed. She hadn't dared to consider the end of today, when they would no longer be working together. She squeezed her eyes closed tightly to rid that dismal thought.

When she opened her lids, salty moisture stung her eyes, and she quickly blinked at the irritating sting. She forced herself to think of the positives. After all, it was Christmas Eve.

The loud timer interrupted Lydia's thoughts, and she straightened to focus on her responsibilities. As a tray of cool rolls was passed to her, she took in the smell. Her mouth watered.

She gave her powdered sugar mixture an extra stir before planting a teaspoonful of white glaze on each roll.

But as voices happily floated around her, she realized something she hadn't recognized before.

That very realization made her lungs pump harder for air. Because she had an additional Christmas wish.

One she must keep secret. And that very wish was to court John King and to be in his life forever.

Later that evening, Lydia stood in front of the red candle in their living room window. With one swift motion, she lit the match and applied it to the wick. As the flame burned, the light fragrance of cinnamon filled her senses.

She should be elated that her Christmas dream had come true. However, a sigh that was a conflicting combination of satisfaction and regret escaped her throat.

Joyful events from the day floated through her mind, finally prompting the corners of her lips to lift into a huge satisfied smile. To think, a month ago she hadn't believed she could make it through December and now, she was experiencing the best Christmas ever. In her entire life, she'd never seen as many smiles. Or heard as many thank yous.

While she took in the special candle and its significance, tears of joy wet her eyes. The burning flame was a valid reminder that she'd achieved her Christmas dream with flying colors.

In deep appreciation, she closed her eyes and pressed her palms together. She breathed in deeply and pushed out the air before lowering her chin in gratitude. "Dear Lord, I give you all the praise and thanks for giving me the most joyous, meaningful Christmas ever. Thank you especially for the King family and John, and bless all of the people I worked with today. I pray you will help me to continue to serve you and only you. Amen."

When she opened her eyelids, the sad reality hit her. The day that had provided her more joy than she'd ever had in her entire life was over. As melted wax began slowly dripping down the sides of the candle, she realized that not only had this day ended, but also her time with John and his siblings.

Of course, from the beginning, she'd known that their time together was temporary. What she hadn't realized was the impact the denouement would have on her.

As she glimpsed the bright, fragile-looking stars that cluttered the unusually dark sky, she parted her lips in awe. She missed the noise. The laughter. She even missed the preparation that had gone into the drive. And she especially missed bumping into each other and the chitchatting as each of them had carried through with their jobs.

Lydia plopped down in the nearest chaise and rested her chin on her right fist, contemplating the complete turnaround her life had taken in the past few weeks. She'd first wondered how she would get through the holiday. Now, she wasn't sure how she'd carry on afterward! How her life had changed.

And her own needs had been tremendously altered by what had recently occurred. Being with the King brood had enlightened her in many ways. More than ever, she yearned for a large family. She imagined little ones running around in the house. Crying. Laughing.

When her thoughts landed on John, her heart fluttered. She'd never had an interest in the boys at church. Hadn't even given thought to falling in love. Mamma had always taught her that love didn't have anything to do with infatuation or looks. Or an unrealistic sensation that could easily confuse a person as to what's right or wrong.

That true love meant helping with the kids or

doing errands. That it was all about being there for your spouse, dependability when things were bad as well as when they were good. Lydia tapped the toe of her black shoe to a nervous, uncertain beat against the wooden floor.

She stiffened. *Does that mean that Mamma's heart never flutters when she looks at Daddy? Is Mamma trying to tell me that their marriage is only about helping each other out?*

Lydia drew her brows together in a deep frown of concentration while she considered that piece of information that was routinely offered. For some strange reason, Lydia wanted her own marriage to be much, much more than her mother's definition. With a hopeful sigh, she contemplated times her parents had looked at each other and tried to recall if she'd ever noticed a special light in their eyes.

Lydia thought about the other couples she'd seen. When she'd attended events in the community, she'd glimpsed English girls and boys holding hands. Even kissing. The Plain Faith wasn't into the public display of affection. Of course, Lydia didn't pass judgment on others. That wasn't her place.

As she sat very still, thinking of John and considering the marriages she'd witnessed within their Amish community, a wave of disappointment floated through her. She didn't know what God had in store for her. And she wouldn't even try to guess.

But deep down inside of her heart, she wished for a husband who truly loved and cherished her for the person she was. *Isn't it okay for my heart to flutter? Given that John is not of the Plain Faith, envisioning a relationship with him can only lead to disappointment. Because we can never be together. But I can dream. And I can pray for God to give me the man I would love to spend my life with.*

* * *

That evening, the King household buzzed with excitement. A great sense of satisfaction and relief filled John's chest while he grabbed his coat.

A nudge on his shoulder stopped his thoughts. He looked down at Hannah's freckled grin and smiled a little. He narrowed a suspicious set of brows. "What?"

"You did a great job leading the drive." A sigh escaped her. "I'll never forget the looks on the faces of those people we gave the cinnamon rolls to."

"Yeah, it was quite a day, wasn't it?"

For several awkward moments, he studied the odd expression on her face. Finally, she smiled a little. "Are you going over to Lydia's house?"

The question gave him pause, and he continued to stuff his arms in his wool jacket. Adjusting for a comfortable fit, he sensed mischief. He knew Hannah well. And he loved her. But she had a subtle way of getting involved in other's people's business.

He tried for a calm tone. "No, I didn't plan on it. Why?"

She hugged her hands to her hips and rolled her eyes. "I was hoping the two of you would see each other after the drive. She likes you, John. And I know you like her. And Lydia and I . . . we're friends now."

John considered his sister's obvious wish and smiled a little. "Don't tell me you're playing matchmaker."

When she didn't reply, he lowered the pitch of his voice to a mere whisper and motioned to the corner of the kitchen. The house was filled with people, and the last thing he wanted was for someone to get wind of this conversation.

"Hannah, you know Lydia and I can't be together. Even if we wanted to."

Hannah pleaded. "Why ever not?" She stepped forward to meet his gaze.

John lifted his palms in a dismissive gesture. "Because she's Amish. To court Lydia, I'd have to join the Plain Faith."

After a long pause, Hannah gave a gentle lift of her shoulders. "And what's so bad about that?"

Moments later, inside of the barn, John couldn't rid his recent conversation with Hannah from his mind. As he filled the water troughs, her words nagged at him.

What's so bad about that?

The question stabbed at him until he finally sat down on the nearest bale of straw. Shoving his hands into his pockets, he focused on Hannah. And Lydia.

The thought of the beautiful Amish girl brought a grin to his lips. Every time she popped into his mind, a warm, happy sensation filled him until he wanted to jump up and down.

Don't be ridiculous. But is being enamored with an Amish girl so ridiculous, really? A girl who's good and honest? Someone who makes me happier than I've ever been? I want to see her. But I've been a Mennonite my entire life. The only way to be with her would be to switch to the Plain Faith. Could I do it?

The doorbell sounded at the Schultz home. Lydia jumped up from her chair. She stepped to the side door, where Daddy was letting John King into the kitchen.

She didn't try to stymie the excitement from her voice. "It's *gut* to see you!"

"Merry Christmas, Lydia. I came by to thank you for all the work you did for our drive."

She motioned him in.

As he removed his coat, she smiled a little. "Come and see the candle I lit to celebrate my Christmas dream coming true."

He followed her into the living room. She eyed him before focusing her attention on the flame from the single red candle.

"My Christmas dream came true, John. And it's all because of you. Since I've been working for the drive, I put serving others before myself, and throughout the month, I've realized the true blessing of Christmas."

She paused to compose her emotions. "Of course, I always knew the significance of the birth of Christ. I've heard it over and over in church and in Scripture. But this year . . ." She drew in a deep breath and pushed it out. "I've truly experienced the true meaning."

A long silence ensued while Lydia took in the powerful significance of what she'd just said. Salty emotional tears of joy filled her eyes.

"Lydia, I have a confession."

She parted her lips and studied him.

He chuckled. "Don't you want to know what it is?"

She offered an eager nod.

"When I drove home after having dinner with you and your parents, I couldn't stop thinking about how you miss your sister and that you needed a Christmas wish. So I came up with my own goal. To bring joy to you as we prepared the celebration of the birth of Jesus. And . . ."

He paused to laugh. "I think God planted you in my life to help me."

"To help you?"

He lowered the pitch of his voice to a more emotional tone. "Lydia, this is the most satisfying Christmas I've ever had. Working with you has brought me joy."

A surprised breath escaped her throat. Speechless, Lydia contemplated what she'd just heard. Without warning, this conversation had catapulted her feelings for him to a whole new level. The surprising admission gave her pause as she faced reality.

"I'm so glad to hear it, John. It means the world to me that I've done something for you. All the time, I thought helping with the drive was for me. For my goal."

"You didn't know that being with you made me happy?"

The question took her breath away. Warmth filled her cheeks until she lowered her gaze to the floor to hide her blushing.

"Lydia?"

Finally, she lifted her chin to look at him.

"Being with you has taught me a lot about myself."

She couldn't find her voice.

He cleared his throat and tapped his shoe against the floor to a nervous beat. "You've taught me to accept change."

"What do you mean?"

After a slight hesitation, he spoke in a soft, gentle tone. "I've learned what it's like to truly care about someone."

"John . . . I don't think . . ."

"Lydia, I'm going to ask your parents' permission to court you."

It took a few moments for his statement to sink in. When she absorbed his unexpected words, she hugged her arms to her chest and closed her eyes. When she opened her lids, she drew in a breath that was a combination of excitement and surprise.

"Oh, John!"

"But before I talk to them, I wanted to make sure it's what you'd like."

She clasped her palms together and breathed in. "I'd love nothing more than to court you, John King! But what about . . ."

"Being Mennonite?"

She nodded.

"I had a very interesting conversation with Hannah this evening. And she made me think. Do you know that my grandmother on my mother's side is Amish?"

She looked at him to continue.

"I admire the Amish faith. And if I'm allowed to court you, I plan to join the Plain Faith."

"Oh, John! You've made my second Christmas wish come true."

"There was a second wish?"

"To spend more time with you. But I didn't think it could happen."

He grinned. His eyes lightened. "Lydia, anything can happen when two Christian people care about each other. Merry Christmas, Lydia."

"Merry Christmas, John. You've made both my Christmas dreams come true."

Cinnamon Rolls

DOUGH

1 envelope fast-rising yeast
½ cup warm water
½ cup scalded whole milk, plus 1 tablespoon half-
    and-half
⅓ cup granulated sugar
⅓ cup real butter, salted
1 egg
3½ cups all-purpose flour, plus about 1 cup for
    kneading

FILLING

1 stick (½ cup) melted butter
1 cup sugar (more, if needed)
Ground cinnamon, as much as desired (I use
    1 tablespoon)

Heat oven to 350 degrees F.

In one bowl, stir yeast in warm water and put to the side. In a second bowl stir milk, sugar, melted butter, and egg. Add about 2 cups of flour. Mix until smooth. Add dissolved yeast. Stir in remaining flour. Knead the dough mixture on floured surface for 8 or 9 minutes. Then place in buttered bowl. Cover, and let rise for a couple of hours or until doubled in size.

Punch dough and roll out onto floured waxed paper. Spread melted butter over dough. Mix sugar and cinnamon and spread onto buttered dough. Slice the dough into straight lines and roll each piece up.

Butter the bottom and sides of the baking pan. Place the rolled-up pieces close together in the pan and let rise until dough is doubled in size. Bake for about 30 minutes. Enjoy!

Lisa Jones Baker's heartwarming series continues as a new generation inherits precious hand-carved chests that bring blessings of faith, love, and happiness . . .

Secret at Pebble Creek
Hope Chest of Dreams, Book 4

Sam Beachy's heart warmed as he added finishing touches to the beautiful piece of oak in front of him. To his right, a hope chest lid he'd started rested on a felt cloth. To his left, another piece for a young grandma-to-be waited for completion.

Inside of his old barn in the quiet countryside of Arthur, Illinois, the bright July sunlight poured in through the opened windows, enabling him to better scrutinize the detailed lines of his newest project.

He held his special work in front of him. Sam gingerly exchanged his carving knife for another tool from the worn holder and continued to hone the fine details.

For years, he'd etched pictures into hope chest lids, and by now, the skill came so naturally to him he could create depth to make his art appear real by using his knife and other tools at different angles.

Only this particular project wasn't a hope chest. With a slow, steady motion, he ran a pointer finger over the rounded smooth edge. A squirrel quietly appeared next to Sam's black sturdy shoes and stood on its hind feet, extended its front paws, and held them in a begging position. As Sam stared into two round, hopeful eyes, he laughed and stopped what he was doing.

"You think I was born to feed you, don't you?"

As the brown mammal stayed very still, Sam got up from his chair, reached into the sack of treats that he kept next to him while he worked, plucked a lone pecan, and bent to give it to the small furry creature.

With two pigeons hovering at the top of the ladder leading up to the hayloft, the squirrel didn't hesitate to accept the morsel before scurrying across the long distance of barn to the opened doors where he finally disappeared. The moment the beggar was gone, a loud whinny filled the air.

A few yards away, Strawberry, Sam's horse, trotted into his stall where he sucked up water from the deep metal trough. Afterwards, he threw back his head and clomped his hoof to an impatient beat.

Letting out a deep breath, Sam put down his work, got up, stepped to the animal stall, and stroked the long nose of his pal with gentleness. "Strawberry, I know you're lookin' for Esther's sponge cakes. But I don't have any."

He extended his fingers in front of him to show empty hands before dropping his arms to his sides. He touched the animal's nose with his pointer finger. "Be patient. Esther's making a fresh batch right now. *Jetzt sofort.*"

In response, the young standardbred nudged Sam's chin with his nose. Automatically, Sam caressed the long, thick reddish-brown mane with his fingers until the horse closed his eyes.

As Sam regarded the loving creature that had been named by his dear wife Esther, he considered his nearly sixty-year marriage. The mere thought of Esther made his heart melt.

As he considered the petite white-haired woman he'd known his entire life, emotional, joy-filled tears filled his eyes, and he blinked at the salty sting. "Pal, God blessed me with Esther, and do you know that next year, we'll celebrate sixty years of marriage? *Sechzig.*"

The only response was a shake of Strawberry's head to rid it of some flies. "I've made her something very special."

He lifted his chin a notch. The buzzing of flies was the only sound. "It's going to be hard to keep the secret for nearly a year."

He furrowed his brows while the horse brushed against Sam's forearm where his shirt sleeve was rolled up. "I know this might come as a surprise, but this time, it's not a hope chest. But . . ." Sam let out a satisfied sigh. "It's the most special gift I've ever made."

The mouth-watering scent of Esther's desserts floated from the opened kitchen windows all the way to the barn. Sam's stomach growled. But right now, there wasn't time to think about food. Even if they were sponge cakes baked by the best cook around.

Whenever Sam focused on a project, and right now it was his hand-carved gift for Esther . . . his mind was one-tracked. He lived and breathed each special story which he captured on wood.

And right now, this present required serious thought. Where to keep it. What clues to write to help Esther find it.

And the hiding place wouldn't be just anywhere. *Nein.* It would be at their special spot. Where Esther had agreed to spend the rest of her life with him. The place they called "their own."

Sam dropped his arm to his side and shoved his

fingers into his deep pants pockets. When Strawberry nudged him, Sam lifted his right hand and continued caressing the spoiled standardbred.

But as Sam stroked the long nose, his thoughts weren't on the needy animal. Or the squirrels that counted on him for treats. Or his Irish Setter who kept Esther company while she baked. Or his next hope chest order.

"Esther." A combination of great affection and emotion edged his voice as he mouthed her name. A loud snort temporarily pulled him from his reverie, and Sam moved his fingers to behind Strawberry's ears. After a satisfied snort, the horse lowered his gaze to the cement floor and held very still.

Feeling the need to talk about his secret plan, Sam began thinking out loud. "Strawberry, I'm going to tell you something that no one else is privy to."

Sam moved the toe of his left shoe up and down to a quick, excited beat. He could hear the long branches of the tall oaks brush the top of the building. In the background, chickens clucked. Through the opened doors, he glimpsed horses in the distant field. He knew the man behind them on a small platform.

"Pal, do you know that Esther and I have been married close to sixty years?"

As Sam acknowledged that very blessing, he shook his head in gratefulness and squeezed his eyes closed to pray. "Dear Lord, I give You all the praise and thanks for my marriage, for our four sons who are with You, and even for our needy four-legged family members."

He paused to clear the uncomfortable knot from his throat before lowering the pitch of his voice to a tone that was barely more than a whisper. "Thank you for helping me to make Esther my most beautiful carving. And *denki* for our sixtieth wedding anniversary that we'll celebrate next year. Amen."

Fully aware of the beautiful day on the other side of the walls, he encouraged his furry friend. "Go on." He patted him with affection. "Summer doesn't last forever. Enjoy the day."

Strawberry snorted, stomped his left hoof twice, turned, and swished his reddish-brown tail back and forth while he trotted out of the opened door leading to the pasture. Once he was outside, the uneven clomp clomping disappeared.

Sam glanced at his work table and smiled. He looked forward to seeing the look on Esther's face when he gave her his very best work of art. But in order to keep his surprise secret, the knowledge of the special hand-carved present couldn't be shared with anyone.

Except for a reddish-brown spoiled horse who enjoyed sponge cakes. The corners of Sam's mouth lifted into an amused grin.

He returned to his work area and lifted the newly finished piece so it was directly in front of him. While he drew it closer to his chest, he imagined Esther's reaction to it. Because their anniversary was still months away, he'd hide it to ensure it stayed a secret. A warm breeze floated into the wide opened doors and gently caressed his fingers.

For a moment, the barn darkened a notch, but not long after, bright rays poured through the windows. Sam closed his eyes a moment to savor the gentle sensation. But his mind worked while he continued to plan his anniversary surprise.

He straightened and pressed his pointer finger against his chin while he thought. He would write a note to Esther to remind her of his undying love for her. In the message, he'd hint about the present and where it was hidden.

But he wasn't about to place it just anywhere. He quickly decided that he'd hide it in their most special place. Where they'd committed to love each other the rest of their lives.

Long strides took him outside where he glimpsed a jet's trail of white. His gaze eventually landed on the out-of-place-looking hill and creek behind his home. Annie Mast and Levi Miller had coined the beautiful scene Pebble Creek. He shoved his hands into his pockets and parted his lips in awe as he marveled at the view.

I love my home. I treasure this land. One of these days, when Esther and I are with the Lord, I don't know who will live here, but I pray that an extension of the Beachy clan will continue to carry on here. God has blessed me with kin, including my brother who chose the Englisch life. But familie is familie, no matter where they live or what church they go to. And familie means love. Just like Pebble Creek.

Books by Bestselling Author
Fern Michaels

___The Jury	0-8217-7878-1	$6.99US/$9.99CAN
___Sweet Revenge	0-8217-7879-X	$6.99US/$9.99CAN
___Lethal Justice	0-8217-7880-3	$6.99US/$9.99CAN
___Free Fall	0-8217-7881-1	$6.99US/$9.99CAN
___Fool Me Once	0-8217-8071-9	$7.99US/$10.99CAN
___Vegas Rich	0-8217-8112-X	$7.99US/$10.99CAN
___Hide and Seek	1-4201-0184-6	$6.99US/$9.99CAN
___Hokus Pokus	1-4201-0185-4	$6.99US/$9.99CAN
___Fast Track	1-4201-0186-2	$6.99US/$9.99CAN
___Collateral Damage	1-4201-0187-0	$6.99US/$9.99CAN
___Final Justice	1-4201-0188-9	$6.99US/$9.99CAN
___Up Close and Personal	0-8217-7956-7	$7.99US/$9.99CAN
___Under the Radar	1-4201-0683-X	$6.99US/$9.99CAN
___Razor Sharp	1-4201-0684-8	$7.99US/$10.99CAN
___Yesterday	1-4201-1494-8	$5.99US/$6.99CAN
___Vanishing Act	1-4201-0685-6	$7.99US/$10.99CAN
___Sara's Song	1-4201-1493-X	$5.99US/$6.99CAN
___Deadly Deals	1-4201-0686-4	$7.99US/$10.99CAN
___Game Over	1-4201-0687-2	$7.99US/$10.99CAN
___Sins of Omission	1-4201-1153-1	$7.99US/$10.99CAN
___Sins of the Flesh	1-4201-1154-X	$7.99US/$10.99CAN
___Cross Roads	1-4201-1192-2	$7.99US/$10.99CAN

Available Wherever Books Are Sold!
Check out our website at www.kensingtonbooks.com

More by Bestselling Author
Hannah Howell

Available Wherever Books Are Sold!

Check out our website at
http://www.kensingtonbooks.com

More from Bestselling Author
JANET DAILEY